"*Project Megalon* is a fast-paced story full of action and twists. Hodes merges past life regression and sci-fi masterfully, giving aficionados plenty to enjoy. A sure winner!"

Lynn McGee,
author of *Woman of the Mists*

Project Megalon

Richard Hodes

Project Megalon
A Book World, Inc. Publication
First Edition: July 1999

This is a work of fiction. The characters, names, incidents, dialogue and plot are a product of the author's imagination.

ISBN 1-881542-36-X

An Original Trade Paperback
Cover Art: Jan A. Sainsbury

Library of Congress Catalog Card Number: 99-62226

Published by Book World, Inc.
9666 E. Riggs Rd, POB 194, Sun Lakes AZ 85248

Printed in the United States of America

Be sure to visit our web site at:
www.bkworld.com

To my wife, Jane,
and daughters, Lisa and Stacy:
Thanks for your encouragement and support of my writing.

Special thanks to the Coral Springs
Creative Writing Workshop

To Betty, Zelda, Roxanne, Joe, Art Millie and Lynn:
Without your editing excellence this book would never
exist. Dinner is on me.

Richard Hodes

Project Megalon

Prologue

Outside the City of Sidon
Kingdom of Phoenicia 3000 Years Ago

ONE HUNDRED THOUSAND EYES WATCHED FOR THE signal. Like a hungry panther stalking its prey, the human mass stood immobile, awaiting the crucial moment.

"Attack," ordered Pharaoh, "by land and sea." He stood upon his golden chariot, held his scepter high and commanded the battle from a hill overlooking the city and the harbor. Three pure white Arabians strained their bridles, awaiting his bidding.

Clouds of arrows rained on the last of the Phoenician perimeter defenders; their bodies littered the plain and the river. Legions of Egyptian foot soldiers and charioteers swiftly overran the stronghold of the enemy. Panic spread through the city with word that the Egyptian army massed outside the walls. The people knew the horrible price they must pay for the ideal location of their city: the Pharaoh required a port in this region. His ships had appeared on the horizon before dawn, crowded with warriors ready to strike.

With the dawn came the thundering sound of the army on one side of the city and a storm of fire unleashed from the ships. The Pharaoh timed his offensive perfectly; the city lay virtually defenseless with the main divisions of the Phoenician army far away, fighting barbarians to the north. The palace guard remained the sole obstacle between the royal court and the Egyptian army.

Unaware of the immediate danger, a young man sat alone in a small study deep in the palace, engrossed in his work for the drawings of a new temple he had promised the Phoenician King. He always shut himself away for days when concentrating on a new project. The sound of screams in the distance brought him out of his cogitation. Suddenly, the door burst open and two soldiers charged in, their bloodied spears threatening.

They spoke in a strange tongue and though their words sounded unintelligible, the meaning was clear. He stood slowly, hands raised in surrender, when a commanding voice from the corridor ordered the soldiers to lower their weapons and retreat. A high ranking officer appeared and surprised him by speaking Phoenician.

"Who are you?" the officer asked in a calm tone, looking at the drawings scattered on the table.

After his breath returned, the young man answered, "My name is Menefter. I am the Royal architect."

The officer shouted an order to his soldiers, who entered the room again and dragged Menefter away.

Distant screams of death echoed through the palace.

"Where are you taking me?" Menefter yelled. The officer laughed and said, "To the Pharaoh himself, my young friend. It seems your designs for the temples to your gods have captured his imagination and he wishes to meet you. I've told my men to treat you well but if you try to escape they will kill you."

Menefter was thrown at the feet of the Egyptian King, and through an interpreter, told the Pharaoh that he did indeed design the buildings of the city. The Pharaoh told of his love of architecture and spoke at length of his dreams of an

Egyptian treasure city and of ideas for his tomb. At the end of the meeting, Menefter was told that the King liked him. He offered Menefter a chance to prove his skills by drawing plans for a temple to be built in Thebes to honor the god Amon-Re.

Thebes, Egypt 3000 Years Ago

Menefter came to the Palace during the time of celebration for the anniversary of Katara's rise to power following the fall of his Aunt, Ti-mon. Pharaoh ordered a great feast in the palace, and the people of the city joined the festivity with sacrifices to the gods. The occasion was interrupted by the palace guard announcing the arrival of strangers from a distant land who wished to honor the Pharaoh with a gift.

A sudden stillness filled the hall as the visitors entered bearing a chest. Even the Pharaoh's body guards remained uncharacteristically silent and allowed the strangers to approach the king.

"We bring greetings," said one of the three men. He bowed and spoke perfect Egyptian. "This gift is meant as an offering of peace from our people to yours." They set the chest at the foot of the throne.

"Who are your people and where do you come from?" asked Katara.

"We come a great distance from across a vast sea. This gift is from our leader. Please accept it in friendship."

Katara ordered his guard to open the chest. Then he stepped from the throne and moved closer to view its contents. Slowly, he withdrew a crown inlaid with colored stones that seemed to glow with life. The Pharaoh touched the smooth stones, fascinated with their radiance. One of the visitors approached and placed the crown on Katara's head.

The stones changed colors and glowed brightly, causing the guests in the room to gasp in amazement.

The visitors stayed with the King for two days, after which, they left, mysteriously as they had appeared. But the King changed. The visitors and the new crown that Katara now wore exclusively had a mystical effect on him.

Thereafter, Katara fulfilled his image as the living god of Egypt. He brought the country to unparalleled heights of power; every battle won, all enemies vanquished, all subjects loyal. Egypt's borders encompassed an empire larger than she ever knew.

Menefter enjoyed the Pharaoh's favor. During one of their long talks on architecture, the King confided the reason for his success. Only Menefter and a select few knew the secret of the King's power.

Twenty years passed, and the king hurried the preparations for his tomb. Menefter had indeed proven his skills and went on to become not only the Royal architect, but friend to Pharaoh. The greatest honor came with the task of designing and building the Royal burial chamber, which now neared completion.

Menefter surveyed the tomb. More of the Pharaoh's spoils of war and treasure arrived each day for the journey into the King's next life. Golden long boats and chariots, pottery casks filled with wine and grain, thousands of statues, some as big as ten men, carvings of rose alabaster and jewel encrusted shrines, all ready for the Pharaoh's trip down the river of eternity.

Menefter grew up around such treasure; first, the treasure of the King of Phoenicia, then the Pharaoh. He never longed for material things as did other men. Katara liked and trusted him for this reason. But the Pharaoh possessed one thing that fascinated him: the Royal crown. The "crown of the visitor's," as it became known. Menefter remembered the day the visitors came to Thebes.

Now, the artists and scribes neared completion of the task set before them so many years ago: recreate the triumphs of the life of the Pharaoh Katara III on the walls and ceiling of his magnificent tomb.

Stone cutters and masons placed the finishing touches on marble columns and statues that must last a hundred lifetimes for the enjoyment of the Pharaoh.

The Pharaoh purposely chose this mountain for his tomb because of its unusual location, far from the many other tombs in the valley of the kings, where the living gods of Egypt had traditionally been housed for their journey into the next life. Though he never had formal architectural training, the Pharaoh gave Menefter many ideas for the tomb that he claimed appeared in a vision.

Menefter stood inside the tomb and supervised the final work of the artisans. He wore the robes of the Royal court and a ring given to him by Pharaoh.

A messenger arrived and stopped short outside the entrance to the tomb, his chariot carried the Pharaoh's seal. He entered the tomb and knelt before the overseer.

"My lord, Menefter, I bring you greetings from the high priest," he said looking at the ground. His outstretched hand held a papyrus scroll.

"I told you before, my friend, there is no need to bow before me. I am but a humble architect."

"For you, my lord," the messenger remained on one knee.

"Very well, let us see what the old priest wants this time." Menefter took the scroll and read it.

"My lord would do well not to insult the high priest. He commands much power."

"I am not afraid. The old Nile snake and I have fought since the Pharaoh appointed me chief architect and put me in charge of building this tomb. I have the Pharaoh's favor and the priest can do nothing."

The architect's smile disappeared. Menefter looked up after he read the note.

"It is time," he ordered his assistants. "Complete the final preparations. The Pharaoh is dead."

My friend is dead.

Menefter watched the royal scribes finishing the last of the hieroglyphics, and wondered if he would ever truly understand their religious meaning.

No matter. With stone walls this thick, surely no one will ever see them again.

Menefter stared at the dome with its brilliant colors depicting the battle against the Phoenicians that had shaped his life. He thought of his service to Pharaoh, and to the tomb construction, to the feelings of frustration as the task at times seemed unattainable. The tomb cost ten years of labor and the king had considered it a masterpiece of engineering, exceeding even his expectations. The Pharaoh had challenged Menefter to design a robber-proof tomb; no easy task given the intricate designs tried unsuccessfully by many of his predecessors. But he had come up with a new idea: a way to seal the tomb automatically from the inside after the sarcophagus was in place.

Initially, the King remained unconvinced, but after Menefter constructed a small working model, he won the task of designing and building a tomb to house the finest treasure the world ever knew.

Menefter insisted the final work continue through the night, and he fell asleep in the sanctuary. A commotion outside the tomb awakened him. He watched as the Royal guard loaded his workers onto carts and hauled them away.

"Where are you taking them?" he asked the guards who herded the workers together.

"Out of my way. All those who built the tomb are to be put to death at once. This is by order of the high priest."

Menefter wondered if the order included him.

The palace guards departed with their screaming victims, but enough guards remained behind to protect the soon -to- be sealed tomb. With his task completed, Menefter gathered his belongings and traveled across the Nile to take his place in the Royal funeral procession.

The Pharaoh's death saddened the people. Preparations for the king's journey to the land of eternal life began on the great sun boat, which always bore Royal remains to the valley of the kings. Fifty Nubian slaves and mourners would accompany the boat across the Nile to the tomb. Three smaller Sun Boats would then bring the final items of treasure, food and wine that the Pharaoh needs for his journey into the next life.

Terrible mourning consumed the people in the following days. But they also celebrated the Pharaoh's immortality. The royal physicians had prepared the king's body according to custom. The funeral procession would pass through the Avenue of the Sphinxes and across the Nile to the west where the tomb awaited.

Menefter received word that the King mentioned him in his will. It pleased him to think that his years of loyalty would be rewarded. He and his wife, Ashanti, waited outside the priest's chamber. The door opened slowly. Menefter and Ashanti entered the sacred hall.

"Sit down," ordered the high priest.

The door slammed and two guards blocked the exit.

"You and I have had our differences through the years, my lord architect. I am willing to forgive you and forget the past. All that is required of you is some information."

Menefter and Ashanti sat silently, though they knew what the priest wanted.

"Tell me the secret of the King's power and I will let you live and prosper."

"Say nothing," said Ashanti.

"Ah, the woman knows the answer," said the priest.

"She knows nothing. Let her go," said Menefter.

The priest motioned to one of the guards, who approached Ashanti and lifted her off the chair.

Still, Menefter said nothing. The guard held a small dagger at Ashanti's throat, the blade tight against her skin.

"Tell me now."

Menefter shared her pain. The sharpened metal penetrated her skin. She screamed as tiny droplets of blood oozed from the incision.

"The scepter," he yelled. "The magic is from the scepter." Menefter lied and kept the vow of secrecy he swore to the King.

The holy man ordered the knife away from Ashanti's throat. The priest approached Menefter and noticed the Pharonic seal on a gold medallion around his neck. He glared at the symbol and ripped it from Menefter's neck.

"We are aware that you were not born to Egyptian parents. We also know that you do not believe in the gods that we worship. It is for these reasons that we tried to convince our King that it was unseemly and inappropriate to bestow upon you the high honor that he insisted belonged to you by way of the deeds and service you rendered to the Royal Court."

Old Nile snake.

Menefter sat on the edge of his seat.

What did the priest mean? What honor?

The priest smiled, then continued reading from the papyrus scroll. "It is my wish that for excellent and unquestioned service in my name, my architect and friend be given a place of honor in the royal funeral procession, that he share with me my joy in the palace of dreams which he has created for my eternal life."

The priest put down the scroll and laughed.

"Those are not the King's words," said Menefter. The color drained from his face, certain the document was forged. He knew that without the King's protection, the high priest must finally have his way. Menefter lunged for the priest, but the guards apprehended him.

"Here, now," ordered the priest, pointing to the floor.

Immediately, the Nubian guard grabbed Menefter. Once on the floor, the guards held his arms and legs while the priest poured a sour, foul smelling, thick liquid down his throat. He gagged at the strong taste, but enough of the foul potion went down to satisfy the priest.

"Ashanti, I love you." Menefter called out to his wife.

"Prepare him for the ceremony and burn her."

"No!," Ashanti cried. She freed herself and ran to Menefter. The guards separated them and dragged her away. They carried Menefter out of the chamber, bound and unable to move his arms or legs but still fully conscious.

Ashanti, my beloved, I will never see you again.

First, the temple servants removed his clothing and bathed him in scented water. Next, he dressed in the finest golden tunic from the East.

Why had I not pretended to believe in the foolish Egyptian gods and their afterlife? Those statues I have become so accustomed to, now seem hateful. If only I had not been so foolish to make an enemy of this priest and sworn to the king to protect the secret of his mind control power.

Paralyzed and helpless, Menefter joined the procession through the city toward the Temple of Karnac. Only those going into the tomb to be buried with the Pharaoh would be allowed onto the great sun boat for the trip west across the Nile into the mountains.

The Egyptian people filled the streets cheering and crying. Slowly, the procession moved through the city and Menefter saw smoke from the fire in the temple courtyard.

Ashanti was dead.

A small boy stood by his mother's side and held onto a goat. Menefter's eyes met his and for an instant, the boy's innocence touched him. Tears welled in the small eyes, then fell onto his cheek as he raised his hand in a quiet wave of farewell. Unable to return the gesture, Menefter watched as the crowd swallowed the boy, trying to get a last glimpse of their dead leader.

Only the low chanting of the priests echoed through the monolithic columns and statues of the gods in the massive Temple of Karnac. The group moved out of the Temple gates, past the Avenue of a Thousand Sphinx's, toward the Nile River.

As the coffin received the Pharaoh's body, Menefter noticed the Crown of the Visitors on his head; the divine crown that came to symbolize his power, the joining of upper and lower Egypt, and the power of the empire that Katara had forged. This, in accordance with a direct order from the King on his death bed.

The cursed crown. I will die because of the secret of the crown.

Still unable to move or speak, Menefter and the priests joined a small number of honored others and the boat slowly made its way across the river, into the desert mountains, to the King's final resting place.

The heat of the sun reflected off the desert sands, rising in waves, distorting the image of the distant mountains and trees. A small village that once housed the tomb workers remained quiet and empty now; its inhabitants slaughtered for what they knew. These simple people had devoted their lives to their king, only to be rewarded by the high priest with a blade through the heart.

The royal assemblage approached its final destination. All the years of work failed to prepare Menefter for this moment. He always tried to separate the purpose of the tomb from the work, and the job of building became a purpose unto itself. It took so long, he forgot that one day it would be finished.

All those years, he never dreamed he had constructed his own tomb.

As they entered the antechamber, Menefter strained for a last glimpse at the sun and blue sky. A swarm of hungry vultures hovered and dove toward the worker's village near the tomb, their dead and rotting human prey lay scattered in the scorching sand that eventually reclaimed even the bones of those who lost the battle of life to the desert.

The tomb's antechamber consisted of a cluster of small rooms designed to look like a tomb. A small amount of treasure placed here attempted to fool trespassers into believing they were looking at the main tomb. Even a decorated sarcophagus completed the picture. Many staircases placed around the entrance might further confuse would-be grave robbers.

With the entire entourage now in the inner chamber, the Nubian slaves returned to the tomb entrance to begin their final job. A small pile of bricks and mortar closed the entryway from the inside. Brick by brick, the last rays of sun grew thinner. One of the priests lit the oil lamps mounted on the walls throughout the tomb. The lamps provided dim light for them to complete their final ceremonial tasks.

Watching the slaves work, Menefter knew that on the other side, a layer of rough, stone-like mortar applied to the outside of the wall rendered the entrance almost invisible. All of this his own design.

Propped up on a carved chair beside the golden chariots and life-size statues of the king, Menefter's leg twitched suddenly and he believed that the drug left him.

If only I could move before the king's body is placed into the giant coffin, I might still fight my way out of here. The mortar is still wet and. . .

"No, no!" he cried out as the paralyzing drug released his vocal cords. He watched in horror as the Nubian slaves lifted the coffin into the sarcophagus.

The platform under the coffin filled with water. As the increased weight of the sarcophagus caused the water to run off, small pipes collected this water and emptied it into another system of pipes near the inner entrance to the tomb. The running water caused a finely balanced valve to open. This in turn allowed sand held in a container to empty. A series of sand filled containers drained in turn until the final one emptied. Once accomplished, the huge stone blocks held in place by the sand slid into place, until the entire inner opening of the tomb sealed with a stone wall two feet thick.

Menefter remembered the day he had presented this design to the Pharaoh. Katara thought it most ingenious, and praised the plan as the first truly robber-proof tomb he had ever seen.

Their job complete, the Pharaoh's personal slaves sat in a corner of the main chamber. The priests chanted, grouped around a giant statue of Horus. Menefter looked at the lively scenes painted on the walls and dome of the chamber.

What if there is an afterlife?

He searched for courage.

The faint sound of running sand brought him out of the trance. He felt a low rumbling and the floor shook. The irreversible process that would seal the tomb forever, began. The silence suddenly broke as the first stones fell into place. A cloud of dust filled the tomb and the inner opening disappeared. The sound of the falling stones so deafened him, that he screamed and held his hands over his ears.

I can move. The drug has worn off.

But it was too late to save himself. Menefter stood and ran to the newly formed wall, pounding on the massive granite edifice.

"I don't want to die!"

The priests turned to look for a moment then returned to their meditation. He sank slowly to his knees, cried softly, and grabbed a small golden statue of Osiris.

Why are the priests unafraid? Perhaps if I believed as they do. . .

He pressed the god to his heart and prayed for strength and acceptance.

The flickering oil lamps cast an eerie glow on the walls of the tomb. The magnificent hieroglyphics and reliefs carved into the tomb walls and dome meant nothing.

The priests filled a silver temple cup with wine and each drank from the cup. Menefter turned away and when he looked back in the next moment, they all lay dead at the foot of the statue.

For a long while he sat motionless, mentally exhausted. He contemplated the poisoned wine, but realized he did not have the courage to drink it.

The air smelled stale and his lungs ached with each forced

breath.

Drifting in and out of consciousness, his mind filled with the deeds of his life. Without the sun, day and night joined as one and time stopped.

He sat on the ground, clutching the golden statue.

"Ashanti. . ."

The last light from the lamps faded.

One

RIPPLING WAVES LAPPED AGAINST THE BOW OF A rusted red and blue tanker docked next to the International Development Corporation oil drilling platform #279 in the middle of the Gulf of Mexico. Jake Parker leaned on the safety rail of the upper level of the oil rig and squinted through his dark glasses into the intense morning sun that reflected off calm, blue water. He watched the rig crew throw the last of the lines to the waiting hands on the ship's deck. Through most of the night, the ship tapped into the pipeline and filled her waiting holds with the black liquid cargo. A school of dolphin at play near the stern of the ship caught Jake's eye. They reminded him of happier times when he and his wife and son spent so much time on their boat in the Florida Keys. They had always seen dolphin jumping, almost inviting them to join in the fun. Now, his only family was the company, or InDevCo as its employee's called it. One of the largest corporations in the world, it handled many government contracts including research and manufacturing anything from weapons to high tech space hardware.

Because of the secretive nature of much of its work, the company maintained a large security force and had no trouble policing itself in matters of internal affairs.

The core of this security force consisted of a cadre of special agents, trained to handle problems in any sector of the company. Many in the elite order were former military personnel, accustomed to rigorous training. Known to the company as Inner Core Agents, or ICA's, their commandments were few: survival, secrecy and loyalty to the company. The word *impossible* did not exist for them.

Jake had joined the crew of the platform three weeks ago, ordered there by an override command directly from the CEO's office. This order had the highest priority; investigate the disappearance of twenty-five percent of the oil produced by the platform. His job as a computer and communications expert allowed him free access to the main computer that coordinated the necessities of life on the rig, and he used this to monitor the lives of everyone on board.

Jake watched the ship pull away from the loading area and made a mental note of the name painted in white on her stern. "Conquistador Del Mar," certainly indicated Latin American origin, but the country of registry was conspicuously absent and she flew a flag he did not recognize. He made a mental note to investigate this later.

The ship distanced herself from the docking area and Jake noticed how low she rode in the water; she'd had her fill of their oil. His morning check of the commander's computer log made no mention of the 'Conquistador,' nor any other ship taking on oil today.

They sure are blatant about this.

Jake rubbed his eyes. He felt exhausted after a fifteen hour shift and his body ached for sleep. In his mind, he reviewed the names of the men responsible for the 'lost oil.' He would transmit his coded report to the ICA office today and join the supply helicopter on its return flight to the mainland tomorrow morning. Central control would take it from there. He'd had enough of oil rig life.

With the Conquistador Del Mar just a speck on the

southern horizon, Jake headed for the communications room on the opposite side of the platform. He watched two special teams as they tested the new mini-sub delivered one week ago. According to the manifest, it was designed to perform rig anchorage maintenance and other lengthy and high risk underwater tasks. The first job of the sub's crew was the assembly of a prefabricated docking base that would allow the sub to stay down for long periods. This underwater facility served as a parking garage for the sub.

Jake passed the open door of the air-conditioned mess hall and felt a blast of cool air escape from the room. The aroma of bacon and sausage reminded him that he'd not yet eaten. Men crowded around the big screen video-television watching an emergency weather bulletin transmitted via satellite from Tampa. He listened for a moment, then moved on.

Jake took advantage of the quiet time and continued on his way to the deserted radio room. Once inside, he sat at the console, placed the headset on his ears, fixed the signal on the satellite and established a radio link with the now distant ship.

"This is InDevCo 279, to Conquistador Del Mar. Do you read?"

The voice reply came in Spanish. "We read you 279. Why do you make contact? Is there a problem?"

"No, I just need your exact time of departure for my log entry," said Jake in his best Spanish.

The voice sounded annoyed. "8:05 hours."

"Thanks. InDevCo out." Jake turned to a computer tracking console next to the radio, and programmed the trace. Instantly, the computer screen lit up with the exact course and speed of the vessel. He entered the command, and waited.

"Most probable destination within given parameters:

Havana, Cuba."

Jake stared at the screen for a moment, then turned his attention to the radio once again.

"This is InDevCo 279 calling central command. Do you read?"

"This is central comm-link. Make your report, 279."

Before Jake could answer, something cold and hard pressed against the back of his neck. He turned around slowly and looked at the point of a weapon he had never seen before.

"Interesting looking gun," Jake said, calmly removing the headset. "What's it called?"

"A Lorestron 'blow your head off' gun. Now, stand up, slowly."

Two men had silently followed Jake and entered the radio room after he'd put the headphones on. Pat Young worked on the drilling lines. Eddie Garcia's title was assistant to the head of operations. Jake suspected Eddie, but he did not know Pat, except for a chance meeting in the mess hall.

Eddie held the gun at Jake's head. He was two hundred pounds of muscle wedged into a black tee-shirt. Jake thought he could beat Eddie in a fair fight, though he outweighed Jake by thirty to forty pounds. Jake was slim, but powerfully built.

"Who's on the other end?" Eddie asked pointing to the computer screen. He saw the words *Havana, Cuba.*

"I just checked on the weather report and I. . . ."

Suddenly, Pat punched Jake in the stomach, knocking the wind out of him. Jake doubled over.

"You been asking a lot of goddamned questions about things that don't concern you, pretty boy," said Pat.

Some of the men gave Jake that nickname because of his boyish good looks. His straight, dark hair complemented his translucent eyes; the left eye blue, and the right one, green.

Two large dimples framed his face when he smiled. He looked much younger than his thirty-five years.

"Maybe he's one of those guys that has to know tomorrow's weather so his *mommy* can put out his clothes," said Eddie. Both howled with laughter. "Now, why don't you tell us who the fuck you really are, mister?"

Jake glanced at the exit door and judged his chances for escape. The radio room had only one door blocked by Eddie. Eddie's finger tightly wrapped around the trigger of the odd gun, and Jake felt he wouldn't hesitate to shoot him if he made a wrong move.

Jake straightened up slowly. "We're all working for the same boss, boys. Let's talk this over. Look at the time. Break's over, time to get back to work." Jake raised his arm to show Pat his watch and hit him in the face with his right hand, breaking his nose. Blood trickled out of Pat's nostrils. At the same time, he kicked the gun out of Eddie's hand sending it flying toward the ceiling. The gun discharged, but missed Jake and blasted a hole in the wall, fusing the entire communication system.

Momentarily distracted, Eddie quickly regained control and caught Jake by the shoulder as he tried to run for the door. Pulling him back, Eddie held Jake in a headlock. Before he could break the hold, Pat recovered sufficiently to join in the fight and gave Jake a snap-kick to the groin. With Eddie holding him down, Pat continued beating Jake. Blinding white pain overpowered him. Finally, his strength gone, he vaguely sensed that the beating had stopped. With the last of his consciousness fading, he felt himself being dragged from the radio room.

When Jake awoke, he found himself locked in a storage

room somewhere in the lower levels of the platform. He was alone and could not hear any activity nearby. He tried to stand, but a searing pain in his abdomen and chest stopped him. Slowly, he got up.

No broken bones.

This level served as a storage area for drilling supplies and large spare parts. The smell of grease hung in the air like a fog. A locked caged area used to store electronic equipment and expensive drill bits held him prisoner.

He called out; no one answered.

Then, as he scanned the open area, he saw something on the column at the far end of the room. A light attached to a timer on a large clump of plastic explosive flashed red.

Jake knew he had to deactivate the bomb to save himself and the other men on the platform. He looked at his watch and realized twenty-four hours had passed in unconsciousness. Suddenly, he felt a strong vibration that came from the foundation of the rig. A loud noise followed, like the sound of twisting metal. Jake wasted no more time, and quickly removed his belt. A locksmith's pick attached to the inside of his belt fit into the lock on the cage door. After a few seconds, the lock sprang open with the door. He ran toward the bomb. The sensitive timer-trigger counted down the minutes until detonation: seventeen minutes. All his training in bomb electronics told him that there was no way to deactivate it.

He ran for the door; a solid steel hatch locked from the outside. There were no other exits. Jake spotted a ventilation grill above the door. He stood on a storage barrel and removed the grill cover. Ignoring the pain that screamed in his side, he crawled into the narrow shaft and pulled himself away from the storage room. Again he felt a strong vibration that shook the entire platform.

After crawling a great distance, he stopped and looked through the nearest opening. The mess area appeared deserted. He kicked the grill out with both feet and slid out into the room. His watch read 9:13 hours, only minutes to go before the blast. Though morning, no light shone through the nearby windows.

He approached the window cautiously and stared in horror as twenty-foot waves battered the structure. The sky was almost totally black and sheets of rain driven by strong winds pounded the windows like tiny nails.

The wind gauge in the mess hall stuck on 120 miles per hour. He tapped on the glass, and the indicator needle darted to the end of the scale; 160 miles per hour.

A large supporting beam beneath the mess area succumbed to the pressure of the pounding sea. Jake ran down the corridor, making his way to the main supply and storage area. With all the windows shattering, the wind swirled around him and doors banged open and closed. Jake reached for one of the many wet suits and tanks that hung neatly on the racks; the air gauge on the tank read full. He stripped off his clothes, suited up quickly, grabbed a waterproof flashlight and glanced at his watch.

Three minutes left. Time to leave.

The door flew fully open and the force of the wind threw him to the floor. Struggling against the power of the wind and torrential rain, he left the supply room and released an emergency escape slide. The wind tossed it around like confetti. Finally, inside the chute, the weight of his body stabilized it somewhat. He let himself go and slid down into the sea, barely missing a support beam that came loose and swung free. Little time remained before the explosion would bring the entire platform crashing down.

In the churning sea, Jake freed himself from the slide and tried to find his directional bearings. He swam away from the doomed rig, but the immense waves pushed him around like a cork. With every advance, the currents forced him halfway back. It was impossible to judge the distance. A flash of lightning cracked the sky apart and illuminated the almost invisible platform.

The rig still posed an immediate danger to him.

Summoning all his strength, he distanced himself from the impending disaster. Through the howling wind and rain, he saw three explosive flashes.

Lightning showed him brief outlines of the platform as it lost all three of its supports, collapsing into the churning sea. Jake floated and tried to regain his spent energy. It would be easy to surrender himself to the sea and end the struggle, but his will to survive prevailed.

No time for self pity. God, I hate the dark, but no choice.

He dove under the mountainous waves and headed for the bottom.

The storm should have little effect at the this depth.

The sea bottom appeared at 78 feet. He snapped the depth finder on his watch to be sure it worked properly. Turbulence stirred up the sandy bottom and caused poor visibility. Light from the flashlight reflected off the particles suspended in the water.

A hammerhead shark nudged his foot. Jake cursed his bad luck as three more sharks circled him. He took out his knife and planned his strategy. The poor visibility worked against him. He knew that once the sharks started a feeding frenzy, there would be no chance. Trying to observe and guard all sides at once, Jake chose his target.

A baby hammerhead passed within inches and Jake sliced open its belly as it swam. Blood surged from the wound sending an olfactory signal to every shark in the area. The other sharks quickly picked up the scent and attacked. Jake swam like a bullet away from the scene.

Safe for the moment, he glanced at his watch again.

Five minutes of air left in the tank.

A distance indicator on the watch read 50 feet, SW. The compass pointed the way and he swam toward his only chance of survival.

Please let it still be there.

In the distance he saw its shape and faint color; round and yellow. The minisub tucked neatly into its berth. He carefully untied the mooring lines and entered the airlock. The air flow from his tank stopped just as he reached the chamber. He held his breath and ripped the mask from his face. The water drained out of the airlock slowly, but the tanks on the sub were full. He removed his wetsuit and equipment and slipped on a dry InDevCo uniform. Then, he sat in the control seat to begin a systems check.

All indicators read green and normal after setting a course for the nearest landfall. He engaged the auto pilot. The engine whirred and came to life, stirring up the sand beneath him. The tiny ship lifted off the sea floor and gradually picked up speed; the purr of the engine the only audible sound.

The sub's headlight illuminated the dark underworld only a short distance in front of him. Jake allowed himself to relax for the first time since the ordeal began. His thoughts drifted to the surface, where mother nature vented her fury against the Earth. In contrast, the gentle swaying of the sea vegetation reminded him of her beauty, even in such an inhospitable place.

Exhaustion crept over him.
Must close my eyes.
Just for a moment.
Just a moment. . .

Two

THE TINY, YELLOW MINI-SUB BOBBED HELPLESSLY IN smooth waters considerably different from the previous day's convulsive weather. Endless blue sea surrounded Jake and tropical sun bathed the eastern gulf of Mexico with intense light and heat through a cloudless sky. Jake awoke and found himself on the surface; the sub's batteries dead. He silently thanked the ship's designers who incorporated an automatic surface program into the computer if battery power failed for any reason. A tiny trickle of energy from back-up batteries fed an emergency transmitter that sent a continuous, though weak, SOS to anyone close enough to receive it. Not enough reserve power remained to transmit a voice message, and Jake guessed at least 200 miles separated him from the west coast of Florida. With power gone, the ship drifted with the prevailing currents.

Jake stayed in the sub to escape the scorching sun. The inside temperature gauge read over one hundred degrees. He stripped off his uniform and kept cool by blotting a sea-water soaked shirt against his skin. He knew the emergency kit in the sub contained enough food and water for two days.

The sun crept across the sky; the scenery unchanged throughout the day except for an occasional flying fish or dolphin. Jake figured he could catch enough fish to keep his stomach quiet, but water was another question. All the survival training in the world couldn't teach the human body to continue to function without fresh water. Still, he busied himself, trying to believe that he would soon be rescued.

The sky reached out and over the clear blue horizon that wrapped around the sea; as if the hurricane had scrubbed the sky clean. With the absence of clouds, a rainbow sheen reflected off the twilight waters.

Thankfully, the temperature dropped to comfortable levels at dusk. Jake fixed a crude fishing line from a spool of electrical wire he found in a tiny storage bin near the airlock. He used a piece of meat from his emergency rations to bait a bent nail, now turned fish hook, sat on the bow of the sub and watched the line and the sunset; thoughts his only companion.

The sun sank below the horizon, and darkness quickly shrouded the ship. There was no moon this night and the stars touched the sea. Jake stared at a sky filled with countless twinkling lights. Only the familiar sight of the stars and the smell of the sea enabled him to overcome the anxiety and loneliness.

There are more stars in the heavens than there are grains of sand on the Earth.

He remembered his father had told him about the stars one summer night on the beach.

Are there other people out there?

His father had shrugged his shoulders.

Jake believed with all his heart that there had to be other intelligent life somewhere in the vastness of the universe.

How arrogant we are to think that we are alone in the cosmos.

He fought a stab of feelings from the past. A tug on the line brought him back to the present. He'd caught a small bluefish. The fish thrashed around and Jake threw it into the open top hatch of the sub.

Never cared much for Sushi.

At dawn, Jake awakened to the sound of a distant helicopter. He searched the clear sky for a sign that it was real. A dot on the horizon stood out against the vast expanse of the sea. Jake retrieved a small piece of aluminum foil from the food kit and smoothed it with his fingernail. Then, he stretched it out and held it flat to reflect the sun's rays. The sound of the aircraft's engine increased with each minute.

They see me.

He waved his arms wildly as the craft approached.

The coast guard helicopter hovered overhead whipping the water, creating gale force winds around the tiny sub. Jake protected his eyes from the gusts but saw the cable that dropped from the ship. He waited a long minute while the harness lowered, grabbed the line and wrapped it around his waist. It lifted him to the aircraft, then the ship's engine increased power and rose slowly. Jake watched the sub bob in the water as it grew smaller.

"Is that you, Harry?" yelled Jake, hanging from the winch just outside the door to the chopper. Once inside, he removed the harness and the two men embraced.

"Of course, little brother. Don't I always come charging to your rescue? What have you gotten yourself into this time that I find you floating in the middle of the sea?"

"You mean up the creek without a paddle? How'd you find me?" Jake asked ignoring the question. He gulped a cup of water as the ship headed east toward the coast of Florida.

"We picked up your distress call, but it was so weak that we kept losing it. Then, your reflector trick caught the pilot's attention." Harry handed Jake a candy bar. "Your sixth sense really saved you again."

"What do you mean?

"You know very well what I mean. You and I have always been tuned to each other. I can sense when you're in danger. It would probably work the other way around, except I don't get involved in these crazy schemes like you."

"This wasn't a scheme. I was on a company assignment."

"Floating in the middle of the sea without food or water is an assignment? I'd turn in my resignation, if I were you."

"No, you don't understand, but I can't talk about it."

"I think for once I agree with Mom. It's time you got a real job."

"Look, my work is important to me and leave Mom out of this, Harry. I don't want to argue. You'll just have to accept the fact that my work is confidential and carries some risks."

"That's fine, except I spend half my life chasing after you to get you out of these risky jobs. If you have a death wish, turn off your mental SOS and leave me alone."

"Harry, we've been through this before. I can't..."

Harry held up his hand as if to say he understood. After all, they were brothers. It didn't matter that Jake couldn't confide in him. He would always be there to pluck him out of danger. Like the time they were diving together off the coast of Key West, searching for Spanish treasure. Jake wandered off and caught his leg in the wreck of an old galleon. After trying unsuccessfully to free himself and almost out of air, Harry found him, and with nothing but brute strength, lifted the rotting timbers that held him. Jake lost consciousness during the return to the surface and remembered nothing of being rescued by Harry.

Jake smiled at Harry and squeezed his shoulder. "All you have to do is come to work for the company and we can share all this fun stuff I do."

Harry laughed. "No thanks. I'm getting too old for your kind of fun."

Harry was older than Jake, but he was still in excellent shape. On the tall side of six feet, he had soft, watchful, dark brown eyes that missed nothing. His rugged good looks belied his soft spoken manner and gentle personality. At forty years old and gray at the temples, he still attracted his share of glances from younger women.

"At least say you'll think about it." Jake tried to stand, and winced in pain.

"What's wrong?" asked Harry.

"It's nothing. I'm a little sore from the workout on the rig. I assume you know about the oil rig." He didn't want to tell Harry about the beating he'd taken from Pat and Eddie. That was a score he'd settle himself.

"Yeah, the platform. I guess the storm destroyed it. It's completely gone. Were there any other survivors?"

"Don't know," Jake said, recalling the events that led to the platform's demise. He smiled at the thought of revenge against Pat and Eddie.

The sight of the Florida coastline caused a flurry of activity in the chopper in preparation for landing, but Jake was unprepared for what he saw below. The hurricane had rained destruction on the entire Tampa Bay area.

"Looks like we just lost some bloody war," Jake said, still in shock. The city took the full force of the storm.

"It was hurricane Diane; the storm of the century. This was the big one that they knew would come some day. Look there." Harry pointed to the port of Tampa, where an abandoned tanker lay on her starboard side in the middle of a nearby downtown street. "We'll land at a small section of the airport that's clear of debris. It'll be a week or more before it can open to commercial traffic."

"Harry, you never did tell me why you were in Tampa."

"I came in to help with the relief effort. You know me Jake, I can't resist a good cause."

Jake remembered too well how Harry always gave away whatever he had. Material things just weren't important to him. Harry seemed so happy that Jake could say nothing.

Who's to say whats right?

"What are your plans now, Jake?"

Jake was engrossed with the scene outside the chopper window as it landed; roofless buildings, shattered glass and trees stripped of all their leaves. "No plans. I have to call my office if I can, but I'm free for the next few days."

"Come with me," said Harry. "These people need all the help they can get. Besides, it'll do you good to work for free for a change. Volunteer work cleanses the soul and Lord knows your's need a bath."

Jake laughed. "If you weren't my brother, I'd..."

Harry slapped him on the back, then hugged him.

"I'm glad you're okay, little brother." He knew Jake hated it when he called him that.

Jake called his office on a cellular phone, then he and Harry wandered through the streets of the city for many hours. Occasionally, they stopped to help a rescue team clearing debris, looking for the dead and injured. The storm surge caught hurricane partygoers by surprise and many had drowned. Despite the desperate pleadings of local officials, these people never believed they were in any danger and stayed in their seaside homes. The tidal wave which engulfed the area was a wall of water twenty feet high, and much of the beach had washed away. So too did the piling foundations of many of the newer high rise buildings, causing their collapse. Anyone who stayed behind died.

Crews of federal soldiers had constructed a tent city where the now homeless population could have a dry place to live until their homes were rebuilt. The officer in charge of the work detail assigned Jake and Harry to a group fixing the roof of a church.

The high humidity, temperature, and sun sizzled in the late summer sky. Ominous, black clouds swelled over the bay and the sound of distant thunder warned of their approach. The first drops splashed out of the sky and the men were called off the roof. Jake was glad for the break. Once on the ground, he took a hose and doused his head with cool water. He joined Harry and the other men inside the church to avoid the tropical lightning. They were soaked to the skin with perspiration and water.

The workers gathered around a tray of sandwiches offered by the priest.

"This is a day for first's," said Harry.

"What do you mean?"

"Well, here you are on a job that has nothing to do with InDevCo and you're inside a church. Could it be the great Jake Parker is getting soft in his old age? You haven't set foot in a church since Dad died."

Just as Jake was about to answer, the priest approached him.

"Are you Mr. Parker?"

Harry and Jake turned and said, "yes."

"I'm looking for Mr. Jake Parker." Jake stepped forward. "There's someone looking for you outside."

Jake and Harry left the church and descended the steps. The sight of a black stretch limousine with the InDevCo company seal on the door greeted them. The driver's door opened and a uniformed chauffeur stepped out and approached them.

"Jake Parker?" he asked.

"That's me. What can I do for you?"

The man handed Jake an envelope with an 18 carat gold border and his name engraved in gold on the front.

"Step into the car, Mr. Parker."

Three

JAKE EXAMINED THE CREAMY-COLORED, ENGRAVED envelope slowly, then he looked at Harry with questioning eyes and opened it.

"What's this about?" he asked Harry.

"Damned if I know. What's it say?"

Jake removed a gold embossed invitation from the envelope, and read aloud. "The pleasure of your company is hereby requested at the season's end Labor Day celebration- The residence of Mrs. Ruth Cromwell, Newport, Rhode Island."

Harry took the card and reread it. "Cromwell, Cromwell, where have I heard that name recently?"

"Philip Cromwell is the CEO of InDevCo," Jake answered. He took the invitation back and dabbed at a drop of sweat that fell onto the card. "Why in the world would they invite me to a fancy society party?"

"Now I remember," said Harry. "I saw an article in the Wall Street Journal last month about Cromwell. Seems he died under mysterious circumstances. I think it said they found his car abandoned and never found the body."

"Philip Cromwell is dead? Wonder why I hadn't heard?"

"Probably because you were in the middle of the Gulf of Mexico. Are you going to accept?"

"What do you think? Your intuition is usually pretty good."

"I never turn down an invite from a lady."

Jake approached the chauffeur, invitation in hand.

"Sorry, but I don't have any clean clothes," he said to the driver. Jake was shirtless and dripping with perspiration.

"Please step into the car, sir."

"I just won't sit on the seat," Jake said.

"Go ahead, little brother. I'll find you somehow and check in with you later." Harry nudged Jake toward the car. The driver opened the back door and Jake stepped in. Given his appearance, he felt uneasy in the luxury of the limousine.

Jake tapped on the glass partition. "Any chance of a hot shower before the trip? I must smell like low tide."

The panel slid open and Jake repeated the question. "Most definitely, sir."

"More like an open cesspool," mumbled Jake.

The stretched car drove onto a newly cleared runway of a private airport and stopped in front of a waiting 767 customized jet with the words "InDevCo." painted in large, red letters on the body of the plane. The driver stepped out and opened the door for Jake.

Jake exited and pointed to the plane. The chauffeur nodded, got back into the car and drove away. Jake stood at the foot of the stairway and tried to see into the plane. He climbed the stairs cautiously until he was at the top. Seemingly alone, he walked into the cabin.

The lavishly decorated interior stunned his senses. It was obviously the VIP jet, yet he wondered, "Why the royal treatment?"

Plush couches formed a conversation area while a conference room contained a large table with several chairs around it. A full kitchen and a bedroom with a private bathroom completed the interior. In the bathroom, a white terrycloth robe hung on a valet next to the shower. It had the initials JP on the pocket.

Jake moved back into the cabin and made his way forward toward the cockpit. He knocked on the door and waited. When there was no response, he opened the door.

Two mechanical men sat at the controls.

They're god damned robots.

They were involved with the preflight check and paid no attention to Jake.

"Hello? Anyone else on board?" The robotic captain and his co-pilot said nothing. "Not much for conversation are you?" Jake returned to the cabin feeling uncomfortable about his decision to get on the mysterious plane.

The aircraft moved onto the runway and taxied into position for takeoff. Jake disregarded the flashing seat belt sign, stripped and stepped into the shower; a hot water chill flashed through him. He felt the plane lift off, but continued to enjoy the soothing sensation of the massaging water on his sore muscles. Suddenly, the plane heaved as a pocket of turbulence tossed Jake around in the shower like a rubber ball. When the disturbance ended, Jake found himself on the floor of the shower.

After the excitement of the shower, Jake wrapped himself in the thick robe and went into the lounge for a drink. A filled ice bucket and fine crystal glasses lined the bar, but there were no bottles. A drink dispenser flashed ready when Jake picked up one of the glasses and filled it with ice. He placed it on the tray and a synthesized voice spoke.

"Please state drink preference."

"Scotch," he answered into the machine. In less than fifteen seconds, an amber liquid filled the glass. Jake tasted the drink and smiled. He'd never seen anything like this before.

Jake sat on the white leather couch and picked up a

handwritten note that was attached to the cover of one of several magazines on the cocktail table.

"Dear Mr. Parker, please read these articles about my husband, Philip." It was signed, "RC."

He selected a six-month-old issue of Time Magazine from several on the cocktail table in front of him. Philip Cromwell's distinctive face graced the cover, posing with his wife, Ruth. Jake scanned the pages, read the stories and brief autobiography of the man that headed one of the largest conglomerates in the world. A newer issue of Money, portrayed Philip Cromwell as a trailblazer in the financial world. "A man who built an empire from humble beginnings," read the caption.

The latest issue of New Yorker Magazine also had devoted their cover to Philip Cromwell, but Jake discovered something more in the in-depth article that chronicled the entire Cromwell family. Jake read about the early days of the company, its phenomenal rise to world class conglomerate and the man that captained this ship of success. But the Cromwell family had its share of problems. The reporter had done his homework. Jake read intently about the Cromwell's two sons, Charles and Andrew.

"The Cromwell family has had great success through the years in maintaining privacy. Until recently, little was known of the wife and two sons of the CEO of InDevCo. Charles, the eldest son, does not seem to fit the image of the Newport elite. His public image is quite different from the recently uncovered truth, when a former Cromwell employee disclosed startling facts that indicate that Charles is a barely tolerated misfit who is shunned by the Newport wealthy, including his own father!" Jake looked up from the page.

What am I getting myself into?

Sunlight streamed into the open curtained windows of the jet as it landed and pulled in front of a free standing building. Jake looked outside and saw a white stretch limousine drive onto the runway and stop at the base of a mobile stairway rolled into place at the exit door of the aircraft. Jake looked in the mirror and fixed his tie. The double breasted suit that hung in the bedroom closet fit him perfectly, as did the shoes and shirt. He waited a moment and opened the hatch.

The door to the limo opened automatically when he reached the bottom of the stairway. The dark tinted window prevented him from seeing the driver and he hesitated, then stepped into the car. The door closed and the car pulled away.

Feeling rested and relaxed, he occupied himself with the ever changing scenery and thought he could cope with any situation. A brisk wind skimmed the sloping hills and the treetops stirred in unison to the early nor-easter. The ride from the airport lasted about an hour.

The car pulled up to a large, wrought iron gate which opened in response to a signal from the driver. The drive to the house revealed immaculately manicured lawns with graceful, sculpted trees lining the road. A legion of gardeners hurried to place the finishing touches on the flower beds and planters.

The car finally stopped in front of a stately Victorian mansion. Imposing white marble columns supported the porte-cochere that led to two enormous etched glass doors with polished brass trim. The car door opened and Jake stepped out.

A uniformed servant approached and greeted him. “Mrs. Cromwell is expecting you, Mr. Parker. Thomas will escort you to the library.”

“Thanks,” said Jake.

Thomas cleared his throat. "This way, sir."

Jake followed him into the house. Fresh flowers filled every corner of the pink marble columned room. Two formal circular stairways wound their way to the upper levels from opposite sides of the foyer. A large C was inlaid into the marble floor just beneath a crystal chandelier. Jake had heard of the homes of the Newport wealthy but he thought this lifestyle disappeared with the depression.

Passing through the marble foyer with its majestic staircase, Jake tried to get a glimpse of some of the other rooms. He purposely lagged behind, and stepped into the grand ballroom. It buzzed with activity; servants prepared for the night's festivities. Two crystal chandeliers hung from ceilings covered with frescoes and ornate gilded carvings. A painting of Napoleon dominated the wall over a white marble mantle.

People actually live here.

"This way, Mr. Parker," Thomas said in an icy tone.

"Oh, sure," Jake responded. "What's the occasion for the party?"

"Mrs. Cromwell always hosts the Labor Day society gathering. Please wait in the library, sir."

Jake nodded and stood in front of two carved, heavy wooden doors that opened slowly. A tall, uniformed servant greeted him by name.

"Please follow me, Mr. Parker."

How the hell do they all know my name?

Jake sat on an antique couch and accepted an offer of champagne. "Mrs. Cromwell will join you shortly, sir. Is there anything else I can get for you?"

"No, I'm fine."

The butler bowed slightly and left the room, closing the doors behind him. Jake was alone. He put the glass down and studied the room. The carved oak walls embraced red silk insets. Wooden columns with Roman capitals stood guard in each corner of the room. A rosewood, antique concert grand piano sat on a six inch platform in one corner of the room. Thousands of books crowded the ceiling high shelves, with a sliding ladder to reach the highest shelves. Thick logs crackled in the fireplace, though the day had been warm. The room smelled of burning pine and freshly polished wood and generated an aura of comfort and life.

Jake sat at the piano and softly touched the yellowed keys. Using one finger, he tested the tone and pitch of the instrument. He closed his eyes and played Tchaikovsky's Sleeping Beauty waltz in b flat minor.

Ruth Cromwell stood in the doorway and listened. Jake looked up and stopped playing when he saw her.

"Mrs. Cromwell?"

"Yes, Mr. Parker. I admire your taste in music. Please continue."

"No, I really couldn't. I only play for myself."

"How unfortunate. The loss is ours. It's a pleasure to finally meet you. I've heard all about you and followed your activities of the past few weeks with much interest. Please, sit."

They sat on the couch and he looked directly into her eyes.

"Your dossier failed to mention anything about classical piano."

"There's a lot about me that's quite private. May I be blunt Mrs. Cromwell?"

She nodded.

"What am I doing here?"

"Well, it's nice to see that some of my information about you is correct. Apparently you're not afraid to speak your mind. All right, Mr. Parker. I too can be blunt. According to my sources, you are the best of the ICA. The fact that you survived the oil rig assignment proves to me that you are the right man. People I trust tell me you can help me with a problem. You're a loyal and honest man, qualities I admire."

Jake listened to the dubious compliments with suspicion. She spoke forcefully but with a gentle, quiet air of authority. He allowed her to lead the conversation.

"I appreciate the compliment." He looked her directly in the eye and she returned the glance.

"Mr. Parker... Jake, I need your help to solve a mystery that's unfolded in the past few weeks. The vanishing oil from our platform in the Gulf of Mexico is just a small part of the problem. There are things going on inside the company which are becoming more uncontrollable with each passing day. The first of which was the disappearance of my husband, Philip."

"I thought Mr. Cromwell was deceased." Jake sat back, crossed one leg over the other and sipped the champagne. His curiosity piqued, he studied the lady beside him. The wall that surrounded her slowly decayed and he detected a touch of softness in the granite strength.

She stood and closed the heavy library doors, then returned to the sofa. She appeared to be deep in thought.

"I believe my husband is still alive. I am prepared to offer you a hundred thousand dollars if you'll help me." Jake raised his left eyebrow. "Fifty-five years ago, my husband Philip founded InDevCo. We put everything we had into the company and came close to failure many times. Eventually, things got better and the company got its first government contract. During the war, we were in position to supply the military and success came rapidly after that. The company grew into the multi-faceted conglomerate it is today.

"About a year ago, Philip mentioned an exciting new

project that the research and development division had begun. He told me very little about it, only that it had tremendous potential for impact in many areas. Philip became personally involved with this project, something he hadn't done for many years. He devoted so much time to this work, that whenever I asked about it, he put me off saying the time would come to tell me all about it. I assumed it was some kind of top secret government job and I didn't press him. About two months ago, Philip and I were to attend a very important social function here in Newport. He never arrived and I haven't seen him since."

"What about the police? Didn't they investigate his disappearance?"

"Yes, of course there was a thorough inquest. Philip was an important man and the local police chief called in the FBI at my insistence, but they were unsuccessful. They found his car abandoned in the woods and nothing more. Philip's body never turned up. I kept hoping that one day he would reappear at my door. Last week, my attorney convinced me to allow my husband's will to be read. Philip left everything to me, but ordered control of the company to my youngest son, Andrew."

"How did Charles react to that?"

"He was furious and stormed out of the house. It shouldn't have come as a surprise to him. Philip had told him on numerous occasions that he'd disowned him."

"Why?"

"Philip was deeply disappointed in Charles and told him so often. There are many things that Charles did throughout his life that I can't discuss at this time, but he was always extremely jealous of Andrew. I suppose now that the will has been read things will get bad again."

"Where is Charles now?"

"I don't know. He stormed out of the house after the will was read and I haven't seen him since. He knows I expect him to be at the party tonight. I seem to be the only one who can get through to him these days."

"What about Andrew?"

"What do you want to know? Andrew graduated at the top of his class at Brown University, always successful in anything he attempted, and recently finished Harvard Law. Andrew and Charles are opposites, Jake."

"Regarding Philip, what's the status of the investigation, and has there been any evidence at all?"

She removed a letter from her pocket.

"This letter was handed to me by my attorney after the will was read. It was written by Philip and addressed to me." She read aloud.

"My darling Ruth, if you are reading this letter, something has happened to me and you are alone. I know you are strong and will survive this difficult time. Ruth, dear, the work I have been doing for the past year has been the most important of my life. I know I've been very secretive, but I had no choice. I could not take a chance and tell anyone about it, not even you. I knew what your reaction would be. The risks were great but the potential for this project is so unbelievable that I deemed them worthwhile. You know me better than anyone. I could not pass this one by.

"I dare not put the details of the project in writing, lest it fall into the wrong hands. If you are interested, seek out Lane Darby.

"I wanted to tell you that our years together were the best of my life. We built an empire and I hope Andrew is up to the task that is now thrust upon him. I think he is ready to take over the helm of the company. As for Charles, I know we have tried through the years, but I admit now that we have failed completely. I know you still love him, but he can't be trusted. Don't give in to him. I have thought long and hard before disinheriting him and I know it is the right decision. Carry on, my darling. I will love you forever."

Tears streamed down her flushed cheeks as Ruth finished the letter.

Jake sat quietly, digesting the flood of facts and emotions. The story intrigued him, but he felt certain there was more to it.

"Who is Lane Darby?" asked Jake.

"The head of Research and Development at InDevCo."

"Have you spoken with her about the project Philip referred to in the letter?"

"No, I haven't been able to contact Lane since I received the letter. She'll be at the party tonight. I'll make it my business to speak to her about it."

Jake was silent for a moment, then he said, "Let me get this straight. Philip is missing and the FBI investigation is inconclusive. His body has not been found and there's no evidence except for an abandoned car. What makes you think I can find Philip if he is alive?"

She stood up. "I've studied you, Mr. Jake Parker. You're relentless. Once you set out to do something, you won't stop until it's done. I want you on my team. Until I see Philip's body in a morgue somewhere, I'll never give up."

Jake studied her words as she spoke. She was a tough but genuine woman who'd had a turbulent life. Years of hardship before the fantastic wealth had molded her into this unusual combination of survival at any cost, tempered with a gentle forcefulness.

"How and when do I meet the players?" asked Jake. "I think Lane Darby sounds like a person I should get to know."

"Oh you will, tonight at the party. By the way, it's Dr.

Darby. She has a doctorate in Bioelectronics. I think you'll find her interesting."

Jake was about to ask a question, when the door opened after a soft knock.

"Excuse the interruption, Mrs. Cromwell, but your presence is required in the ballroom."

"Very well." She extended her hand to Jake, who also stood. "I feel good about your being here, Jake. I have confidence in you. By the way, feel free to look around and we'll talk again later."

She left the room.

Jake took the half full glass of champagne and swallowed the remaining wine in one gulp.

Four

THE LIBRARY DOORS OPENED. JAKE WAS DEEP IN thought and did not see a butler enter. Many questions remained unanswered, but at least now Jake better understood the magazine articles he read on the plane.

I must have another meeting with Ruth Cromwell.

"Excuse me, sir. If you will follow me, I'll show you to your suite."

Jake eased out of his trance and followed the uniformed man through the library doors. They climbed the prodigious marble staircase to the second floor. Jake paused a few times to admire the paintings that covered the walls, only to be subtly reminded to move faster by the butler's throaty noises. The house and its occupants spoke softly of wealth and class. The second floor in this wing of the mansion housed the guest suites. Antiques and oriental rugs decorated a long corridor. They entered a high ceilinged bedroom filled with French style furnishings: a veiled canopy bed with a thick down mattress, a roll top desk inlaid with Mother of Pearl, and a wash basin stand complete with pitcher and basin.

The butler disappeared into the closet, emerged with a black tuxedo and hung it on the valet next to the bathroom.

"I hope this will be suitable for this evening, sir. You'll find additional clothing if you wish to change before dinner. Will there be anything else?"

Jake shook his head. "Can't think of anything right

now."

"Cocktails begin at eight, and dinner is at nine. My name is Patrick. Please call me if you need anything."

"There is one thing, Pat. I must speak with Mrs. Cromwell again before the party. Can you arrange it?"

"I'll mention it, sir, but she is very busy." He stiffened at the informality.

"I'm sure you'll do your best, Pat."

Patrick left and closed the door.

Jake waited a minute, then tried the door. It was unlocked.

It's foolish to be so suspicious. This is safe territory.

But then he reminded himself of his own first law of survival: *Jake's rule #1 — Trust no one.*

The only thing he wore that belonged to him was his watch. The 'secret agent watch,' Harry had called it when he gave it to Jake after he was hired by InDevCo and placed in ICA. It had some unexpected capabilities. Jake pushed a tiny button on the side of the watch and a green light flashed on the face. The immediate area was clear. Jake moved slowly around the room and stopped at the bathroom. The green light turned red. There was an electronic 'bug' close by. The light turned back to green if he retreated from that spot. The device was somewhere in or near the bathroom. A quick search of the lamps and telephone revealed nothing, as did the medicine cabinet in the bathroom. Finally, the red glow flashed; he was next to the valet with the tuxedo. Jake examined it carefully and noticed the top button was sewn with different thread than the others. He had found his transmitter, but now the question: who put it there? Mrs. Cromwell had just confided her darkest secrets to him and offered him a fortune to join her.

Someone else. Someone who doesn't want me here. Patrick brought out the tux. Perhaps something could be learned by speaking to the other servants.

For now, he decided to leave the button transmitter alone. *All the elements are in place. A mansion, a wealthy widow who suspects foul play in the death of her husband and a butler with a wired tuxedo. What a perfect setting for an Agatha Christie mystery novel.*

Jake picked up an orange from a bowl of fresh fruit and tossed it from his left hand to the right as he paced the room.

Plenty of time before the party.

The deserted corridor beckoned; he grabbed a small paring knife from the fruit bowl on his way out the door.

All the suites along this section were ready to receive the guests and VIP's that were to arrive later today for the evening's festivities. Jake guessed that the servants were busy in the ballroom. After finishing the fruit, the orange peel and paring knife went into his pocket for later disposal.

Jake noticed the carpet in his room and the corridor just outside appeared new and brightly colored. As he walked farther from his room, the rug appeared worn, though still immaculate. At the end of the hallway, a slight but definite wear in the carpet indicated a subtle traffic pattern leading directly into the wall. He examined the rug closely, and had no doubt about the flattening of the carpet nap in the direction of the wall. But there was no door, nor a sensible explanation.

All this and now a secret passageway. Too much to believe.

Nevertheless, his fingers reached around the frame of the wall panel looking for a switch or some indication of a door. The house would not give up its secrets easily.

Jake tried moving the panel, the painting and the lamp

that stood on a small Chippendale table next to the wall. Nothing. The pattern in the carpet glared at him. It was real and so too, the hidden door switch he was now determined to find.

Jake heard voices at the other end of the corridor. Guests arrived and servants escorted them to their rooms. He flattened himself against the wall as though fastened to it.

Mrs. C did say to feel free to explore the house.

The voices grew muffled as the door to the suite closed and the butler returned to his duties on the lower level. Jake relaxed and noticed a small landscape oil painting overshadowed by a larger, much more impressive colorful primitive painting just above it. But something was odd about the landscape painting...something different. Then, it struck him. Every other painting he'd seen in the house was perfectly straight, but this one hung slightly off center. In seconds, his fingers explored the tiny masterpiece and found their mark: two micro-switches carefully placed into the design of the frame, camouflaged as part of the decoration. Jake hesitated, deciding which switch to push, then, touched the top button. Within seconds, through the corner of his eye, he saw a tiny projector move and discharge an intense beam of red light. Instantly, he fell to the floor and rolled away as the thin laser beam impacted on the wall just above the rigged painting.

Wrong one.

Jake returned to the painting and more carefully now, touched the other micro-switch. A wall panel slid silently open, revealing the inner sanctum. After making certain his activities were unobserved, he slipped into the secret passage. The door closed behind him and he stood there, fists clenched and body rigid. A single bulb activated by the opening of the door panel lit the narrow chamber. He touched a switch on the wall and the door opened, quieting his apprehension, but his training always overruled his feelings and his senses remained heightened. Before him stood an elevator barely large enough for two people.

Strange combination of old and high tech.

He stepped in and pushed the only button on the control box. The creaking of the car gave away its age, but a sense of mystery filled its confines; which occupants of the house had used the elevator? How many clandestine rendezvous took place here, forbidden lovers delivered to secluded encounters? What ghosts inhabited the this old secret passage? The abrupt stop of the tiny car jolted Jake back to reality.

The door opened and he looked out into a vestibule filled with barrels and crates. From their state of decay, he guessed they were many years old. In the middle of the wall stood a substantial wooden door with rusted hinges. Given the dampness and cold, a stale odor of mold and rot pervaded the air. Jake thought this must be under the basement level of the old house.

The door looked imposing, but not enough to thwart his curiosity. Dozens of mice scurried around his feet, startling him as he stepped closer. To his surprise, the door opened easily. A closet sized chamber appeared, with solid, shiny white walls and no other apparent openings. The door slammed loudly shut behind him after he walked in. Darkness enveloped the chamber. His fear of dark, closed places began to dominate his mind until a bright light blinded him momentarily and the words blinked in front of him: DECONTAMINATION-PLEASE WAIT. The sign ceased blinking its message and the wall in front of him slid silently away.

Jake left the decontamination chamber and stood at the entrance to a modern research laboratory. His entry into the chamber activated the power in the lab. Unfamiliar, sophisticated, but dusty, computer equipment, looked as though it had not been used for some time. In all his years of electronics training he had never seen advanced computers such as these. A helmet shaped headset lay on top of the large monitor screen. The equipment had no keyboard. He resisted the temptation to activate what appeared to be the main terminal, lest an alarm be activated.

Next to the computer area was a room filled with empty animal cages. By the size of the cages, Jake surmised they once housed monkeys or gorillas. Surgical and anesthesia equipment completed the picture and his mind ran with the possibilities. The equipment fascinated him. He let down his guard and failed to notice a video camera mounted behind the last cage near the ceiling. In fact, a camera like this followed his movements since he entered the lab.

A long corridor adjoined the cage room, with empty storage rooms on each side. At the end of the hallway, a door marked PRIVATE, invited Jake to enter. In the next minute, he picked the lock and stood in an office with a large Victorian desk in the center. Oriental rugs wore colorful patterns, overstuffed brown leather chairs sat unused and more of the curious computer terminals completed the picture. Photos of Ruth Cromwell and Andrew Cromwell crowded the top of the desk. Only one small picture of Charles as a young child could be found among the photos.

Philip's private office.

The large padded chair behind the desk swivelled around to command the panel of computers and video terminals that surrounded the desk. Jake pictured Philip sitting there, barking orders to his lab tech's about some top secret project. What connection existed between this last all-engrossing project and his disappearance or demise?

Jake searched the desk. The drawers contained nothing unusual: letters from suppliers, books and paper goods. One drawer seemed subtly different. The bottom right drawer appeared somewhat smaller inside than it should given its outer dimensions. (Jake finally forgave his spatial relations teacher for forcing him to study the dreaded subject) He cleared the contents of the drawer, then searched more carefully. A clever sliding panel revealed a hidden compartment in the base of the drawer. It opened only halfway, enough to expose part of its contents. Jake pulled out a triangular shaped object and a small, blue jewel box. He opened the box. It contained two objects, each no bigger than the eraser of a pencil. The letters CCEM were printed inside the box. He closed the box, slipped it into his pocket, and examined the odd shaped item. Jake turned to the terminal on the desk. The shape matched the opening in the machine. It was a computer disc which fit perfectly.

The screen lit up with a three dimensional image of Philip Cromwell.

Five

DETAILED FEATURES OF PHILIP'S FACE LEAPED FROM the screen. A date appeared in the corner of the monitor: July 27.

The image spoke.

"A research breakthrough today. Our people tell me they have perfected an entirely new and different type of ceramic material that can carry a superconductive current at room temperature. The ceramic offers virtually no resistance to the current. I know the Japanese are working on a similar project, but my people at ICA tell me the Japanese are not even close to this kind of success. The possibilities are staggering. I will meet with the lab scientists tomorrow to confirm their findings."

Philip spoke about his excitement and how he hoped the discovery was valid, and not a repeat of disappointments he'd had before. There were no additional entries until one month later.

August 29:

"My head is still spinning from the past week's activities. The discovery has far exceeded my expectations. Trying to keep all of this secret has been difficult, but I think we have good security. Ruth is becoming concerned at the amount of time I've spent on this project. I believe she senses my enthusiasm and has not pressed me for information. The R&D boys tell me they will be ready for a full presentation at tomorrow's board meeting."

September 5:

"Someone leaked the story to the press and they stormed the InDevCo Building the day of the meeting. I guess we can't keep discoveries like this to ourselves very long. Even I can't believe the scope of applications for our new materials. They may be utilized as the basis for a totally different type of superconductive-electronics. Using it for computer applications, we can make all other systems obsolete and revolutionize the electronics industry."

Jake looked at the odd terminal on the desk and only now understood the magnitude of what he had found.

September 21:

"The R&D people are working around the clock to find practical applications for the new materials. Some of them are comparing the discovery to the electric light. Anything using the old style microprocessors and integrated circuits will be a dinosaur. The capabilities of the new superconductive computers seem limitless. We are calling the system, Lorestronics, for low resistance electronics." Jake thought about the oil rig and the gun Pat and Eddie had used on him. They had called it a Lorestron gun.

October 6:

"The FTC has ordered all work on Lorestronics to cease immediately. 'In the interest of national security,' they said, 'until we can assess the impact on the economy.' I know there are those out there who are jealous of my successes and fear that we will take over the electronics industry. I must fight them with every means at my disposal."

November 10:

"We have been unsuccessful in our attempts to lift the ban on Lorestronics research. All my so called friends in Washington have deserted me. My corporate enemies have joined together to stop me from marketing the wondrous products we were close to developing. The Lorestronics lab at Subterra is shut down and I have no choice but to continue the research in secret. Toward that end, I have ordered work to begin on a fully equipped lab to be built in the sub-basement of my Newport home. My engineers have informed me this lab could be operational in three months. I have ordered that no expense be spared to ensure the full capacity of this facility. During the construction, we will continue our efforts in Washington to influence the right people to allow this important work."

February 2:

"The Newport lab is finally operational. Test animals will be used to try a radical idea using a lorestron module designed to be implanted in the brain. Other experiments using Lorestronics are now also ongoing, but this one is by far the most fascinating. I have always believed that only a small fraction of the total capacity of the human brain is ever used by the average person."

March 15:

"My love of old science fiction movies has given me an idea for a name for this experiment. One of my favorites is a Japanese movie called Godzilla verses Megalon. Therefore, I name this experiment Project Megalon.

"The lorestron brain module is finally ready for our first trial in a living animal. If it is a success, it will immediately propel mankind and technology years into the future. Are we ready for this? I don't know, but we cannot turn away from the knowledge that is at our fingertips. Preliminary neuronal testing using a lorestronic computer has shown that proper application of a superconductive current can actually increase the efficiency of the neuronal transmitter chemicals (so they tell me), thus greatly strengthening that neuron. Since the brain is made up of billions of neurons, theoretically, applying this type of current to the entire brain should effectively boost the power and capacity of that organ to previously impossible levels."

Jake reclined in the chair and tried to fully comprehend the story that unfolded. The idea of a supercharged brain was unbelievable. Visions of a Frankenstein-like monster flashed in his mind. Further entries in the diary described other new marvels resulting from the Lorestronics revolution. Mentioned in detail were a new solar cell, a powerful electric motor which required very little battery capacity, (this one could change the automotive industry overnight) and a deadly particle beam weapon.

Philip seemed to understand the far reaching implications this technology would have on society. Every fabric of daily life would be changed in some way by the discoveries they made here. But the excitement in his voice when he spoke about Megalon was unmistakable.

April 11:

"Earlier failures with Megalon have taught us much. Most of the animals have had strokes or never awakened from the general anesthesia. The superconductive current needed to accomplish our goal is much less than originally thought. It seems the neurons of the brain have the capacity to magnify the superconductive current. The scientists can explain it in medical terms but the end result is that we have effectively been short circuiting the brain with an overload of power. We have developed a new, lower power module and it should be ready for testing in a week."

May 29:

"Success at last. All of the test animals survived the implantation procedure. Results show some promise, but not what I expected. It was decided that one of the reasons for the failure was the limited capacity of the animal brain. The doctors speculate that the module would give us the desired effect only if used on a brain with adequate cerebral cortex tissue. Of course, we know the only animal that fits this description is man himself. I have ordered the R and D people to come up with a module suitable for human use."

May 30:

"Many hundreds of hours of work have given us CCEM, the Cerebral Cortex Expansion Module."

Jake sat back again and paused the program. He took the tiny jewel box from his pocket and opened it, the meaning of CCEM now clear. In this small box, Jake held mankind's greatest discovery. He stared at the modules for a moment, then returned to the diary.

Jake sensed a change in the tone of Philip's voice. Something subtle, but a definite difference in the feeling of the recording. As though Philip felt greatly excited and anguished at the same time, and the decisions he made concerning the project weighed heavily on him.

June 4:

"We are at a crossroads with Megalon and I have ordered the work transferred to the Subterra lab, where the facilities are better. The ban on the work has not been lifted but the attention we were getting before has died down and I feel it is worth the risk to move the operation. All of the dedicated scientists involved with the evolution of the modules all the way to CCEM, know the time has come to try the unit on a human subject. The ethical and moral questions raised by this need are far reaching. I have met with the department heads and we decided that a volunteer should be found, preferably someone with a terminal illness whose nervous system is intact."

June 21:

"Dr. Darby has found a suitable subject. The man has a fatal viral cardiac myopathy. The specialists give him one to two weeks to live and there is no treatment or cure. We have approached him and his family, given them the facts of our experiment along with an offer of a generous gift. After a short time to consider, they have agreed to allow the CCEM to be implanted. The procedure is scheduled for tomorrow morning. Time is of the essence."

June 22:

"The doctors performed the implantation surgery without a problem. After the local anesthetic wore off, the patient reported a slight headache and dizziness, but no other change. Every system is constantly being monitored. (For what, we don't exactly know) A cardiologist is standing by to observe the cardiac symptoms."

June 24:

"We almost overlooked the first change. The patient asked for reading materials to pass the time. A nurse gave him the newspaper, then left the room for a moment. When she returned, she asked the patient why he did not read the paper he requested. "Indeed," he said. "I have just read it cover to cover." When asked if he ever learned to speed read, he replied that he had not, and in fact, had little formal education and reading was always difficult for him.

Excitement spread through the lab. The CCEM worked. EEG's revealed a tremendous increase in brain activity compared with pre-implantation tests. Memory span, reading comprehension, linguistic capabilities, and a general IQ test were ordered, but never given. The subject weakened and the virus overtook his heart. He lapsed into a coma and was dead twelve hours later. Our brave volunteer proved that the CCEM can be safely implanted. The next step is obvious-a healthy subject must be found. I see no alternative but to offer myself for this duty. I could never in good conscious allow anyone else to do that which I would not do first. Besides, I must admit to a certain curiosity about how it would feel to become a genius at my age."

That was the final entry in the diary, dated almost one year from the start of the experiment.

Just around the time Mrs. Cromwell first reported her husband missing. I must show her the diary and the lab.

He stood and left the office. A previously unnoticed video camera in the corridor surprised him.

"Stupid," he said, and quickened his pace.

Without warning, he felt a sudden and sharp pain in the right side of his neck, like a wasp sting. Automatically, his hand reached up and he pulled a small tranquilizer dart out of his skin.

A dark curtain of unconsciousness closed in fast. Nothing could be done to prevent the blurred vision, then dizziness and disorientation. Far away, Jake heard the sound of a man laughing. Through the growing buzz in his head, he felt the disc and the jewel box pulled from his hand.

Wild laughter reverberated in his ears. Jake fell hard and lay on the threshold of oblivion.

For a split second before falling away, his vision cleared and Jake glimpsed the face that owned the malevolent smile.

Six

Darkness closing in . . . the stench of death . . . no escape . . . trapped.

No more sun or clouds. No pleasure or pain.

Empty blackness.

No feeling at all . . . worse than pain.

The king is dead.

Can't breath . . . no more air . . . no . . . air.

JAKE WOKE FROM THE DREAM WITH A START. THIS WAS not the first time he had nearly choked and vividly dreamed about his death. Although it was always in a different setting, many of the dreams took place in a dark crypt. He knew these dreams had an important connection to his fear of the dark.

Jake had spoken to a psychologist about the problem of the recurring nightmares. "The most probable explanation is that these dreams are experiences that are only known to your psychic subconscious."

Jake recalled the sessions that followed, but even tape recordings of the encounters failed to convince him of a past existence dating back three thousand years.

Nonetheless, the detail and realism of the dreams was

sometimes too great to be mere coincidence.

Jake felt a twinge of pain in his neck and remembered the dart and heavy sleep that followed. Now, different sensations: dizziness and nausea. He tried to move, only to discover his hands tied tightly behind him and secured to a column. A blinding white light shone in his eyes.

Jake sat on the floor with his legs stretched in front of him and pulled against the ropes that bound him to the column.

Suddenly, the bright light disappeared; white spots danced before his eyes.

Now, the only source of light in the room was a small candle on the floor about twenty feet from him; its faint light cast a soft glow on the empty storage room and outlined an animal cage. Directly above the flame, a rope stretched tightly to a hook on the wall, the other end tied to an elastic cord attached to the cage door. A weight kept tension on the rope and it was obvious that after the rope sufficiently scorched, the weight would drop and the thick elastic band would open the door.

Jake strained to see the contents of the cage, but the dim light prevented it.

Someone went to a great deal of trouble to design this elaborate setting. Maybe, I can loosen the ropes.

He continued his efforts, but only earned a rope burn.

A putrid smell permeated the room. Jake suppressed the nausea that grew in the pit of his stomach.

Something on the floor of the cage moved toward the door.

For a moment, the candlelight revealed its smooth, spotted skin, piercing eyes and searching tongue.

A python!

His mind raced in a hundred different directions, sorry now that his eyes had adjusted so well to the dim light.

Jake's Rule 45 — Escape: the only option.

He renewed his efforts, but the ropes gouged the flesh on his wrists. He had to get free before the flame burned through the rope, and released the snake. The scent of his sweat would surely attract the snake.

Perspiration streamed from every pore as thoughts of suffocation at the mercy of this creature filled his mind.

The sound of the weight dropping halted his escape efforts, and he watched the cage door slide open. The snake remained motionless.

Calculations of how long it took to suffocate to death rolled around in his mind. Release of the bonds that secured his hands took on new meaning. His skin blistered beneath the ropes, but there was no pain. Sweat soaked palms supplied the needed lubrication to allow some small progress in the fight to free himself.

Jake guessed that only ten minutes had passed, though it seemed like an hour.

Then, the candle burned out throwing the room into complete darkness.

Jake stopped moving and held his breath, the darkness and silence unnerving. His heart raced. Whoever planned this seemed to somehow know of his secret fear of darkness and snakes.

The candle tipped over; the creature was loose and on the move. Jake's eyes fully dilated and he strained to see in the dark.

Trying desperately to fight the growing panic, he continued to work on the ropes. Sweat poured off his body and lubricated his wrists. The ropes loosened slightly.

Something lightly brushed his leg.

Shit.

The giant reptile found him. Jake stayed perfectly still. The snake did not move. It sensed that Jake was helpless, and waited to move in for the kill. The Python lay motionless for a long time, judging his opponent.

Jake sensed his presence.

Cool and smooth, Jake felt the first of the snake's movements around his legs.

It wrapped itself around his body.

The pressure increased as it coiled slowly and steadily.

Finally and with a great effort, Jake managed to free his right hand. He reached down and grabbed the body of the snake and tried to free himself from the beast. It held tight. He needed something to pry free from the grip; the crushing grip that would soon squeeze the life from him. The ropes from his left hand fell free and the column no longer held him. With the snake wrapped tightly around his legs, he rolled into the middle of the room. The snake sensed his new freedom and tightened its hold. Jake lost the feeling in his feet. He writhed on the floor and used both hands to try to undo the death grip.

Something fell from his pocket.

The paring knife.

His hands reached out in the darkness.

Nothing.

It has to be here. It's my only chance.

The serpent continued its gradual suffocation ritual. A thin, moist tendril repeatedly touched his arm, sending waves of nausea through him.

It's tasting me.

He overcame his revulsion and grabbed the beast, trying to uncoil the body. The slimy tongue darted in and out, judging its prey. The darkness disoriented him and Jake could not remove the creature.

Jake could sense the monster's eyes.

Could they see in the dark? The giant eyes are there.

Jake took his finger and plunged it into the snake's eye socket. He felt the gelatinous eye fluid ooze from the wound and onto him, but the vice-like grip persisted.

Jake's searching hand brushed against the knife and he grabbed it, while still attempting to free himself. With the knife firmly in his grasp, he thrust it into the reptile's neck and opened its throat. The creatures blood spattered over Jake.

Finally, the hold loosened.

The body of the once powerful behemoth fell to the floor next to him. Relieved and exhausted, Jake waited until the feeling returned to his legs, then stood up; the twitching remains at his feet.

He felt his way around in the dark until he located the door. It was unlocked. Bright light from the corridor illuminated the grizzly scene.

Jake realized he had lived through another death scene, but this one was not a dream.

Seven

HOT WATER CHILLS SPARKED THROUGH JAKE'S BODY. The shower eased his tight muscles and he enjoyed the sensations, but wished it could cleanse the memory of the recent horrifying episode. His wrists ached where the ropes had denuded the outer layers of skin. The dried blood on his body slowly washed away, turning the shower floor an unnatural shade of crimson.

After the snake incident, he escaped easily from the deserted lab. He had almost reached his room unseen when a chambermaid entered the hallway and came face to face with him. She screamed, dropped a stack of towels and ran sobbing toward the stairway. Jake made it to his room, slammed the door behind him, stripped and jumped into the shower.

Feeling cleansed, he sat naked on his bed.

The diary.

Would anyone believe him now that the evidence disappeared? Who was responsible for the tranquilizer and the snake? One thing was certain: he must speak with Mrs. Cromwell. He lay on the bed and stared at the ceiling. His eyes closed slowly and his exhausted body relaxed, accepting sleep. Before drifting away, his hand touched a tiny alarm set button on his watch.

Will the strange dreams return again?

Exactly two hours later, the chimes on his watch rang

softly. Jake had a dreamless sleep which he knew would leave him feeling refreshed after the initial grogginess. Instinctively, his eyes opened only slightly and scanned the deserted room. He stood and checked the single strand of hair that he placed across the door frame before entering the shower. He smiled at the undisturbed hair, then thought of the dinner jacket. Jake took the jacket, pulled the top button from its attachments, and threw it into the toilet.

With his clothes in hand, a soft knock on the door distracted him. Wearing only a small towel around his waist, he opened the door quickly, startling the young maid, who was just about to knock again.

"Pardon me, sir."

Jake recognized her as the same girl who saw him walking down the hall covered with blood and torn clothes.

"Yes?"

She stared in silence for a moment. "Forgive me for intruding, but the guests are arriving for the party and I wondered if you needed anything before dinner."

"Would you ask Mrs. Cromwell if I could have five minutes of her time before the party?"

"I'll ask, but she's greeting the guests. Perhaps later would be better."

"Tell her it's urgent." Jake fidgeted with the towel, which unfastened.

The maid nodded and stood there.

Jake stood at the top of the grand stairway and surveyed the scene below. He pulled the tight sleeves of the tuxedo jacket away from his irritated wrists. Excitement charged the house as Mrs. Cromwell headed a receiving line that greeted the arriving guests. She spotted him descending the stairs and he made his way toward her.

"I must speak with you immediately," Jake whispered to her. She looked at him blankly for a moment, trying to interpret the urgency in his voice.

"It will have to wait until the guests are seated. Meet me in the library at ten." She returned to her duties as hostess.

A woman who had just entered the foyer shot Jake a long look after he spoke to Ruth Cromwell.

"Ruth, darling, how dare you keep this gorgeous stranger to yourself."

"Forgive me. Francesca Campbell, this is Mr. Jake Parker, the head of security for InDevCo. Francesca is newly married to our good friend George who sits on the InDevCo board and has known Philip and me for many years."

Jake looked inquisitively at Ruth Cromwell. She never mentioned anything about chief of security.

"The pleasure is mine." He took Francesca's hand and kissed it gently, hiding the surprise on his face. Her ring-laden fingers matched almost every other area of exposed flesh which was covered with gold and jewels. The snugly fitted sequined gown accentuated her slender but voluptuous body, with bounteous breasts that spilled over the plunging V neckline.

"Francesca has rescued George from the grief he suffered at the recent death of his wife and my dearest friend, Molly. Isn't that right, dear?"

Francesca ignored Ruth's cutting remark, looked at Jake with covetous eyes and grabbed his arm.

"George will be along shortly. Poor old dear always has to make sure the Rolls is parked in a safe spot. So, Mr. Parker, Jake, you must tell me every single interesting thing about yourself." Francesca led Jake into the ballroom, where the party was in progress.

Servants carried champagne and trays of canapes amongst the guests who stood in small groups in the lavishly decorated ballroom. A ten-piece orchestra played from a raised platform, creating a formal but friendly mood. Jake guessed that no European Royal Ball could ever be presented on a grander scale.

"May I have this dance?" Jake asked Francesca, bowing slightly. He enjoyed the surroundings and felt as if he acted in a movie he had seen in his youth about the life of the Czars in pre-revolutionary Russia.

"I thought you'd never ask," she replied.

They joined the couples on the dance floor.

Jake's Rule 24 — When in Rome. . .

"So, tell me Jake, how did you manage to convince Andrew to make you head of security? I understand that position was held by someone else." She surprised him with her knowledge of the company.

"Jake's Rule #49 — Never discuss business with a beautiful woman."

His hand explored the bare flesh exposed by her backless dress as they moved around the marbled dance floor. Jake bristled his nose at the strong smell of her sweet perfume. Francesca laughed and Jake felt her skin tighten.

"I'd love to hear the first forty-eight rules." They danced around the room. "You seem to be missing a button, Jake," she said, toying with the remaining button on his tuxedo. "You really should complain to the butler who gave you a jacket in this condition." She slipped her hand under the jacket and opened a button on his shirt.

Then her hand disappeared.

How did she know the butler gave me this coat?

For the moment, Jake wondered how far she would go.

The music stopped and everyone applauded softly. Jake and Francesca separated and she spotted her husband at the door.

"Well, its been most interesting, Mr. Parker. My dance card is open later in the evening. Until then. . ." Jake lightly kissed her outstretched hand. Francesca Campbell joined her husband, but glanced at Jake twice while speaking with him. Jake grabbed a glass of champagne from a butler's tray and decided to mingle. Francesca continued to stare at him, but averted her eyes when he returned the look.

A man wearing a white silk dinner jacket walked through the foyer and into the ballroom. He stood tall and slim, with thick sandy hair, a well trimmed beard, high cheek bones, and large, blue eyes. Most heads in the room turned toward him, and Ruth Cromwell stopped what she was doing to greet him. She kissed him on the cheek, spoke with him for a moment, looked around the room until spotting Jake next to the bar, then took his arm and led him toward Jake.

"I'd like you to meet my son, Andrew. I've told him all about our little chat this afternoon, Jake, but Andy doesn't agree with my feeling about his father."

They shook hands. "Why is that?" asked Jake.

Andrew looked stern. "For one, I don't think father is still alive. Second, I don't think someone like you could find him if he was. No offense intended, Mr. Parker."

"None taken, but you underestimate me."

"Perhaps, but if it were up to me, I'd let him rest in peace. Mother has apparently made up her mind, and I know better than to try to change it."

"Andrew, I insist you cooperate with Mr. Parker."

"See what I mean? All right, Mother. What can I do to

help?"

"Introduce him to Lane. There are some questions that only she can answer. I thought I saw her talking with Professor Flint."

"The astronomer? Why did you invite him? The only thing he ever talks about is alien civilizations."

"He's fun. Besides, Lane loves science fiction as did your father. Those two can talk for hours. Be a dear and do as I ask. I've got to check on Madeline Crosby. She always gets into a fight with Francesca."

Andrew grasped Jake's arm firmly and pulled him to the side of the room. "Mother told me she confided in you and that she trusts you. I respect her wishes, but be forewarned. I won't tolerate anyone taking advantage of my mother's good nature and vulnerability. She has this fantasy that my father is still alive, but I'm a realist. I love my mother, Mr. Parker, so I've agreed to help you, with her promise that if you fail, there will be no further attempts in this direction."

Jake took Andrew's hand off of his arm.

"Your mother seems like an intelligent and rational woman. If she believes your father is alive, I'm sure she has a good reason."

"I'll be watching you, Mr. Parker."

Jake looked deeply into Andrew's eyes. He was young, but fiercely protective and strong, the product of years of grooming to take over control of the InDevCo empire.

Jake's Rule #11 — Choose your enemies carefully.

Jake followed Andrew as he walked toward a man with white hair and a woman in her late thirties who were engaged in an energetic discussion. The woman wore a black silk gown that showed off her well proportioned figure. Her honey gold hair fell to shoulder length, and her green eyes sparkled like chipped emeralds.

"Prove it," she said waving her right hand toward the ceiling. "Prove to me that there is life on other worlds and I'll stop calling you a fanatic." She turned toward Andrew. "Tell him, Andrew. We can't devote the kind of resources needed for a galactic search project like this without proof of extraterrestrial intelligence."

"Whatever you say, Lane. Perhaps Dr. Flint would be interested in the Search for Alien Intelligent Life Project in New Mexico. I know the project director. Oh, Dr. Lane Darby and Dr. Byron Flint, this is InDevCo's new security chief, Jake Parker."

She shook Jake's hand. "Welcome aboard, Mr. Parker. There's only one thing to remember in that job: Always watch your back. The previous occupant of your position didn't like the idea of being fired."

Andrew and Lane laughed.

"Sorry, but I missed the joke. Who was the chief of security before me?"

"My brother, Charles. Another one of Mother's wonderful ideas to try to make amends to him for the loss of his inheritance," said Andrew.

"I see. What happened?" asked Jake.

Andrew intervened, and led Dr. Flint away. "I'd love to hear this story for the hundredth time, but I have to greet the CEO of Fuji Electronics. You might find him interesting, Professor. I understand his company is doing research in space station technology."

"Don't mind Andrew, Mr. Parker," said Lane. "He's really a nice kid when you get to know him. It's Charles you have to watch."

"Who fired him?" asked Jake.

"Andrew, of course. He's head of the company even though Mrs. Cromwell still has a lot of input into decisions, like hiring you. Charles caused a great deal of trouble in the board room and Andrew was right to dismiss him. I understand you're an inner core agent, Mr. Parker."

"It's Jake, and yes, I'm ICA, though it's supposed to be a big secret. How did you know?"

"There isn't much that goes on in the company that I don't know about."

"I'm impressed. What else do you know about me?" Jake asked.

"That you're intelligent and capable of defending yourself."

"This is intriguing."

"You live by rules that are numbered, have an older brother named Harry that you idolize, a tattoo of a butterfly on your left butt cheek, you're as good on the piano as you are with your fists and you have a lot of questions for me about my relationship with Philip Cromwell. Want to know more?"

"Remarkable. I had no idea my file was so complete. Since you brought it up, I do have questions about a certain project you and Philip Cromwell worked on before he disappeared."

"Philip and I worked on many projects. Which one did you have in mind?"

Before Jake could answer, a butler approached Lane and handed her a folded note. She read it, crumpled it and jammed it into her pocket.

"Can we continue this conversation another time? I must have a word with one of the other guests."

"Of course. Is everything all right?"

Ignoring the question, Lane placed her unfinished drink on a nearby table and stormed off toward the foyer. Jake waited a moment, then followed.

She left the ballroom and walked toward a stairway that led to the second floor of the north wing of the house. (The guest suites were in the south wing). All of the servants were occupied in the ballroom, and no one saw Jake follow Lane into the wing of the mansion occupied by the Cromwell family. Jake stayed cautiously behind her and moved closer only when certain she reached her final destination.

The door to a small sitting room was ajar as he edged slowly nearer. The two made no effort to quiet their conversation.

"No, I won't help you. The project's been shut down for months," Lane said in a distressed tone. Jake could not see either of them.

"The equipment is still there waiting to be activated. It would be a simple matter for you to. . ."

"No, that project died with your father. I'm sorry, Charles, what you ask is impossible right now. I must get back to the party as should you. I know your mother is expecting you to put in an appearance."

"My mother is a weak fool. Even she can't stand up to my brother. I must have the power of Megalon."

There was silence for the next moment.

"No, Charles, don't. . ."

Jake almost charged into the room when the door burst open and Lane ran into the corridor toward the stairs. Jake hid behind a large antique hutch as Charles followed after her. She was halfway down the stairs when he reached the railing. Jake dared not move. He knew Charles would see him if he returned to the room, but Charles ran down the steps without turning, and continued out the front door.

Jake followed Lane into the ballroom and joined her at the bar.

"White Russian," she said to the bartender.

"Stoli on the rocks with a lime twist," ordered Jake. "You okay?"

Lane finished the drink and ordered another.

"Fine. Why?"

"We've only just met, but you seem upset," Jake said, stirring his vodka.

"I'm a scientist, Mr. Parker. I don't get upset over someone like. . ."

Jake finished the sentence, "Charles Cromwell?"

"How could you know about Charles?"

"Ah, I too have my sources. Don't you think it's time we had a long talk about what's really going on here?"

Before Lane could answer, a butler announced dinner.

"Seems like these interruptions are timed perfectly, Dr. Darby."

"Coincidence. Sheer coincidence," she said, walking toward the dining room.

The banquet hall was smaller than the ballroom, but large enough to seat 125 people in comfort. The tables were set with the finest Oriental linens, Rosenthal china and Bacharrat glassware. Jake circled the room, looking for his name on a place card. He hoped Mrs. Cromwell had thought to seat him next to Lane.

"Jake darling, you're sitting next to me," said Francesca, calling to Jake and patting the seat of an empty chair. Jake forced a smile and looked for Lane, who sat on the far end of the table.

"Foolish me, I thought I was supposed to sit at that end

of the table."

"Oh, you were, but I switched your card. It'll be much more fun sitting next to me."

"I'm sure," he said, and sat in the only remaining seat. Francesca moved her chair so close to Jake, that the butler had to reach around to serve Jake. Francesca grabbed Jake's napkin and placed it in his lap, allowing her hand to linger there. Jake tried to stay calm but she was unrelenting.

He removed her hand. "Thanks, I can manage the napkin."

She looked at her husband, who sat next to her and talked with his neighbor, leaned over and whispered in Jake's ear.

"I want you."

Jake stared at her for a moment, then moved closer and whispered, "I can't blame you."

Francesca laughed so loudly that the guests around her stopped talking to look at her.

"I love a man with a sense of humor, but watch out Jake, I always get what I want."

"We'll see," said Jake.

Dinner consisted of several courses and as the main entree plates were cleared, Francesca seemed increasingly uneasy. Jake noticed she continually looked at her watch."

"Do you have another appointment?" he asked.

"No, of course not. I think I'll go to the powder room."

Jake stood and helped her move her chair, then sat down. The highlight of every Cromwell banquet has always been dessert. Known in Newport society circles as a superb hostess, every guest in the room now waited with anticipation for the crowning glory to a perfect party.

Suddenly, the lights went out and the room was completely dark. No one spoke, expecting a flaming treat to be carried in by a parade of butlers.

Minutes later the lights came on, but there was no Baked Alaska. Ten men dressed in black Ninja-like clothing stood throughout the room pointing automatic weapons at the seated guests. Over screams and protests, one of the intruders nearest the door finally spoke.

"No one move and there will be no need for bloodshed. Put your hands on the table NOW."

The guests obeyed. Jake looked around and realized there was no hope of escape. He placed his hands on the table.

The man who gave the order stood with gun in hand while his men moved around the room, stripping the guests of their jewelry and watches. Then, the lights extinguished again and they were gone.

Eight

Luxor, Egypt
The Present

COERCING THE DESERT SANDS TO SURRENDER SECRETS of the distant past required a formidable effort. Local Egyptian men hired to dig for artifacts and tombs viewed the slow progress as completely normal. Dr. Stanley Lawrence, an archeologist and Egyptologist, took charge of a dig in the Valley of the Kings on the west bank of the Nile just outside the ancient city of Thebes, now called Luxor. He had recently discovered the three thousand year old tomb of an important priest named Imhotek on the outskirts of the valley, where non-royal persons of importance were buried.

Dr. Lawrence wandered from the dig site and sat on a sandy hill overlooking the narrow road that led to the Pharonic tombs, now open to the public. He always enjoyed being alone among the tombs, where the specter of the long dead kings called out and comforted him. Lately, the noise and pollution from the tourist busses had stolen this pleasure.

The years of working in the dry desert took its toll on him, and he looked much older than his years. Though he appeared robust and carried a few extra pounds, his health was poor. Dust from the tombs also had its way with his lungs, the emphysema getting worse as each year the doctors warned him to abandon the work.

Bus loads of eager tourists arrived from the city, as they did each day. Hoards of faceless foreigners tramped the timeless desert to get a momentary look at the specter of the Egyptian gods. Local merchants lined the road with hastily built booths cloaked with colorful canvases, hawking their miniature King Tut death masks and tee shirts to visitors that hungered for anything Egyptian. He resented this intrusion of the masses into *his* domain, and wondered what each of them thought as they scurried in and around the various sacred tombs. These great men, the Pharaohs, had cheated time and become immortal. The idea captivated him and he was obsessed with unlocking their secrets, working closely with the Department of Antiquities to find undiscovered tombs in the Valley of the Kings.

Do they understand what they see?

Dr. Lawrence watched the swirling sand of the desert caught in an intensely hot wind, the barren mountains shimmering in the distance. The summer temperatures bothered him at first, but the years provided him with a tolerance and he no longer minded the heat. Movement from behind brought him out of his contemplation. A man wearing a white and gold embroidered Galabeya approached, climbing the steep hill with little effort.

"I thought I might find you here, Aton," said the man, using the nick-name the workers gave Dr. Lawrence after the discovery of the tomb of the Sun King, Akhenaton. It was a name fondly given. "I see the tourists come in larger numbers each day to view the great ones we uncovered from sleep."

"Yes, but it seems meaningless now. They don't understand the beauty or the power as we do. It's been five years since we unearthed the empty tomb of King Akhenaton. I had hoped to find an intact tomb, but that dream is failing with my health." Dr. Lawrence took a small medicine bottle from his pocket and swallowed a pill. Then, he turned to his friend and grabbed his shoulder as they both stood. "You have been an encouraging assistant, my friend, but I think this project will be my last. Once this priest surrenders the secrets of his tomb, I must leave the desert."

"That is what you said after the last tomb. You cannot leave this place any more than I can. The spirits of the dead kings command us and guide our thoughts and actions."

"I never could fool you, Gammal. You're right. I'll probably die here. Why have you come for me?"

"Lighting has been connected and the final chamber is ready for your inspection. I'm afraid the writings are in poor condition. I know you were counting on the inner sanctuary walls to solve the mystery of Imhotek's master."

"We shall see. Lead the way."

A group of twenty men worked busily around what looked like nothing more than a large hole in the desert with a hastily constructed wooden entry to prevent the wind-blown sand from reclaiming the site. They discovered the tomb of the priest Imhotek by using a sophisticated sonar device that detected a cavern twenty feet beneath the desert floor. Dr. Lawrence directed the team that dug grain by grain until they reached a mud brick door that typified the tombs of the period. Now, months later, the tomb was open and ready for translation of the wall reliefs.

As with most tombs, they found it empty, robbed of its contents in ancient times. Gammal yelled orders to his men who prepared the equipment for loading on the trucks that waited near the tomb entrance. In a few days, the site would be sealed until the Department of Antiquities decided whether to open it to the public or not.

Dr. Lawrence cataloged and photographed the wall paintings, sure that the poor quality of the reliefs would doom them to three thousand more years of solitude. Suddenly, one of the better preserved hieroglyphs next to a platform that had held the plundered sarcophagus surprised him with a long sought reference to an undiscovered tomb.

"Gammal, come quickly," he called.

"What is it? Are you ill, Aton?"

"This is what I have searched for. Our priest, Imhotek, was indeed the high priest for Katara. The King's name is mentioned in numerous places, and there are references that I don't quite understand." Dr. Lawrence pointed to paintings of mountains, and he read from the wall. "The mountain of the living god, Katara, lies beneath the star of power." The wall painting showed a bright star shining directly over the tallest of the pyramid-shaped desert mountains. The scene also depicted the Nile river flooding its banks and the Avenue of Sphinxes leading to the Temple of Karnac. "The Nile always flooded in summer, so if the season is right, the star should appear and guide us to the location of Katara's tomb by standing on the east bank of the river near the Temple of Karnac. What is the date today, Gammal?"

"The fifth of September, Aton."

The next day, Dr. Lawrence crossed the Nile on a felluca and wandered into the Temple of Karnac. The sunset flamed over the mountains to the west, casting an orange hue on the massive columns and statues. Even now, after all the years of living among the ruins and temples, their majesty and grandeur never ceased to impress him. As the last of the tourists left the temple, the guards, whom he knew well, allowed him to remain and wander alone through the halls of ancient Egyptian history. Unique in all of Egypt, the Temple of Karnac was continually constructed for thousands of years, each Pharaoh re-designing the existing structure and adding his own unique addition, claiming the entire complex exclusively for royal worship.

Dr. Lawrence sat on the base of a colossal statue of Ramses II which overlooked the Nile to the west and the mountains, and waited for the sky to darken. The temperature dropped as the sun sank behind the mountains, but the change offered a welcome relief from the scorching heat of the day. He wrapped a colorful blanket around his shoulders to keep the night air from his weary body. The wrap sparked memories of the many friendships he had forged with the local people and it warmed his spirit.

The moonless, crystal night sky offered only a faint glow on the horizon as a final hint of the sunset lingered. A knot formed in his stomach as the stars appeared with the darkness and the outline of the mountains grew dim in the distance.

The season is right, though the Nile no longer floods its banks. Surely the stars will point the way to Katara's tomb. This is what I have waited thirty five years to find. . .

But there was no guiding light, no magical spirit to give away the king's long buried secrets. Not yet.

Disappointed by Imhotek's seeming misinformation, Dr. Lawrence fell asleep among the ghosts of five thousand years of Egyptian royalty.

Something startled him awake. The lights of nearby Luxor dimmed now, and the sky crowned itself with bright stars. Slowly, standing next to Ramses, Dr. Lawrence turned toward the river and the mountains beyond. There was no sound or breeze, as if even the air held its breath. There was no doubt in his mind when the brightest star in the sky signaled to him. Full of anticipatory adrenaline, frantically noting the familiar landmarks nearest the *mountain of power,* Dr. Lawrence knew he found the answer to the greatest mystery of his life.

The sun had hardly risen when Gammal shouted orders to his men. Ten teams of men walked in different directions around the base of the mountain, holding machines that looked like metal detectors, taking readings off the sensitive instruments that measured the density of the soil and rock. Dr. Lawrence had called in many favors in the Department of Antiquities to have this much equipment and man power on one project and on such short notice.

"Number three has a reading worth looking at," Gammal said to Dr. Lawrence, who sat at a portable desk under a billowy white canvas canopy, plotting the paths of each team. He divided the mountain into ten grids, each one painstakingly probed by a team of men for any type of underground cave or defect.

"Tell him to transmit his data to me."

Moments later, a computer printer delivered the information to the command post. Dr. Lawrence examined the printout and turned to Gammal.

"No good. There are too many jagged walls. It's probably just a small cave. Record the location and have number three continue on his assigned grid search."

Gammal barked the orders into the radio microphone, then returned to the desk.

After a week of searching and four cave citings, Dr. Lawrence wondered if the wall reliefs in the priest's tomb were indeed believable. The news from Cairo was also not good: funding for the search would last only two more days. On the final day, Gammal and Dr. Lawrence sat in the makeshift tent and sipped black Egyptian coffee from tiny pottery cups made in the workers nearby village.

Dr. Lawrence held up a cup. "A toast to a shattered dream." His face betrayed a great disappointment.

"I will not drink to defeat," said Gammal. "I drink to

loyalty and respect." Dr. Lawrence looked puzzled. "I have spoken with the men and all are in agreement. They will continue the search without pay until all the grids are completed."

"I don't know what to say. . ."

"No need. Most of these men have worked with you for years. They have seen your selfless dedication and love for their history. They pray to god that you will achieve your goal."

"Tell them they will be paid for their labor if I have to sell the shirt off my back."

Exactly two weeks after sighting the star above the mountain, a weary Dr. Lawrence listened as another report came in from the field. The excitement in the man's voice transmitted with his message and Gammal looked up as he noted the coordinates of the citing. Dr. Lawrence stopped writing in his journal and joined Gammal.

"The machine is going crazy. Northwestern section of grid seven," said Gammal, pointing to a map. "I think we should have a look at this one."

The Land Rover spewed sand as Dr. Lawrence floored the accelerator. Within minutes they reached the site.

Gammal called in the neighboring teams, hoping to use their equipment to verify the information in case of a faulty sensor. Now, a small group of men gathered around the depth finding devices as the Rover pulled up.

"The readings are confirmed by the other sensors," said one of the field men.

Dr. Lawrence checked the data and smiled.

For nearly three weeks, a dozen men dug slowly toward their instrument directed destination. Despite his ill health, Dr.

Lawrence joined in the digging, an act that gave his men the encouragement they needed to continue. Gammal was first to discover evidence that they were in the correct area.

"Aton," he called out. "You must see this."

Dr. Lawrence dropped a small tool and joined Gammal, who dug from a different direction. Gammal had dug four feet down and used a fine brush to uncover a smooth, flat stone. Dr. Lawrence immediately knew what it was.

"Congratulations, my friend. You've uncovered the top step of the tomb entrance. If my calculations are correct, according to the instruments, there are approximately twenty steps to go until we reach the door to the tomb."

Twenty-six steps and two weeks later, they stood before a familiar looking mud brick door that resembled the entrance to many of the tombs in the valley of the kings.

"I must admit, I'm a little disappointed," said Dr. Lawrence to Gammal. "I thought it would look different than the other tombs, especially for such an important king."

"We are not there yet, Aton."

Gammal was allowed the honor of drilling a hole through the brick door. The ancient mortar crumbled as the powerful drill passed through it with ease. A thin tube was inserted and air samples obtained. Then, the hole was enlarged and a small fiberoptic infrared video camera was inserted. Dr. Lawrence activated the monitor and held his breath momentarily as the camera panned the interior.

Nine

JAKE TOSSED IN HIS BED, TURNED ONTO HIS BACK, FOLDED his hands behind his head and stared at the ceiling. A blast of cold air from the open window chilled the room and forced him to retrieve a previously kicked-off blanket. His watch read 2:30 a.m.. The curtains flapped against the wall, responding to a sudden windy squall that pelted the open window with large rain drops. Jake got out of bed and closed the window, then jumped under the warm quilt. The extraordinary events of the day kept sleep at a distance.

Was it the encounter with the snake, or the excitement at the party, or meeting Lane Darby. . .

After the intruders left the dining room, Jake and several guests followed, but the stealth figures seemed to disappear into the walls of the old mansion. Mrs. Cromwell was quickly ushered out of the room by the servants and that was the last time he saw her. Their meeting never happened, despite his repeated requests for an audience. Finally, a servant told him that Mrs. Cromwell had left the house, and traveled to her home in Manhattan. He would be permitted to speak with her tomorrow and arrangements were made to fly to New York in the morning.

Jake slipped out of bed and walked into the bathroom. His body ached for sleep, but his mind refused. The radiator next to the sink clanked as the first steam of the season heated its pipes. He rubbed a soothing cream into the reddened areas on his wrists.

Jake's Rule 29 — Relax, organize your thoughts, plan for tomorrow.

Hot water splashed into the brass and white porcelain tub. Jake stretched his arms and legs, clearing his mind of the confusion and clutter that caused the anxiety. Feelings of frustration remained with his inability to remember the face he saw before passing out in the lab.

He stepped into the tub and felt his muscles relax. The meditative state came quickly to his practiced mind as the subconscious took over and blocked the worries and fears of daily life. In that place between wakefulness and sleep, his thoughts wandered to another time and place. . .

The river overflowed its banks and white water rapids erupted from the heavy rains of the east African monsoon. The Kush tribe responded to the floods and relocated their village further away from the beach, away from the muddy, rising waters, closer each day to the dense tropical rain forest. Okapi, the king, and his wife, Ajaya, watched the medicine man ceremoniously moving the Water of Fire to the new sacred spot he chose next to his own hearth. This was the key to the great power Okapi commanded over his enemies. With this weapon he had conquered all the tribes along the river.

Okapi and Ajaya had a daughter, Iroka, who had reached the age of three rains. She was the only royal child to survive a plague that had decimated the children of the tribe. Ajaya protected her, with a watchful eye always upon her. The royal family was now without a male heir, a fact that occupied Okapi's thoughts since the death of his only son. But he put this aside as a small group of his generals approached the king.

They bowed, touched their heads to the floor, then one man stood and spoke.

"Great one, our enemies gather and grow stronger at the mouth of the river. They will attack us with the passing of the rains."

"They are fools if they think they can overcome the fire that I will spread on the river as they cross to attack us." He turned to the medicine man. "How many moons before the end of the rains?" asked Okapi.

The old medicine man looked up at the sky for a long while, then said, "One moon circle."

"We will be ready for them," answered the king raising his spear high into the air. "The gods of war are with us."

The old man shook his beads, grabbed the king's spear and said, "The spirits do not smile. They tell me the Nubian and the Aksum tribes have joined together for the first time. Even the liquid fire will not be enough if you do not use it wisely. Their leader is. . ." he hesitated, averting his eyes.

"Speak. Who dares to lead these tribes against me?"

"Duala, your brother."

The king looked at the old man , not wanting to believe him, but knowing that he spoke the truth.

"My youngest brother will taste his own blood when this battle is over."

The king pushed the old medicine man aside and returned to his hut to plan the battle.

Finally, the sun broke through the clouds and the rains ended. The weather prediction was correct and this gave Okapi the time he needed. The hour of battle had arrived, and his warriors were anxious for the fight that would determine control of the river. Two men of his personal guard were chosen and given direct orders by the king for a special mission. They kneeled before him and listened to his command.

"Gather the women and children and take them in the

Great canoe to the middle of the upper river, where the fishing boats tie up in the still waters. Stay there until the battle is over. After the enemy is beaten, I will signal you to return." Secretly, he had given them additional orders. If the battle was lost, they were to take his wife and daughter to a village on the other side of the mountain. No one was to know of their royal identities.

Ajaya and Okapi said their farewells when the scouts brought word of the advancing enemy warriors.

The king knelt next to his daughter. "Do not cry, Iroka my little goddess. Soon I will hold you in my arms again and tell you I love you." The little girl cried despite her father's orders. She clung to a small beaded necklace that Okapi gave her. Iroka hugged her father, then removed the beads and placed them around his neck.

Ajaya stood close. She turned away and wiped the tears from her eyes, not wanting Iroka to see her weakness. She took Okapi's hand and held it next to her cheek. Her tears fell into his hand.

"I will never leave you. The spirits have told me we are mated forever," said Ajaya, holding him tightly.

"There is nothing to fear," he said, stroking her hair. Okapi smelled the smoke of his warriors fires as they readied for battle. "The fire of the gods will give us victory as it has in the past. The Kush will rule the river and all who live along her banks and I rule the Kush. Now go."

Ajaya and Iroka stepped into the royal boat and sat silently as the long canoe glided slowly into the river's current. Iroka clung to her mother and waved her tiny hand as the boats fled for safety. The skill of the oarsmen easily directed the boats upstream to the place of the still waters as ordered by the king.

With the women and children safely away, Okapi turned

his attention to the impending battle and gave orders to his men. Each man stood on the river bank ready to empty his pouch of sacred water into the river and set it ablaze. The old medicine man approached the king, who stood on the edge of the river ready to give the order and observe the battle. He knew he must wait until the enemy was close.

Thunder in the distance heralded the approach of a storm. The king ordered the medicine man brought to the river's edge.

"You said the rains were over. Why is the god of thunder angry? Did you make the sacrifice as I have ordered?"

"The gods no longer listen to me. Abandon the battle now before it is too late. The wind is your enemy now. Do not set the fire upon the water."

"Abandon my people and my lands? I would sooner die with my warriors. You told me the fire would destroy our enemies. Why do you now tell me not to set the river on fire?"

"I did not know the god of the wind would turn against us and blow the fire upon our own women and children," said the medicine man.

"You are to blame for this. The gods distrust you and the wind helps our enemies."

Furious, Okapi ordered his guard to take the old man away. Suddenly, he took his spear and thrust it into the medicine man. With the tip of the weapon protruding from his chest, the old man collapsed to the ground.

Okapi looked at his men, poised to pour the liquid fire into the river. He knew that this was the only way the battle could be won. For the first time in his life, he was unsure of himself.

Okapi heard the whoops of the enemy warriors as they massed on the other side of the river, then launched their canoes and approached the Kush warriors.

Without hesitation, the king climbed on the royal platform, and sat on the throne. The order was given to pour the fire into the river and ignite it.

Within minutes, the river was ablaze. Screams of agony from the men caught in the fire blended with the whoops of his own men at the joy of their victory.

True to the old man's prediction, the wind changed direction and carried the flames upstream, away from the attackers. In the distance, Okapi's mind's eye envisioned Ajaya and his daughter caught in the monstrous flames, choking for air, then burning to death in the blazing water.

"Ajaya," he called out, then, yanked Iroko's necklace from his neck, held it next to his heart and fell to his knees.

His men waited for the signal to attack that never came. seized by grief, Okapi never heard the war cries of his enemy as they waited for the flames to abate and overrun the leaderless Kush warriors. He looked up into the eyes of a familiar face painted with strange markings.

"Duala, my brother. The spirits have turned against me. Why have you painted yourself with the colors of our enemies?" The Nubian warriors gathered around the royal platform. Duala held up Okapi's shield and spear.

"I claim the lands of the river." His warriors whopped until he held up his hand. "Bring the basket of truth. My brother must take the test."

Two warriors brought a covered basket and set it in front of Okapi.

"If he survives the test, the gods will allow him to live."

Duala gave the signal and the guards forced Okapi's arm into the basket.

Before he could protest, Okapi felt the sharp sting of a snake bite, then the intense burning sensation as the poison entered his bloodstream. . .

Jake jolted out of his trance by a sharp pain in his arm, which disappeared when he opened his eyes.

God, I hate snakes.

The bath water drained silently as Jake returned to the warm bed. He felt calm and relaxed, his head cushioned by the cool, down pillow as he thought of the dream he'd had while meditating. It seemed so real, so disturbing; not the first time he'd dreamed about death. His thoughts shifted to the present and the tiny Megalon modules that had the power to expand the mind to unimagined heights. Sleep drifted over him and filled his dreams with visions of events that would change his life forever.

Jake buckled the seatbelt and waited patiently in one of the two rear passenger seats of the InDevCo helicopter. The delay annoyed him and he called to the pilot. "What's the problem?"

"Another passenger. Supposed to be here any minute."

Jake glanced at his watch, anxious to begin the trip to New York and share the new information of the basement lab and the diary with Mrs. Cromwell. A lone figure carrying an attache case emerged from the back of the mansion and ran the length of the closely manicured lawn toward the helicopter. She stopped just next to the aircraft as the pilot took the case and helped her into the seat next to Jake.

"Good morning, Jake," said Lane. She spoke loudly to be heard over the increasing noise of the engine.

"You're late," Jake said, hiding both his surprise and pleasure at seeing her again.

"Sorry, but the police seemed to have endless questions."

"Did you have answers?"

"Not many," she said settling into her seat. Jake noted

the reflection of sunlight through Lane's golden hair. "Hell of a time to be in charge of security. Here's a copy of the police report." She reached into her case and handed him a red file folder marked confidential. The chopper lifted off and the file slipped from her hand onto the floor between them. Jake instinctively reached down to retrieve it at the same time as Lane and they lightly bumped heads, then laughed. Jake scanned the file but his mind could not focus on it. The craft reached its cruising altitude and floated through the clouds. Many minutes passed in silence. Jake looked at her, then out the window.

"Tell me about Philip," he said.

She placed a folder in her brief case then looked pensive and said, "What do you want to know?"

"Were you two close?"

"Yes, but our relationship was strictly business. He treated me more like a friend than an employee. In a way, I came to feel like he was the father I never had. We had a special feeling for each other but it was not sexual. I've become very protective of his memory and anything we did together."

"I only meant. . ."

"No, it's okay. You're just doing your job, I understand. Philip was a brilliant man, Jake. He had insight and intuition that enabled him to build an empire. With his business genius, he could put his finger on the trends of the market, or create a new market for one of our products. Of course, much of our work is classified and top secret. But Philip was happiest when he worked on something new and exciting. Something that had the potential to change the old ways of doing things."

"Like the Megalon Project," said Jake.

The expression on Lane's face changed as if all her defenses suddenly activated.

"How could you possibly know about Megalon?" she asked, the softness gone from her voice.

"*Jake's Rule 109 — never divulge trade secrets,*" said Jake.

"Do you just make up these preposterous rules as you go along or is there a handbook called Jake's Jerky Jingles?" she asked.

"Catchy title. I'll have to remember it when I publish my autobiography."

"How much do you know about Megalon?" she asked, the sarcasm gone from her voice.

The helicopter landed on the roof of the InDevCo building and the door swung open. Without answering, Jake stood and offered his hand to help Lane with the case.

"Shall we go?" he asked.

She ignored him, stepped off the aircraft and quickly walked toward the elevator. Jake grabbed his case and hurried to catch up. She wore a stern look.

"Was it something I said?" he asked.

"I asked you a question."

"Did you know you have the cutest dimple on your left cheek when you frown?"

Her expression was unchanged. They entered the elevator together. Jake straightened his tie and looked at his watch.

"Why are we here? I'm supposed to see Mrs. Cromwell at noon."

"Oh, I forgot to tell you. She called this morning and postponed that appointment. She said she'll notify you when another meeting would be convenient."

"How does she expect me to help without her cooperation? Guess I'll have to go on what I have."

"Which is?"

The door slid open and they stepped into a plushly carpeted lobby. On one side, a secretary sat at a round reception desk in front of a computer console that wrapped around the entire surface of the desk. Low chairs lined up against the walls except for a glass wall that overlooked the ground floor lobby far below. Jake stepped up to the glass and whistled. A stained glass skylight lit a forty story atrium.

"Very impressive." Jake said, looking at the pressurized bullet elevators that whisked InDevCo employees from the ground floor lobby to their offices in seconds. "Never seen anything like that."

"There are many innovations here. Follow me," she ordered. Jake turned from the glass wall and followed Lane into a corridor that led to a smaller lobby. "Your office is through here."

Jake grabbed Lane's arm and spun her around.

"Look, we're going to be working together for a while so why not call a truce?"

"Tell me how you know about one of our most secret projects and I may acknowledge your existence here."

"First tell me if Philip's disappearance has anything to do with Megalon."

"Don't get too comfortable in your new office, Mr. Parker. I don't think you'll be staying long." Lane turned to walk away.

"It's Jake, and you win on one condition."

"I'm listening."

"After I tell you how I know about Megalon, you tell me what I want to know."

"No deal. You have the balls to dictate terms to me? As far as I'm concerned, you have no security clearance and your title is a paper one given to you by Madame Cromwell who should have kept her nose out of this." She repeatedly stuck her finger in his shoulder as she spoke backing him up against the door to his office until they were face to face. He could smell her perfume and looked directly into a flame of defiance in her eyes.

Jake suddenly kissed her on the mouth. She took a quick breath of utter astonishment and was speechless for a moment, then raised her arm to slap him on the face.

"Remind me never to have you as my enemy," he said, blocking her meager attempt. "Now what do you want to know?"

Lane turned and tried to hide that fact that the kiss disarmed her.

"You really are exasperating. I want to know where you got your information."

"From Philip Cromwell," said Jake, entering his office. He whistled again. "Wow. I always wanted an office like this."

"Impossible," she followed him in and turned to face him again, this time keeping her distance.

"Scouts honor," he said, crossing his heart with one finger. "I found the basement lab in the mansion. Philip's diary told all. Is it true that you sleep in the nude?"

"Yes. . .no. . .I mean none of your business. What else did you find out. I must know."

"Why?"

"Your life could depend on it."

"That's sweet of you but I'm a big boy, Lane. By the way, I sleep naked too. We should get together and compare notes on that subject," Jake said, swiveling in the black leather executive chair like a kid on an amusement ride.

"I'd rather wrestle a mother grizzly bear after taking a cub from her."

"Nice office. Who occupied it before me?" he asked.

"Charles Cromwell."

"A man I'd very much like to meet. Can you arrange it?"

"Me? What makes you think I could do that?"

"I know about your affair with him."

"You really are full of endless surprises, Jake. I'm changing my mind about you. Maybe you are the one who can find out about Philip's death. Just how do you know about Charles and me?"

"*Jake's Rule #40 — Knowledge is power.* I love that one, though I didn't make it up. Can you do it?"

"What?"

"Arrange an appointment with Charles."

"No one arranges anything with Charles. If he wants to meet you, it'll be on his terms."

"Sounds ominous."

"Charles is insane, Jake. You're better off keeping your distance."

"Somehow, he's a part of this and I'll have to meet him eventually. Now, about Megalon and these computers. You promised if I. . ."

She stood in front of the console and pointed to the controls. "These computers utilize the new superconductive circuits that we developed in our main lab. We call it Lorestronics, which is short for low resistance electronics. Comparing a traditional integrated circuit to an intelligent lorestron logic pathway is like comparing cave writings to satellite communications." She looked at her watch. "Since I seem to have no choice in this matter, I think your questions will be better answered if I take you to the Megalon lab in Subterra. Everything you need to know is there." Jake smiled and nodded his head as she spoke. "I'll meet you on the helipad in two hours. Have my secretary call for a pilot."

"No need. I can fly the helicopter. Just get the co-ordinates."

"All this brainpower and he flies a plane too. What else can you do that's not in your file?"

"You sure you want to know?"

"No. See you on the roof," said Lane turning to leave the room.

Jake toyed with the controls on the desk console. He had only seen equipment like this once before.

The Newport lab. . .

Forty stories below in the atrium lobby, a man wearing dark, wire rimmed sunglasses sat in the Concourse Cafe, pretending to enjoy an espresso coffee and a half-eaten croissant as he watched the growing lunch time crowd hurry through the fountained courtyard. A giant sculptured clock dominated the largest of the fountains and chimed the noon hour. Feeling comfortably lost in the crowd, the man finished his coffee and stood, carefully surveying the area. He picked up a brief case and walked toward a bank of elevators. As each car discharged its many passengers, the tumult grew worse, allowing him to slip unnoticed to the last elevator marked "Security Clearance Required." He stood in front of the scanner and produced an InDevCo badge with the number 001 on it, and swiped it through the security slot. Seconds later, the elevator door slid open, he stepped inside and it closed rapidly. A low hissing sound was the only sign that the car pressurized, ready for its almost instantaneous ascent to the roof of the building.

The InDevCo helicopter sat on its rooftop pad while two maintenance men checked her systems for flight readiness. In the shadows, the man stood and watched the crew until they finished their work and left the helipad area. Satisfied that all was clear, he approached the aircraft. He removed a small package from the brief case and carefully attached an electronic device to the underside of the copter's main rotor. After inspecting his work and being certain that it was small enough to escape detection, he set a remote control microswitch that activated the altimeter for four thousand feet.

The waiting elevator delivered him to the crowded lobby where he exited the building and crossed the street. Now, out of danger, he allowed himself the luxury of relaxing, turned to look up and smiled, certain that his mission would be a success.

Ten

A CLOUD OF SMOG HOVERED OVER THE CITY LIKE A shroud, obliterating skyscrapers that extended to the river. Jake stood near the thick plate glass window of his office and stared at endless stream of cars and people that clogged the streets below. His electronic sweep scan of the office detected a 'bug' in the Ficus tree next to the window. Uncertain as to its ownership, he decided to leave the transmitter in place and say nothing to Lane. Jake returned to his desk and admired the display; the video screen panel measured barely one inch thick and had appeared from a hidden place in the desk. Automatically, he searched for the keyboard, then remembered Lane's description of the advanced capability of the system.

"Intelligent computers", she had said.

"Are you there, computer?" Jake asked.

"Affirmative," answered a synthesized voice. "Please identify. Voice frequency does not correspond with security coded individuals."

"Me? I'm Jake Parker. Ruth Cromwell appointed me chief of security yesterday. Do you have that order on file?"

"Affirmative. Good morning Mr. Parker. How may I assist you?"

Jake sat back in his seat and smiled. "God damn, it really

works. Computer, do I have access to all InDevCo classified project information?"

"All except those with zone ten classification."

"List all classified projects in progress within the last six months."

"Project Sea Titan, Project Andromeda, Project Glastic, Project Atlantia, Project Solarwind, Project Lorestron Particle Beam, Project Megalon, Project. . ."

"Computer, stop," Jake ordered , looking at the list on the screen in front of him. "Display data on Project Megalon."

"Information on this project is tied to zone ten security and is unavailable."

"Computer, who has level ten security clearance?"

"Philip Cromwell, Andrew Cromwell, Charles Cromwell, Dr. Lane Darby and Dr. Eric Fontaine."

Jake was about to question the computer again, when there was a quiet knock at the door.

"Well, I see it didn't take you very long to figure out how everything works," Lane said.

Jake stared at her for a moment. "I've been reviewing some of the company projects, and I can't seem to gain access to one of the files."

Lane entered the office wearing a loose white lab coat that only partially hid her tight jeans and western shirt with the top three buttons open.

"Well, let me guess which file you're after. Could it be the Megalon project?"

"Your bio didn't list telepathy as one of your talents. I'm impressed."

"I've just spoken with Ruth Cromwell and she's confirmed that you're working directly for her. She's instructed me to cooperate with you, even though I don't quite trust you. What do you want to know about Megalon?"

"Start from the beginning."

"It started as a research study but became a continuation of the work begun in Germany at the Munich Institute of Biotechnology on brain function. The Germans were studying that part of the brain that sets humans above all other animals on the evolutionary scale, the cerebral cortex." Lane pushed a series of console controls on Jake's desk and a three dimensional image of a human brain appeared on the screen. As she spoke it rotated to illustrate the cerebral cortex. "Much of it has been well charted and mapped, but there are still many mysteries concerning the brain. As you know from Philip's diary, our recent discoveries in superconductive electronics led to the development of the cerebral cortex expansion modules. Our initial experiments were promising, but after Philip's death, we abandoned the project."

Jake believed Lane told the truth as she knew it, but he couldn't accept the cancellation of a project with the potential impact of Megalon.

"May I see the data on the project up until the time it was canceled?" he asked.

Lane looked at her watch and walked toward the door. "You will when we get to Subterra and the Megalon lab. I've got to pick up the prototype of an experiment Dr. Fontaine worked on for the past month, and then we can leave. Meet me in my office."

Jake busied himself with the intricacies of his first intelligent computer, then made his way to Lane's office and introduced himself to her secretary, an attractive red haired woman with more freckles than Jake had ever seen on one face.

"Dr. Darby is expecting you, Mr. Parker. You can go right in."

Jake opened the door, entered and stopped short. The office was empty.

"Lane?" he called out.

"Back here," answered a voice from a room adjacent to the office. Jake walked toward the voice.

The room was a small testing lab crammed full of electronic gear and equipment. Lane stood and aimed a lorestron gun at a life-size manikin that emanated a blue, glowing aura.

"Thank God I'm in time," Jake said, trying to suppress a smile. "The governor just called with a stay of execution."

"Stand in back of me," she said, ignoring his humor. "In case the beams ricochet in this direction, the shield will protect us. I wouldn't want anything to happen to our new chief of security."

Jake huddled close to her in back of a clear, plexiglass shield. The aura around the dummy fascinated Jake, but her perfume distracted him.

"Why are we doing this?" he whispered in her ear. The fresh smell of her hair reminded him of a distant memory.

"Watch."

She fired all the rounds of the gun into the manikin, but the beams bounced off.

"Nice shooting, but you missed the target. You smell terrific. How did you know Shalimar was my favorite?"

Lane moved around the shield and toward the manikin, pushed a button on the control console and the blue aura disappeared. Then, she unhooked a thick belt around its waist.

"It's a force field we've worked on for months. Dr. Fontaine is going to finish the testing in the Subterra facility. I'll call for a pilot and we'll be on our way."

"Don't bother. I already told you I can fly the chopper."

"Is there anything you can't do?" Lane asked while packing the belt in a specially prepared transport container.

"Nothing I care to talk about."

"Aha, the truth revealed. Doest thou play amongst the gods or be mortal as we?" she asked, only half expecting an answer.

"I can't stand the dark," Jake said in a low voice.

"What?" She was surprised at the humorless answer.

"The dark. I hate the dark and I don't know why. Your turn. Now, you tell me a secret."

"This is ridiculous. I'm not going to. . . "

"Oh, come on and loosen up. Surely there's something."

"The smell of smoke," she said after a long pause.

"What about it?"

"Even the slightest smell of smoke makes my throat close and I choke."

"There now, don't you feel closer for having shared that?"

She sighed. "I'm a new woman. Let's get to the roof. Dr. Fontaine is waiting. We can play lets be vulnerable later."

"This could be a very interesting day. Lead the way," he said.

The elevator delivered them to the roof and they climbed aboard the InDevCo helicopter.

"These are the coordinates of the lab," she said handing him what looked like a computer disc. Jake took the disc, inserted it into a slot in the console, then completed the preflight check list and engaged the computer auto-pilot. The aircraft lifted effortlessly and sailed over the rooftops of the city. Lane checked the transport case secured in the rear seat. Satisfied with its condition, she relaxed for the first time since the morning. Jake sensed her stare and their eyes met.

"I. . .I'm sorry," she said.

"For what?"

"I acted like a fool earlier. I realize now that we're both on the same side. I'm more upset by Philip's death than I thought."

"It's okay. *Jake's Rule 23 — Don't sweat the small stuff.*"

"Those damn rules again. I'd better start writing them down since you don't have a book of them. Who knows, maybe we can get them published?"

Jake laughed. "How far to the lab?"

"Around one hundred and fifty miles," she said.

The flight took them out of the city, north, over Westchester county. Rolling hills and lush, green forest replaced dense population. Soon the landscape changed again to sprawling farmland and fertile valleys that stretched to the horizon. Like a giant checkerboard, great square plots of corn and wheat swayed in the gentle breezes, with only the occasional red roofed barn to disrupt the vista.

A barely audible noise interrupted the drone of the engine.

"What was that?" asked Lane.

"Something's happened to the main rotor. I can't control the altitude."

Just as Jake spoke, the copter dove into the clouds; all efforts at stabilization unsuccessful. Jake knew a controlled landing was impossible. They were going to crash.

"We're going down. We'll have to chance it and jump," she said.

"That's a crazy idea. There's no chance of surviving a fall from this height with no chute."

"Just follow my lead."

Suddenly, Lane turned around, reached for the lab transport box and pulled out the belt. She fastened it around her waist and grabbed Jake's arm.

"Come on," she yelled, pulling his arm. She flung open the door and they jumped from the spinning craft.

Jake clung to Lane and they were face to face.

"I have the feeling we've done this before," he said loudly. The wind howled as they free-fell at great speed.

"Shut up and hold on to me."

Lane touched a button on the belt and the blue aura enclosed them.

"This will be its first field test," she said. "I'm sure it wasn't designed to do this kind of a job."

"It better work. I have a ten dollar winning lottery ticket in my pocket."

The ground approached fast.

Seconds later, they impacted with the upper branches of

a pine tree, snapping its limbs. The lower branches also gave way and they hit the ground. Dazed, Jake could see Lane lying nearby, unconscious. His vision blurred, then he too lost consciousness.

Eleven

LANE DRIFTED BETWEEN IMAGES OF HAZY, GRAY clouds and momentary flashes of bright light. Something pulled her toward the clouds and away from the light, though she felt a strong attraction for the calm feeling stimulated by the brightness. The feeling of falling persisted and the clouds engulfed her. There was no sensation of fear or pain, just weightlessness and falling. Visions of strangely familiar people filled her mind and she was freed from the boundaries of her consciousness. . .

Hundreds of eyes looked right through her as if she were transparent. These were not the faces of her friends, who only last week complimented her appearance at the church function she and her husband, Chauncey, attended to honor his appointment as chief magistrate. These were strangers, though they looked the same as the people she knew before, they acted hateful and passed whispered rumors about her.

Rumors she knew were true.

It was impossible to deny to herself. The feelings she had for James were profound, even though they only just met one month ago when he arrived to take his place as the newly appointed vice-magistrate, she felt like she knew him for years. Their clandestine meetings took on a sense of urgency when she thought Chauncey suspected the truth, but that only served to sweeten the ecstasy she relished in the passionate meetings she and James shared when and where ever possible.

"Lara Devy, you stand accused of witchcraft and adultery. How do you plead?" asked the court scribe.

"I am not guilty. As the wife of the chief magistrate, I demand you release my bonds and free me. Where is my husband? He will help me." The crowded courtroom quieted as the magistrate entered and sat in his chair on the podium. He did not look at his wife.

"Chauncey, tell them this is a mistake. I've done nothing."

She struggled to free her hands.

"Read the charges," ordered the magistrate.

The scribe opened a large book and read aloud.

"Lara Devy stands accused of practicing witchcraft. Using spells and potions with magical powers, she compelled her accomplice, James Palmer, to fall in love with her and perform unnatural acts of sexual perversion. When discovered, the defendant tried to turn herself into a bird to escape punishment, but was caught."

"I'm no witch." The crowd gasped and pulled back as she screamed in exasperation. "If I were, why wouldn't I escape now?"

Chauncey Devy ignored her ravings. "If the defendant pleads not guilty, she is entitled to a trial. How pleads the co-defendant?"

"No plea," said James Palmer, who had his wrists and ankles bound together with chains. "I do not recognize the power of this court to judge me. I can be judged only by the governor. I demand the chance to speak with him."

The magistrate ignored the statement. "Trial is set for tomorrow morning. Defendants will have the entire night to think about the true events in this case." Without looking at his wife, the magistrate stood and left the room.

James and Lara were taken to a dungeon deep beneath the courtroom. Lara was forced onto a flat table with each hand and foot tied tightly to their respective corners. She cringed at the coldness of the stone table, though the narrow blood collecting troughs carved into the surface bothered her even more. James was placed in a tight body-shaped cage and suspended from a rope over a pool of foul smelling sludge. Lara vomited from the stench of rotting flesh and raw sewage. The jailer looked at her, laughed and left them alone.

"Oh, James, tell me you love me and this will end with us running away together as we planned."

She struggled to free herself from the tightly fastened bonds.

"Your husband has another ending in mind for this story. Our only hope is that your father gets word of what Chauncey has done. Only he, as governor, can save us now."

Before James could continue, the door opened and the jailer returned with the magistrate.

"Oh, Chauncey, thank God you're here. Untie me and we'll straighten this out right now."

"Still giving orders, Lara? You don't seem to understand. It's over."

"You filthy pig. If it wasn't for me, you'd still be cleaning fish in the market where I found you. I made you what you are. You're nothing without me."

"Harsh words, my love, but I no longer have need of you. I know all about your plan for Master Palmer to take my place as magistrate. Did you really think I would do nothing while the two of you schemed and plotted my demise?"

"When my father hears what you've done to me, he'll have you drawn and quartered. Let us out of here."

"Ah, your father. If all goes well, he should be dead by now. Even you must admit it's a neat little plan. The only regret I have is that it took six years of hellish marriage to you to carry it out. By this time tomorrow, I'll be the new governor of the territory. Goodbye, my dear. This man has work to do here with you and James. Do cooperate with him and he'll be much easier with you."

She spat at him.

Chauncey looked at the jailer, who nodded and smiled.

The screams from the dungeon throughout the night went unheard by the town's people. After Lara could endure no further pain, she lost consciousness.

Lara opened her eyes and squinted in the bright sunshine. She was surprised to find herself in the middle of the town square. Her hands were bound behind her to a large wooden stake. All around her were piles of dry wood and kindling; her memory of the previous night, unclear. She did remember James' cries for help as the jailer submerged him in the sewage. Then, unconscious but still breathing, he was thrown into a coffin and taken away. She blocked most of the torture from her mind, though the puncture wounds throbbed and the taste of blood lingered in her mouth. She remembered saying whatever was required to stop the torture, even admitting to witchcraft. Someone in the crowd noticed her eyes open.

"The witch is awake. Burn her."

Lara noticed Chauncey in the distance holding onto a black book she recognized as her financial accounts book. He held the book up and waved. In his other hand, he held Hannah, Lara's favorite Persian cat. She was dead.

The people looked to Chauncey, who gave the signal.

"No, I'm no witch," she screamed. "I'm innocent."

A single flame touched the tinder dry wood and it quickly encircled her. Her wrists ached and bled from the futile struggle to free herself before the fire devoured her. Lara coughed as the hot smoke seared her lungs. The flames roared and grew in size, fueled by the wind and the dry wood. Smoke poured over her forcing the people back. Her tears boiled as they fell onto her blistered cheeks and the flesh fell away from her body.

All at once the excruciating pain and heat ceased, exchanged for a feeling of floating and pleasure. Lara watched the entire scene from above the smoke, no longer concerned about the lost wealth, the flames, or any earthly worry. With a thought, she was at the cemetery and watched two men lower a plain wooden coffin into the ground.

Red dirt covered the coffin and a simple cross was placed on the grave. Hard as she tried, she could not stop them or tell them that James still lived. She looked into the coffin and saw him struggle, heard his cries.

But it was too late.

Soon, they would be together again.

Twelve

A SPIDER EXPLORED JAKE'S NOSE AND HE TWITCHED. Slowly, his eyes opened. Crimson and yellow streaked the blue sky of early sunset. Jake lay on a soft bed of pine needles beneath the tree that broke their fall. Many of its branches were stripped by the impact and lay scattered around him. He sat up, still shocked by the experience, wondering how many hours had passed since the crash. Jake noticed Lane a few feet from him, unconscious but breathing.

Visions of the fall flashed before him and he shook his head to clear his thoughts. He moved, slowly at first, then stood and knelt next to Lane. Her pulse was strong and regular. She moaned as her head moved in response to his touch, then her eyes opened.

"We made it," he said. "Can you move?"

"I think so. I'm a little dizzy." Jake helped her stand and she collapsed into his arms. "My right ankle hurts like hell."

"We're lucky to be alive. We'll have to thank Dr. Fontaine and tell him we found a new use for his force field." Lane sat on a rock and stretched her right leg. Jake examined her foot. "The ankle looks pretty bad. I don't know if it's broken, but you won't be square dancing any time soon."

"Is that your prescription, Dr. Parker?"

"That and plenty of bed rest. I can help you with that part."

She scowled, then winced in pain after trying to move.

"It's getting dark. We've got to find shelter. Any idea how far we are from the lab?" he asked.

"I'd guess about twenty miles. What do you think happened to the helicopter?"

"No idea, but rotor blades don't came apart like that by themselves."

"Sabotage?"

"A definite possibility. But let's leave that to the authorities. Lean on me and try to stand." He lifted her.

"It's no good," she said. "I can't put any weight on it."

"Then we have no choice." Jake pitched her over his shoulder.

"Do you intend to carry me like this all the way to the lab?"

"Only if it's over the next hill. Before we jumped, I spotted a building in that direction. Let's try for it."

Jake steadied himself and walked slowly through the grassy field. Bursts of yellow and purple wild flowers complimented the last of the sun's rays. The hill that looked small from the distance may as well have been a mountain to Jake. He struggled, but did not complain. At the top, Jake gently lowered Lane onto a grassy mound.

"There's our hotel," Jake said, pointing to an abandoned barn. "I'm afraid they might not have room service, but the price is right. I'd say it's about a quarter of a mile. There's a stream on the other side of the barn, so at least we won't be thirsty. How's the foot?" Jake said nothing about the sharp pain in his shoulder. Carrying Lane had irritated an old rotator cuff injury.

The expression on Lane's face answered the question as she rubbed the swollen ankle. The injured foot was twice the size of her other ankle.

"Let's go, princess. There's only a bit of light left, and the temperature's dropping."

Lane took his arm and stood on her good foot, then Jake slung her over his good shoulder. He winced from the sudden move, but was sure she didn't see his expression.

Within twenty minutes, the abandoned remains of a barn composed of decayed and rotted wood stood before them. Most of the roof was gone, exposing the front section. Only a small area toward the back had its walls and roof intact and offered the best protection from the elements. Jake carried Lane through the broken doors to the covered area. He lowered her onto the dirt floor, avoiding her bad foot and the pain in his shoulder at the same time.

"I'll gather hay from the other stalls and make a cushion for your foot," he said, unconsciously massaging his aching shoulder.

"What's the matter with you?" she asked, propping herself on her hands.

"Just an old war injury acting up."

"You were never in the war."

"I forgot you know more about me than I do. Never mind me, we've got to reduce the swelling in that foot."

"Maybe I should just call down to the front desk for a bucket of ice."

"Do that. Ask for champagne and caviar while your at it.

In the meantime, I have another idea. Don't go away."

The first beams of moonlight transformed the countryside with a magical aura. Owls hooted into the crisp night air. Jake gathered kindling and logs, then walked to the bottom of the hill to the stream he'd seen earlier. He ripped the sleeves from his shirt and immersed them in the icy water. In minutes, he returned to the barn and piled the logs onto the smaller, dry kindling.

"Wrap this around the ankle," he said, placing the cold compress on her swollen foot. Now, watch this. I used to be boy scout."

Jake took two pencil thin branches and rubbed them together on a flat, dry piece of wood with a knot in it.

"This works. Just give me a minute," he said, twirling the branches together.

Lane sat back and watched him. The cold compress eased the pain and she relaxed. After five minutes, Jake stopped what he was doing, and sat with his back against the wall. Lane reached into her pocket and removed a cigarette lighter.

"You could have said something sooner," he said.

"And spoil your fun? Never."

Jake took the lighter and read the inscription by the light of the full moon. "Yours to command. . . Love always, CC. Anyone I know?" asked Jake.

"Not really. Actually, I'm trying hard to forget him."

"Then why carry it around?"

"To remind me of the past, so I don't make the same mistake. The inscription tells all except, it's a lie. He wanted to control me and was insanely jealous. The relationship was doomed from the start, only I didn't realize it until it was too late."

"Did you love him?" Jake asked, starting the fire with the lighter.

"I thought I did. But that's all in the past. Let's talk about you. What's the real Jake Parker like?"

Jake knelt on one knee and stoked the fire. An orange glow bathed them with its warmth. He sat close to her.

"Just a down to Earth guy who knows a little about a lot of things. Pretty ordinary, actually."

"I don't think so."

"Do I detect a crack in the ice? Maybe there's a real person in there after all." He looked at her then stared into the fire.

"I suppose I deserved that. How's the shoulder?" she asked.

"I'll live."

"Let me see it," she said. "I've had some medical training." She unbuttoned and removed his shirt. "Quite a collection of scars. I'll bet each one has a fascinating history."

The fire crackled and a shower of sparks rocketed into the air.

"How's this?" she asked, gently massaging the tense muscles in his shoulder and chest.

Jake gazed at the reflection of the fire in her eyes. He liked the curve of her nose and mouth, the graceful outline of her breasts against her blouse.

"Feels better already." He grasped her hands together and kissed them softly. "You have a magical touch. The pain is gone."

She pulled away.

"What's the matter?"

"It's not you. I can't explain."

"Is it CC?"

"I always believed happiness could be worked out. I was a fool. Now, the only thing that makes my life bearable are my fantasies."

Jake stared into the fire, his thoughts far away. "I've lived with a different sort of pain. My wife and son were killed in an accident as I watched helplessly. The words come easily to me now, but for a long time, that day of terror was locked deep inside of me. I lived my life as an illusion of normalcy, working and going through the motions, but I was an empty shell. If it weren't for my brother, Harry, I. . . well, he made me realize that tormenting myself wasn't going to bring them back to life, and I had to get on with mine."

"I'm sorry. I didn't know."

Jake continued to peer into the fire. A single tear fell onto his cheek. Lane turned to him and brushed it with her finger.

Her lips touched his, featherlike.

"Thank you," she whispered.

"For what?"

"I know it wasn't easy for you to share that with me."

"It'll always be a part of me."

She moved against him in a suggestive body caress. Her mouth moved over his in a sensuous exploration. The kiss left them breathless. Jake felt passion rekindled in him.

"Are you sure you're ready for this?" he asked.

"Lane's rule #1—never throw away a good thing when

you find it."

Sunrise signaled the new day for birds, and they sang noisily as they went about their morning task of food gathering. The sounds reached Jake and he awoke first. Lane soon stirred and opened her eyes.

"Good morning," he said, and kissed her lightly on the forehead.

"What time is it?" she asked.

"Time to leave. We should find a main road and hitch a ride to the nearest town. I'm starved, but there's nothing. Maybe we can find some berries on the way. Think you can walk today? Seems like the swelling is down a bit."

"No need for any of that." Lane activated a microswitch on her watch.

"Mind telling me what you're doing?"

"Calling for help, of course. Fortunately, it wasn't damaged in the fall. Another helicopter will be on its way. It's an emergency signal and homing device. They should have no difficulty finding us."

"I think I've been set up."

Lane smiled as she held onto Jake and stood. They walked slowly out of the barn into the bright sunshine.

Lane toyed with the cigarette lighter in her pocket and let it fall to the ground.

Thirteen

Albuquerque, New Mexico

THE JEEP TIRES SPUN AIMLESSLY IN THE LOOSE DESERT sand beside the narrow road. Even four wheel drive could not save Julia Welles from the overpowering feeling of dread that rooted in the pit of her stomach.

"Shit," she yelled aloud, banging her fist on the steering wheel, knowing no one could hear her. "An easy first assignment," she muttered, mimicking her boss, who only two hours ago, handed her the keys to the company jeep. "Just follow the route marked in yellow on the map," she continued, and reached into the back seat to retrieve her purse, a tape recorder and a plastic container full of water. "No one said anything about snakes in the middle of the damn road."

Julia put on silk brimmed safari hat, checked her make up in the rear view mirror, and picked up the tape recorder.

"Note to me. Trash the crimson rose eye shadow." She quickly took a pair of dark glasses from the glove compartment, then placed the recorder and water into her purse and glared at the road. "Don't they know I hate snakes," she repeated. The sound of her own voice made her feel not so alone.

The dirt road stretched for miles through the dry lake bed.

Guessing the major distance lay behind her, she left the jeep. An hour later, Julia sat on a large rock and finished the last of the water. She tossed the container onto the road and rubbed her feet. The outstretched map flapped in the dry wind and she placed her high heel shoes on either side to anchor it while studying the yellow line her editor had drawn.

"What was I thinking when I left Bloomingdales and Saks for this?" Blisters throbbed on the bottom of each foot as did the sun reddened skin on her arms and neck. But two large, black birds circling overhead bothered her most.

The sight of a growing cloud of dust in the distance distracted Julia from her misery.

"Oh, thank you daddy. I knew you were watching out for me from up there."

Julia stood in the middle of the road and waved her arms at the approaching car. She was not about to take a chance on missing the only available ride. The dusty Chevy pick-up stopped in front of her.

"That your Jeep off the side of the road back there?" asked the driver with a slight southern drawl.

"You're a lifesaver. I was about to be lunch for those black pigeons up there?"

"They're buzzards and they wouldn't bother you until after you're dead. I can take you to a phone to have your Jeep towed out of the sand. Hop in."

"I can't thank you enough. I was actually perspiring out there."

"What are you doing here, miss. . ."

"Oh, Julia Welles, but most people call me Jewels. I'm a fashion reporter with the Albuquerque Gazette."

"I didn't realize desert fashion was front page news these days."

"Well, the guy in charge of the science stories is out of town. I just moved here from New York and I guess no one else wanted this assignment. So here I am. I swerved the Jeep off the road to avoid a huge snake. The rest you can figure out."

"You've a lot to learn about desert survival," he said pointing to the high heels.

Julia ignored him and pulled a note pad from her purse. "I'm supposed to interview a Mr. Gordon York, the director of an organization called S.A.I.L."

"This is your lucky day. I know Gordon and I'm headed to the S.A.I.L. headquarters. Look over that hill."

A white, concrete block bunker extended over the side of a low mountain. It overlooked a protected crater about a half mile in diameter filled with hundreds of solar collectors and parabolic satellite dishes.

"What is it?" Julia asked as they pulled into the crowded parking lot of a building with the letters S.A.I.L. painted on the front.

"Don't you know anything about S.A.I.L.?"

"I know a good sale when I find one, but I get the feeling this is not about bargains."

"Search for alien intelligent life. S.A.I.L."

"Alien intelligence? This is the ridiculous reason I almost got killed?"

"What did you think this was all about?"

"Something about a new type of computer."

He drove into the only open parking spot. The posted

sign read, "Reserved for Gordon York, Director."

"I wouldn't park here. It says it's reserved."

"It's okay. It's my spot."

"You're Gordon? Oh no. Look, I'm sorry about what I said. I only meant that. . ."

"It's okay. I'm used to it. Let's go in and call a truck to tow your Jeep over here."

Gordon grabbed a carved wooden cane and exited the car. He walked with a limp.

"What happened to you?" she asked.

"Don't be shy," he said. "Just ask anything that comes to mind."

"Sorry, but that's me. My friends say whatever's on my mind is on my lips. I seem to be apologizing too much. Can we start again? My name is Julia Welles." She held out her hand. "I work for the Albuquerque Gazette and I have an appointment with the director of S.A.I.L.."

"Follow me and we'll see if he's in."

They entered a small lobby, signed in with the security guard and Julia followed Gordon through a narrow corridor until they stood in front of a door with his name and title. His small office overlooked a vast control room with dozens of men and women at computer consoles. Beyond the control room, a wall of glass opened onto an unobstructed view of the entire crater with its intelligence gathering equipment.

"I suppose I should do my job. May I?" She took the recorder from her purse.

He nodded and sat behind his desk.

"Mr. York . . . Gordon, what is the purpose of your organization?"

"To collect and process extraterrestrial data. Specifically, we're looking for a message from someone that we are not alone in the universe."

"How long have you been listening to the heavens and have you had any success?"

"Five years and no."

"One of the reasons I'm here today is to learn more about your new computer system. Can you tell me how it's different?"

"This network of equipment is a gift from a company called the International Development Corporation. The CEO was a classmate of mine and he also has a fascination with the idea that it is highly unlikely we are the only intelligent life in the universe. When his company developed a new superconductive computer, I hounded him until he agreed to subsidize this project. It's taken the InDevCo technicians six months to install and train my people on the new unit. They claim it will boost our ability to receive and send messages to the stars by 500 percent over our previous equipment. The network consists of 10 Lorestronic mainframes connected in a series with 250 solar collectors and parabolic dishes giving us a total output of 40 trillion terrawatts."

"Certainly sounds impressive. What kind of results have you had with it."

"None, yet. We're scheduled to have the first full power test today. Anything's possible. How fortunate that you may have the story of a lifetime for your very first assignment."

Julia looked up from her note pad and envisioned herself receiving the Pulitzer prize for journalism.

* * *

Julia sat opposite Gordon at a small table in the cafeteria and picked at a salad.

"You were saying how you never knew your father and your mother died when you were very young," said Gordon.

"I always had the best of everything. Up until a year ago, there was always plenty of money but I never knew where it came from. I was raised by a woman named Soni who loved me as if I were her own daughter. Suddenly, the money stopped. Soni finally admitted to me that my father had hired her to raise me and he supported us all those years. She assumed that he had died when the money stopped, but was never certain. I tried to find him, but there was no trail to follow. Nothing. When the money ran out, I left graduate school and came out here to accept my only job offer."

"If this works as planned, you should have no trouble getting a job with the New York Times if you want it."

"I'm afraid I have to apologize again. I came here to interview you and we wound up talking about me. I do tend to run at the mouth sometimes."

"I grew up with five sisters, so think nothing of it. I suppose that was good training for my job."

"You never did tell me why you need the cane."

"Off the record?"

She nodded.

"Automobile accident my senior year in college. A group of friends and I celebrated my acceptance into the astronaut training program at NASA. A drunk driver plowed into us head on. My best friend was killed and I. . .well, now you know. This place is the closest I'll ever come to going to the stars. Shall we go? The test is set to begin in fifteen minutes."

Julia followed Gordon to the main control room. She took copious notes and drew a sketch of him as he stood at the command computer panel. The clock counted down the minutes.

"Tension thick," she wrote. "Time zero and the only sound is the clicking of the computer as it calibrates the collecting dishes. I can see them turning and adjusting as the computer makes its calculations."

Gordon looked at Julia and gave her the thumbs up sign. "Primary system active and nominal," said the synthesized computer voice over the PA. Julia had never heard a computer speak. "Primary circuits engaged to capacity. Secondary stations activated to receive continued incoming data. Directional complex activated."

Julia moved next to Gordon and whispered, "What's happening?"

"The primary computers are receiving so much data that the back-up system has kicked in. It should tell us the source of the signal."

"Strongest signal emanates from the Alpha Centauri star system, 4.3 light years, specifically from planet PC27 orbiting Proxima Centauri."

All eyes focused on the large monitor screen in the center of the room. The computer continued to calibrate but the screen was blank. It flashed red to blue, then the celestial message took shape in the form of large, white block letters. "ENERGY CONTROLS MATTER."

Fourteen

Luxor, Egypt

SUNLIGHT BREACHED THE ANCIENT ROOM FOR THE FIRST time in 3000 years. Dr. Lawrence peered at the monitor while the video camera panned the area. There was no sign of a sarcophagus or a royal treasure.

"Extract the toxic air and remove the mud brick door," he ordered. "The room may be empty, but I have a feeling about this place. What do you think, Gammal?"

"There's no choice. Do you still think it is Katara's tomb?"

"None other."

After exposing the opening, Dr. Lawrence stood by the entrance and removed his hat. Gammal and the workers each said a silent prayer for the dead who occupied the tomb; a ritual they repeated with the opening of each newly found tomb.

Dr. Lawrence entered the barren chamber carrying an electric torch. Gammal stayed a few feet behind him. It was a rule that Dr. Lawrence always entered first. He approached a colorful wall relief and held the light closer.

"Gammal, come and look. I've only seen hieroglyphics

like this in one other place." He scanned the entire room. "All the writings in here match those we found in the priest's tomb. They make reference to the most powerful Pharaoh drawing and sustaining his power from the heavens. It must be Katara III. The time references are the same as well."

"But the tomb is empty, Aton. There is nothing here but ancient dust and some strange writings." Gammal turned to his men.

"Photograph each wall and take exact measurements. Is there anything else, Aton?"

"Send your men away after they complete their tasks. I will spend the night here. Today will be the last day I torment myself about Katara III and his imagined undisturbed tomb."

Four electric torches stood guard in the center of the room and illuminated the vivid wall murals depicting the life of the Pharaoh. Dr. Lawrence studied each scene and character, taking careful notes and photos. He paused, stretched and rubbed his eyes. Lack of sleep caused his head and muscles to ache. Only a lone cricket disturbed the silence of the night. He sat cross legged, closed his eyes and opened his mind. In a moment, a meditative state shrouded his thoughts.

"Let go of yourself and see beyond your eyes."

"Who's there?" he asked.

But there was no one.

So my friend, have you worked through the night?" asked Gammal as he entered the tomb with two of his workers. Outside, the Egyptian sun cast long shadows as it prodded the night, promising another scorching day.

"Is it morning already? Time stands still for me in here." Lawrence stood.

"Have you learned any more about our illusive king?" Gammal asked, handing him a cup of strong Egyptian coffee.

"Some of these writings are riddles without answers. There is something, however. Look at this wall." Dr. Lawrence led Gammal to the wall at the back of the tomb.

"It appears as the others," said Gammal. "What is it, Aton?"

"I have studied the walls all night and this one is different. Notice how the other walls are carved out of the mountain limestone? This one is man made. It is a stone wall cleverly mortared and painted to appear as the others. The Egyptian designers were skillful, my friend, but simplicity was always their goal. This is a puzzle that beckons us to solve it. Have the men bring the scanners.

"As you wish, but it looks like a solid stone wall to me." Gammal ordered the equipment brought in. Dr. Lawrence activated a spectral densometer and walked the perimeter of the room.

"Look at the reading near the carved entrance, Gammal. Now, as I walk toward the rear wall watch the indicator."

Dr. Lawrence held the sensor directly next to the wall. The instrument reached beyond the stone.

"This wall is two feet thick and a large cavern or cave exists beyond it. From the subtleties in the writings, I've surmised that this room is an ante-room set up to fool tomb robbers into thinking it is the actual tomb. I'll wager the real tomb is intact beyond this wall."

"The fulfillment of your dream, Aton. I can hardly believe it."

"The years of labor will be justified if it is true. Have the men bring in the stone cutting equipment. We begin immediately."

Diamond tipped saw blades sliced through the outer mortared layers with ease, raising Dr. Lawrence's hopes that the task would be completed within a reasonable time. After hours of unsuccessfully attempting to penetrate the inner wall's stone core, Gammal supervised the attachment of the last saw blade.

"Is this the best we can do?" asked Dr. Lawrence looking at a pile of shattered saw blades laying on the floor.

Gammal threw his hands in the air and said, "If this is the way into heaven, we would all burn in hell. There are no sharper stone cutting saws in all of Egypt. I have never before seen an Egyptian stone that resists these blades."

"Tell the men to put down the saws. You are right, my friend. I shall have to find another way if we are to cut through this stone. I'll not admit failure when my dream lies a mere two feet away."

"I agree, Aton, but right now, these are the longest two feet in the world."

The Luxor bazaar brimmed with life at night when its narrow streets filled with natives and tourists, each looking to the other for sustenance. Goats cried out in protest as they were painted with bright colors in readiness for the yearly festival when their wealthy owners gave them as gifts to the poor of the town.

Dr. Lawrence wandered through the merchants stalls, attracting little attention in his tan and black embroidered Galabeya. Smells of grilled meats and spices permeated the air. Women lowered their pottery jugs to fill them in the public fountain, then carried them away on their heads as their ancestors had done for three thousand years. He stopped in front of a shop called the Golden Scepter. Two women dressed in western clothes rummaged through a pile of painted papyrus' on a display table in front of the shop.

"Good evening , ladies,' he said. They greeted him, then continued their search for the perfect souvenir.

He entered the store. Cheap Egyptian artifacts lined the walls to the tall ceiling. Replicas of King Tut statues and death masks, plastic golden sphinx and pyramids and hundreds of tee shirts covered every inch of available space. The proprietor, a heavy man with tight curly hair and a pock marked, olive-color face sat in the back of the shop smoking a filterless Arabian cigarette.

"May I help you?" asked the man. A cloud of thick smoke spewed from his nose.

"I'm looking for Omar," said Dr. Lawrence.

"Who wants to find him and why?"

Dr. Lawrence handed him a ten pound note.

"I'm Dr. Stanley Lawrence. I was told Omar might be able to help me."

The man took the note.

"What can I do for you?"

"I need special equipment. I understand you have knowledge of where I might obtain it."

"Perhaps. What sort of equipment?"

"Heavy cutting apparatus. Specifically, a laser cutting tool. Can you help me?" Dr. Lawrence chose his words with care. He dared not give away the discovery of a new tomb.

"Possibly."

Dr. Lawrence handed Omar a one hundred pound note.

"There is another one of these for you if I get what I want."

Omar's eyes met Lawrence's.

He handed him another note.

"Give me a phone number where I can reach you. I make no promises."

Dr. Lawrence lay in bed, unable to sleep. A dog barked outside the window of his modest house in the worker's village just outside the Valley of the Kings on the west bank of the Nile. The sheer white netting around his bed stirred in the dry breeze from the nearby open window.

The Pharaoh has won. The crypt is impregnable.

He got up and went into the darkroom where rows of recently developed pictures hung from wooden clothes pins. Photos of the hieroglyphics taken in the tomb antechamber revealed startling scenes never seen in all his years of study. Scenes of the people looking toward the sky as strange objects loomed overhead; the Pharaoh wearing a very un-Egyptian crown; beings resembling humans, but with exaggerated heads and small arms and legs.

That part of his mind traditionally educated, rejected the obvious meaning of these scenes, but the dreamer and idealist in him wanted to believe in the story that unfolded.

* * *

The sound was unreachable and far away. Another time or dimension perhaps. Gradually, it came closer and more undeniable. He opened his eyes, but the room was dark. The phone was ringing. Still drunk with sleep, Lawrence reached for the receiver.

"Dr. Lawrence?" Static weakened the connection, the voice barely audible.

"Speaking."

"Good morning. Hope I didn't wake you."

"No, it's all right," he said. "Who is this?"

"My name is Dr. Lloyd Roberts. I work for a company called The International Development Corporation in New York. I understand you need a particular type of equipment. How can I be of assistance?"

Dr. Lawrence sat up fully awake now.

"Thank you for calling. I need an instrument to cut through two feet of very dense stone. I believe a laser could do it."

"We have such a tool, but it's in Switzerland undergoing tests. I'll agree to switch the test site to Luxor on one condition."

"What?"

"Egyptology has always been a hobby of mine and if you're going to open a tomb, I want to be there. Besides, I can keep an eye on my equipment. Agreed?"

"I never said anything about a tomb."

"Dr. Lawrence, do you want the laser?"

"Take the noon flight from Cairo to Luxor tomorrow. I'll have my car at the airport. I look forward to meeting you."

Dr. Lawrence clicked the receiver until he heard a tone, then dialed a local number. The voice on the other end was choked with sleep.

"Gammal, assemble the men. We resume the cutting tomorrow."

Fifteen

WIND GUSTS STIRRED LEAVES AND DEBRIS FROM THE forest floor and forced nearby trees to dance in the man-made storm. The rescue helicopter had arrived and the old barn disappeared from sight as the aircraft rose above the tallest trees. Jake and Lane said very little to each other after they belted themselves into their seats.

Lane felt confused.

Damn you, Charles. Get out of my mind.

Lane reached into her pocket for the cigarette lighter that was no longer there.

Her mind raced to the past and back again. Comparing Jake and Charles was unfair. Both had vitality and a certain mystery. Jake had compassion and passion. Charles had only passion.

Not enough.

Now, she wanted to forget Charles. Jake ignited a new spark in her. Strong feelings of desire and excitement. And an unexplainable familiarity and comfort.

"I never thought I'd be sorry to leave that place," Jake said, not realizing Lane was wrapped in reflection. He handed her half of a sandwich the pilot offered to share.

"We could've stayed longer," she said.

"I understand the next flight out is full. Besides, we've

got to get you to a doctor. That inflatable cast is just temporary. How far to the lab?"

"Twenty minutes,' she said staring out the window at the passing landscape.

"Just enough time to tell me about this place you're taking me."

"It'll make more sense if I show you rather than tell you."

Their eyes met.

"What's wrong?" he asked. "You're disturbed about something."

"It's nothing."

Jake is a different person.

She broke away from the past.

The helicopter landed in a grassy meadow surrounded on all sides by low mountains. A white concrete and glass two story building with an angled roof line stood nestled in the trees at the foot of a mountain not more than 500 yards from the landing site. Jake and Lane entered a waiting tram that took them to the entrance of the building.

"InDevCo Terran Research Division," Jake read the sign aloud. "Subterra?"

"Be patient," she said.

The tram stopped and Jake helped Lane up the steps to the entrance.

"I'm fine," she said, walking on her own. "The neuro-stim pack built into the cast blocks the pain. It'll last until we get to the med-center. Follow me."

The lobby was divided; the front section devoted to security and check-in, while the rear contained banks of various sized elevators, some designed to carry large containers, while others conveyed passengers. Lane avoided a line of people at the central desk and approached an armed guard at a security station near the entry point. She showed her security clearance ID, punched a code into a key pad and signed her name.

"He's with me, Andy."

"What happened?" asked the security guard pointing to the cast.

"Nothing the boys in Med-Center can't fix. Everything okay below?"

Andy nodded. "Number twelve is ready for you, Dr. Darby."

"Thanks. Come on, Jake. I can't wait to show you Subterra."

Lane grabbed his hand and they entered the elevator, but Jake pulled her back. "Why does it say 'women only' over the door?"

"Never mind that. We don't have time for gender segregated elevators. I always thought it was a stupid idea anyway."

The door closed and Jake's ears popped. He felt a gentle falling sensation, but it was not unpleasant.

"I think it's time you explained all of this."

Lane smiled. "Twenty years ago, Philip bought this land from the government to build a research center devoted to the preservation of nature and the planet's resources. He always had a love for animals. Thus, the Terran research division of InDevCo was founded. He took a personal interest in the project and spent a lot of time here during the initial planning and construction phases. A year after it was built, a team was assigned to test the purity of the underground water supply and they made a startling discovery."

A tone and a synthesized voice interrupted her.

"Prepare for superficial disinfection."

A panel in the wall opened. Lane took out two sets of head gear resembling motorcycle helmets with dark visors, put one on and handed Jake the other.

"Put this on," she said. "Take your clothes off and put them in this receptacle. You can keep your watch on."

"I wasn't aware that Subterra was a nudist camp. Is this routine procedure?"

"Actually, I'm dying to see the butterfly tattooed on your butt."

They laughed, and stripped while wearing the protective helmets. A bright light encircled them, traveling floor to ceiling and back again.

Through the dark tinted visor, Jake could see only the outline of Lane's body. He lifted the visor momentarily and reached out to touch the hardened nipple on her breast.

"I wouldn't do that if you value your eyesight. The light burns the first layer of skin and anything else exposed. Most skin bacteria are killed with this procedure. It's been a very effective technique in controlling surface contamination."

The light went out and a powerful fan blew the powdery film from their bodies, leaving slightly reddened, exposed new skin.

A second wall panel revealed a dispenser filled with sealed pouches labeled, 'InDevCo Subterran uniform — sterile.'

Lane handed Jake a pouch and took one for herself. They removed the headsets.

"Now what?" he asked, knowing the answer.

They stared at each other for a moment.

"The uniforms. We're supposed to put them on."

After they dressed, Lane touched a control button marked ready, and the door opened. Lane stepped out and led Jake to a second security check point.

After clearing this station, they walked through a corridor into an area that resembled an airport waiting lounge. Jake counted two dozen people sitting in comfortable chairs, divided into small groups. At one end of the lounge on a raised circular platform, a man sat at a complex control panel. The area was well lit and the ceiling sloped down toward the farthest wall. Ten glass enclosed cylindrical stations sat three feet apart, each with a sliding door. Just above the bank of glass tubes, a large sign read, "InDevCo — Welcome to Subterra."

Lane spoke to the security officer behind the control desk, then turned to Jake.

"I've arranged transport."

"I suppose being transported means getting into one of those tubes?" Jake asked.

"Sort of like 'beam me up, Scotty,' except we'll be going in the opposite direction."

"I'm still waiting for that explanation."

"Well, we do have about five minutes before the tube is clear. Let's sit away from the others. After the project on subterranean water purity got under way, the teams found alarming amounts of toxins in the underground water. They kept digging deeper to try to discover how far down they would have to drill before the water was pure. One of the teams drilling in this area discovered a series of huge caverns under the site of the research building. They continued the experiment and at the same time, mapped the caverns that literally honeycombed this region. Word of the caverns spread through the company and Philip learned of it. He had an idea to build a high security lab in the largest cavern, one or two miles deep, and had plans drawn for its construction. Initially, the project was bogged down with problems and abandoned. But Philip was in love with the idea and he pushed until our experts found the solutions. By then, the project had changed. No longer was it a small lab dedicated to top secret government jobs, but it turned into a place where people could live and work. A totally self-sustained underground city. Philip named it Subterra."

"Like Disney's EPCOT Center," Jake said.

"Only underground and it's real, not an amusement park."

The guard motioned to Lane.

"There's the signal. Tubes 7 and 8 are ready for us."

Lane led the way toward the transport tubes. Green lights flashed over tubes 7 and 8. The glass doors slid silently open as the pods arrived. Jake felt the rush of air as the vacuum in the tube was neutralized. Two uniformed InDevCo guards directed Jake into the tube and placed a safety helmet over his head. Lane went through the same procedure in the next tube. A video monitor read SURFACE on the console in front of him.

"Can you hear me, Jake?" Lane asked through her communicator.

"Yes."

"Good. Now look at me. Fasten the seat belts across your chest and make sure your head gear is locked in place. The pod will automatically pressurize in a minute."

The door slid shut and Jake felt his ears pop as the interior pressure changed.

"Enjoy the ride. We won't be able to communicate during transport. See you in Subterra."

Lane disappeared as her capsule was drawn into the tube at great speed.

The screen on his console counted down, then the pod launched and it fell in total darkness. The only light came from the monitor in front of him. Jake felt as if he were in a free fall again. The numbers on the screen were unreadable. The ride was quiet and smooth, though the sensation of speed was clear.

Hopefully, this thing won't need a force field and a tree to break its fall.

The rate of decent slowed and Jake read the monitor with disbelief. "7,527 feet — Approaching Subterra entry level. Prepare for disembarkation."

The screen read 8,189 feet when the capsule came to a complete stop.

The door slid open.

Sixteen

THE CAPSULE DOOR SLID OPEN, JAKE REMOVED HIS HEAD gear and stood.

"How do you feel?" asked Lane.

"After these past two days, ready for anything."

"Jake, this is Dr. Eric Fontaine, my assistant. I've asked him to show you around Subterra until I finish my treatment at the Med center."

Jake and Fontaine shook hands.

"We've a new technique for repairing this sprained ankle of mine. It should take about an hour. Pick me up at the Med Center at noon and we'll go on to the Megalon lab from there."

Dr. Fontaine blanched and his expression changed from friendly to disturbed. "May I remind you that project is classified under zone ten security, Dr. Darby?"

"It's all right, Eric. Jake has top security clearance and knows all about Megalon." She kissed Jake. "Don't forget, noon at the hospital."

"Well, Jake, why do you want to open the files on Megalon?" Eric asked. "We haven't done any work on that project for a long while. There are other interesting projects you should see, like the recently completed power generating plant at the Subterran hot springs."

"I'm sure there'll be time for that. Right now I'd like that tour I was promised."

"I'll have to speak to Lane about reopening Megalon. It doesn't make sense."

"The tour?"

"This way." Eric said, tapping his fingers on his leg.

Jake made a mental note to question Lane about her nervous assistant.

"You're clear to go through, Mr. Parker," said a security officer sitting at a control panel.

A sign at the entrance read, Lateral TransTubes ahead. Jake and Eric walked past the check point into a short corridor. Jake felt a strong, cool breeze against his face. A bright light at the end of the walkway piqued his curiosity. They emerged from the passageway into a vast, underground world of caverns and waterfalls.

"Welcome to Subterra," said Eric.

An open, circular observation terrace fifty feet in diameter was bordered by a red guard rail. The observation terrace overlooked a cavern thousands of feet deep that stretched for miles from one end to the other. In the distance, a cluster of buildings on the floor of the cavern consisted of geodesic domes and spires that comprised a city unlike any he had ever seen. A brilliant light emanated from the ceiling of the cavern that lit every corner of the complex.

"What do you think?" asked Eric.

"Wonderful."

"The lateral tubes are one level down. I'll answer your questions on the way into town."

Jake followed Eric down a short stairway to a platform directly beneath the terrace. There were four, clear transport tubes built flush into the stone floor about three feet apart.

A security guard appeared on a monitor. Eric entered a code into a key pad.

"You and Mr. Parker are clear for tube three," said the man.

There was the sound of pressurized air escaping and a clear panel slid open revealing the travel pod. Within seconds, the pod had risen above the floor and its door opened. Eric and Jake stepped in and sat on padded seats in front of a small computer monitor. The door slid closed and the capsule dropped into its tube. The capsule enclosed them in total silence and isolation from the outside. Jake tapped on the clear material.

"It's called Glastic," said Eric. "Our engineers developed it. Sort of a combination of the best qualities of glass and plastic without the disadvantages. It's virtually indestructible and very lightweight. You'll see it used here in many different applications."

Entering the capsule activated the computer monitor.

"Please state destination, you bastard," said the female synthesized voice.

"Damn computer glitch. It was supposed to be fixed by now. Computer, Med Center via perimeter tubes. Do you copy?"

"Affirmative, asshole."

Jake burst out laughing. "A cursing computer. How intriguing"

"The programmer had a fight with his wife and the

computer picked up a few new words. Remember these computers are intelligent."

"Can we trust it?" asked Jake.

"Probably not, but we have no choice. Computer, pressurize and initiate transport when ready."

"I do everything around here. You're just a lazy son of a bitch. Do it yourself for a change."

"Computer, I'll send you to the junkyard if you don't. . ."

The pod lurched forward into the tube at great speed. Jake's head was forced against the padded seat but soon the sensation eased.

"That's better," said Eric. "I'm sure Lane told you all about Subterra, so I won't bore you. This transport tube can take us anywhere, that is when the computer is working. This is the main cavern and there are many smaller caves which are connected to this one through tunnels via the tube system. We've placed some of the top security projects in the smaller caverns away from the main population."

"Like Megalon?" asked Jake.

"I'd like to know why you're so interested in that particular project."

"Sorry, I can't say. What's the light on the cave ceiling and its power source?"

Eric clenched his teeth and worked the muscles in his jaw. "The Megalon project was dangerous and should not be reopened."

"I asked about the light."

For a moment there was only the wispy sound of the pod as it floated in its tube descending toward the city.

Eric activated a command override control. "That should

do it. The computer will answer your questions."

"Computer, tell me about the bright light on the ceiling of the cavern."

"It is called the Subterran 'sun' and has all the natural light bands, simulates the light of the real sun and changes its intensity and position depending on the season and the time of day. Our sun is computer controlled to give the appearance of sunrise and sunset and the inhabitants get a natural feel for day and night to set their biological clocks. All of the electricity for the city is generated at the new Hot Spring power plant. It also provides unlimited free hot water."

"What about fresh air?" Jake asked.

"A system of surface vents with high power turbo fans deliver enough fresh air to exchange all the air in Subterra every five minutes."

Eric looked at his watch. "I must warn you. Tampering with Megalon can have serious repercussions. Please don't."

"Sorry, Eric. I have no alternative."

"Computer, disregard previous routing instructions. Terminate transport at station delta nine." The pod veered at a junction into a different tube and headed away from the city. Eric grabbed a lorestron revolver from his pocket and pointed it at Jake. "The tour is over. You'll get out at the next stop."

The computer interrupted. "All is forgiven, darling. You were terrific. Can I have a cigarette?"

"Computer, go to hell," Eric yelled. Perspiration beaded on his forehead. The hand holding the gun shook.

"You're making a mistake, Eric. Let's talk about this," said Jake.

The pod slowed and stopped, then rose above the tube

and the door slid open.

"Out."

Jake turned to step out of the pod, but grabbed the gun and at the same time punched Eric squarely in the jaw. Surprised by the rapid maneuver, Eric lost consciousness. Jake put the gun in his pocket and tried unsuccessfully to operate the pod control.

"Computer, I want to go to the Med center."

"Transport codes are required for travel anywhere in Subterra."

"Where are we now?"

"Maintenance and storage delta nine."

"Display map of Subterra with present location and Med center."

Jake looked at the display.

"Eric, wake up. Come on, I hardly hit you. Damn it."

Jake stepped out of the capsule and walked the short distance to the maintenance building. It appeared deserted and contained equipment used for cleaning the pods. There was no sign of any type of communication device. When he exited the building, the transport pod was gone.

The Subterran sun approached high noon position.

Got to get to Med center. Follow the tube system back to the city.

Jake found the tube and walked toward the junction. A narrow tunnel that the pod traversed in seconds took him twenty minutes to walk, stooped at the waist to avoid the low ceiling.

Jake emerged from the tunnel and saw the comforting

sight of the spires of the city. Now all he had to do was find the hospital and tell Lane about her traitorous assistant.

What if they're partners? I'll say nothing about Eric and let her play her hand.

Signs for the hospital were clearly marked and Jake had no difficulty finding the Med center. By now, he was forty minutes late for his rendezvous with Lane. Jake climbed a few steps to the lobby and the door opened. A directory posted the Med center's services and listed orthopedics on the tenth floor.

The waiting elevator took seconds to deliver him to ten.

Jake noticed the button for the eleventh floor was locked.

Funny. I don't remember an eleventh floor on the directory.

The doors opened on ten and a sign welcomed all patients and visitors.

Jake slipped into the stairwell next to the elevator and climbed one flight up. The door was sealed and a sign read, KEEP OUT. He looked through a small glass window, but saw nothing in the darkness.

Back on ten, he noticed Lane standing at a distant control station, chatting with two of the floor nurses. She smiled and waved at Jake, then walked toward him.

"Looks like you're cured," he said.

"It feels terrific. I was just about to send security to look for you. Did you and Eric get lost?"

"You might say that. Let's get out of here."

Lane pushed the elevator call button.

"What happened on the eleventh floor?" Jake asked.

"It's a former genetics research lab. They tell me there was a nasty accident with a new strain of a virulent virus awhile ago. It's been sealed ever since. I've ordered a special team to check it out."

Jake stared at the locked eleventh floor button in the elevator. The skin on his forehead tightened. He closed his eyes for a moment.

"What is it, Jake?"

"I don't know. For a minute I thought, no, it's nothing. Enough distractions. Let's get to the Megalon lab."

Jake belted himself into the now familiar transport capsule and watched Lane operate the control.

"Please state destination."

"Megalon research facility," Lane said.

"Prepare for DNA security scan," answered the computer.

"Keep your head perfectly still, Jake. You won't feel a thing."

A pinpoint beam of laser light emanated from the control panel and penetrated the surface skin on his earlobe. Lane experienced the same probing scan.

"All passengers are cleared for access to secured areas."

The pod moved silently into the tube and the hospital complex disappeared.

"Did Eric show you the important sights?"

"Why, yes. It was a most interesting experience. How long has he been your assistant?"

"About three years. He's a genius with Lorestronics. I've placed him in charge of certain projects that deal heavily with the new superconductive electronics."

"Like Megalon?"

"Yes. He headed the team that first discovered the Megalon technology. Why all the questions about Eric, Jake?"

"Just curious. What's that blue, domed structure?"

"The core control building. From there, we control all the systems that make Subterra work. Did you miss that one on the tour?"

Before Jake answered, the pod entered a tunnel and it's internal lights came on. The distant glow from the end of the dark passage soon opened into a small cavern. The capsule stopped, rose above the tube and they stepped out. A thin waterfall splashed into a pond spraying a fine mist that quickly dissipated in the cool air. Stalactites hung from the ceiling and formed a jagged display of dripping rock art. The only light in the cave came from a floodlight mounted over the front door of the white modular concrete lab building. The area appeared deserted.

Jake followed Lane to the front entryway, where she entered a code in a key pad. The door opened and they walked into the building. She switched on the main power and the computer room glistened with light.

"How long since you abandoned the project?" Jake asked.

Lane sat at a computer terminal. Jake recognized the apparatus as similar to the equipment he had seen in the Newport lab.

"Months," she said, "after Philip disappeared. But this is impossible."

"What is it?"

"Someone's tampered with the files. The only thing that prevented access is the new code I entered when I closed the project."

Jake heard the distant sound of shattering glass. Lane looked up at him. He put his finger to his lips.

"What's in the next room?" he whispered.

"The operating room and more computers. The actual insertion of the brain module took place in there."

"Stay here and don't make a sound."

"But I can. . ."

"No. Stay put." Jake pulled the lorestron pistol from his pocket.

"Where'd you get that?"

But Jake did not hear her and moved toward the door of the lab, hugging the wall. The only light in the lab came from the computer room.

The shadows moved.

He froze and listened.

Nothing.

The noise moved further away now.

Jake penetrated deeper into the building through the lab and found himself in front of a half open double door at the end of a carpeted corridor. The sign on the door read, PHILIP CROMWELL-PRIVATE.

Poised and ready to fire, he pushed the door open with his foot and slipped into the room.

Seventeen

TWO FIGURES WRESTLED IN THE SHADOWS AND FELL to the floor. Jake moved cautiously into the room. "Stop," he ordered, aiming the pistol. Jake thumbed the light switch.

Eric had Lane pinned behind the desk. When light flooded the room, he ran for the door.

"Freeze," ordered Jake.

Eric reached the door and Jake fired.

"What the hell are you doing here, Lane?" He held the gun aimed at Eric. "I thought I told you to stay in the computer room. How'd you get in?"

"Back door. I tried to tell you but you didn't hear me." Lane grabbed Jake's outstretched hand and stood up.

"I'm fine. It's him we need to worry about."

She knelt and felt the pulse in Eric's neck. "He's okay. You've just stunned him. He was at Philip's computer console when I surprised him. I guess he panicked. Where'd you get the lorestron pistol?"

"From him. I have a lot of questions for your assistant."

"Uh uh. I get him first. But I'm afraid he'll be out for a while. Maybe the computer file he tried to access can tell us what we want to know. Eric sure was anxious to get into this file. Computer, display Cromwell Megalon video log, last entry. Password, Alpha Centauri."

"Interesting choice of passwords," said Jake.

"Password accepted. File date, August 13."

"That's after the final entry in the Newport Log," Jake said. "Philip was here before he disappeared."

Philip's face appeared on the monitor. Lane touched the screen, then sat in his chair and listened.

"The implantation of the CCEM in a human subject was a success, although the patient died of unrelated complications. We now know that the procedure can be done with complete safety. I have dreamed of something like this for a long time and have offered myself as the next test subject. All the members of the Megalon team have refused to allow me to have the implantation. They feel additional testing must come first and other volunteers should be found. I suppose my age has something to do with it also. Even Lane Darby is opposed to it, though she knows it is my dream. I've made them all believe that I'm convinced it's too dangerous, but secretly, I've decided to proceed with the operation. Lane's assistant, Eric Fontaine is capable of performing the procedure and I have 'persuaded' him to do it. The truth is, I would never have fired him, as I threatened, if he refused. He'll do the implantation tomorrow, and I swore him to secrecy. I can't wait to tell Ruth about my adventure. The next entry I make will be with my newly supercharged brain. I haven't felt this excited about a project for a long time, and I doubt I will be able to sleep tonight."

"Program terminated," stated the computer.

"That's it," Lane said. "Philip disappeared right after Eric implanted the modules into him. Eric murdered Philip."

"We can't be sure he went through with the operation. Are there any other entries?"

"Let's find out. Computer, scan Megalon file for any data entered after final Cromwell log."

"Working. Two files exists with entries on or after specified date."

"Activate the first."

Eric Fontaine appeared on the screen. The date was August 13.

"Mr. Cromwell is obsessed with this project and spends inordinate amounts of time in the Megalon lab. He wants to be the next subject for implantation of the modules but we have all refused. Lane knows nothing of his persistent attempts to have the operation and is on the surface for important unrelated business. Since I am in charge in her absence, I've told him that more testing is required to ensure safety, but he is most insistent."

August 14.

"Mr. Cromwell has threatened to fire me if I don't follow his instructions. I've never seen him so unremitting. I have no choice. This is my life's work. The procedure is scheduled for tomorrow."

August 15.

"The implantation operation went well, without complications. I wish to go on record as being against the entire thing. Mr. Cromwell sat up on the table with a smile. All his vital signs were good, and he appeared fine. He told me he had an awareness and clarity of thought that he never imagined possible. The only ill effect was a slight headache. I left the room for a moment to verify the EEG results on the main computer and when I returned, Mr. Cromwell was gone."

August 16.

"Mr. Cromwell is still missing. I've searched everywhere. No one suspects the truth. I decided to anonymously alert security. I can only assume the worst, but I'm too scared to come forward. I'm going to contact Lane and recommend that Megalon is too dangerous. It should be abandoned and the files sealed. I hope this video log will vindicate me if and when Philip is found."

"Termination of program," said computer.

"I'm such a fool," said Lane looking at Eric. "I never thought to scan the files before I sealed them."

"It's not your fault. Philip was in control. How long after did you seal the project?"

"About a week. Eric called me in New York and sounded quite upset about Philip's disappearance. Little did I know he was partly responsible for it. I returned to Subterra shortly after that."

"The computer mentioned a second entry. Let's see it."

"Computer, display additional data entered into this file after August 16."

"Unable to comply. Files are security coded and unavailable."

"Impossible. I locked the entire project under the same password."

"Someone else was in here during the week before you coded the file and that data is evidently protected under a different password. Who else had access to this area during that time?"

"Someone with only the highest security clearance."

Jake gave the computer a command. "Display all InDevCo personnel with security clearance high enough to enter the Megalon complex on August 16."

Jake and Lane scanned the list that appeared on the screen. The chief of security was included without a name.

"Looks like the pieces are coming together. Computer, verify identity of chief of security during the specified period?"

"Charles Cromwell."

"It fits," Jake said. "Charles knew he was disinherited and his only chance to run the company was to get rid of his father."

"Are you saying that Charles killed his father?"

"We have to consider the possibility."

"But, how does Eric fit into that?"

"Maybe the answers are locked in the next file."

"Wait a minute. Why didn't I think of this? Computer, run Philip Cromwell override program Alpha-LD."

"Working."

"When we first started Megalon, Philip and I designed a resident program intended to override any password in case of an emergency. I'd forgotten about it. Computer, now run previously requested data."

The screen filled with data on an improved CCEM module.

Lane pursed her lips and pounded her clenched fist on the desk. "Damn. Someone worked on the microchip without my knowledge. Look at this new circuit pathway. Computer, state functional difference between original design and final CCEM specifications."

"Latest design allows fine tuned adjustment and automatic fluctuation of the electromagnetic CCEM frequency bands to match precise output pattern of subject's brain. This change allows a 74.61% improvement in efficiency. Subjects tested with properly integrated CCEM have exhibited increased IQ, sensory perception and telekinesis."

"Mind translating that?" asked Jake.

"It means that the improved brain implant is more efficient because it matches the exact brain wave patterns of the recipient. I never expected telekinesis. . ."

Eric moaned and moved his hand.

"Put him in Philip's chair."

Jake lifted Eric, placed him in the chair and he regained consciousness.

Lane slapped him in the face and he suddenly awoke.

"That's for lying to me."

She slapped the other cheek.

"That's for Philip."

Jake pulled her back. "Whoa, calm down. We'll never get anywhere if he's unconscious again. Okay, Eric, we know about you and Philip, and the improved modules. Did you see Philip again after the operation?"

Eric rubbed his neck. "No. I haven't seen him. I never wanted any part in this. Why couldn't they have left me alone with my work. It was stupid of me to make the video log, but if something happened to me, I had to make sure the truth was known. I admit I was trying to erase it, but it's too late now. The day after Philip disappeared, Charles Cromwell came to me and told me he knew what I had done to his father. He blackmailed me into working secretly with him to improve the modules and then forced me to perform the operation on him."

"Charles has the power of the CCEM?" asked Jake.

"That explains a lot," said Lane. "We found that the CCEM enhances the subjects own personality traits. In Charles' case, his schizophrenia only intensified."

"If Charles has all this brain power, what's he up to?" asked Jake.

Eric shook off the last effects of the stun. "I saw him the day after the operation. He came to me with a severe headache. I told him it was unusual to have that much pain. I told him I could run a diagnostic on the CCEM and hooked him into the Med computers."

"Then what?" asked Jake.

"I told him the only way to cure it was to remove the implant. He stormed out of here in a rage."

"Charles is unpredictable, Jake. I believe he's capable of anything."

"We have no choice," Jake said. "You must give me the same power that Charles has. I want the CCEM implant."

Eighteen

THERE'S A ONE IN TEN CHANCE THAT YOU'LL HAVE A stroke, or suffer permanent brain damage," Lane said. Eric left the room and went into the lab to prepare the equipment. She and Jake were alone in Philip's office.

"I'll take those odds. Let's get on with it before I change my mind."

"That's exactly what I'm trying to do. This is not something to take lightly. It will change your life. Our lives." She took his hand.

"How can I hope to face Charles if he has the power and I don't? You know I'm right."

"We've done this before, you know," she said.

"I've never been here until today."

"No, I mean you and I against Charles."

"What was the outcome? I hope the good guys won."

"Don't mock me. I mean it. I've experienced deja vu since we first met. Haven't you felt an unexplainable familiarity?"

"Only every time I look at you."

Eric opened the door. "Ready."

"We'll be there in a minute." The door closed. "I don't trust him."

"Eric's on our side, Jake. He's a victim just like Philip."

"And Charles is a modern 'edipus.'"

"Let's hope this Greek tragedy has a happy ending."

They entered the operating room where Eric programed the controls of an eight foot robot with four arms that extended into thin projections resembling fingers.

"Jake, meet Maggie."

Jake touched one of the fingers. "Pleased to meet you, ma'am."

"Greetings," said the robot.

"How do you know it's a she?" Jake whispered in Lane's ear.

"References to gender are erroneous as I do not possess sexual reproductive organs. The name designation is meant as an endearment."

"Sorry, Maggie. I didn't mean to offend you," said Jake.

"Greetings, Dr. Darby. Is this male Homo sapiens to be our next subject?"

"Is he suitable?" asked Lane.

"Please have the subject lie supine on the sensor array and remain immobile."

Jake followed Maggie's instructions and within seconds, the robot moved skull restraints into position that held Jake's head tightly. He winced as Maggie inserted a large bore needle into a vein in his arm.

"It's not too late to reverse the program," Lane said.

"No."

"Maggie will perform the actual implantation, Jake. She can process and implement the computer's instructions in a fraction of the time it would take a human surgeon. Maggie will administer the local anesthetic, prep and map the target area and insert both modules at the exact same time."

"What happens if one is inserted and activated before the other?"

"Then, that side of your brain will overtake the weaker half. We've never seen the result of such an event. It would be most interesting to study."

"No thanks. Test uncharted waters another time."

Maggie circled the sensor table and absorbed the incoming scanner information through a link with the central computer.

"Well, Maggie, is this male a good candidate for the CCEM implantation?"

"Scans of all major systems appear within normal limits. Abnormalities include scar tissue formation in various organs indicating previous trauma. Epidermal scarring is noted including the image of a red, permanently imprinted, three centimeter lepidoptera on the left upper gluteus maximus."

"She's getting personal, Lane. Next, she'll be describing the size of my. . ."

"Okay, Maggie. Proceed with phase one."

". . .feet."

The robot stood over Jake with two of its arms extended on each side of Jake's head. Exact measurements indicated the insertion spot and Maggie deposited a local anesthetic just under the skin.

"That's all you'll feel, Jake. When the anesthetic takes effect, it'll be over before you can say lepidoptera. Phase three, Maggie." Lane and Eric monitored Jake's life signs even though the robot was programmed to abort the operation if there were any abnormal readings. "According to the new program, this is the phase where the modules are conformed to the unique frequency of your brain," said Lane.

"Phase three complete," Maggie said.

"Initiate phase four," ordered Lane.

Maggie made a half centimeter incision midway between Jake's eye and ear on both sides, inserted the CCEM, then used a laser to close the puncture. The entire procedure lasted thirty seconds.

The robots arms retracted and Maggie moved away from the table.

"Eric, check the EEG telemetry while I disconnect him. How do you feel, Jake?" Lane removed the IV needle and released the head restraint.

"A little dizzy. What's supposed to happen?"

"Over the next couple of days, the number of active neurons in your brain will expand from eighty billion to two hundred billion."

"Post-op data is within normal limits," said Eric.

Lane helped him off the sensor array.

"I'm ready for anything."

Jake stood up, his knees buckled and he fainted.

Nineteen
Luxor, Egypt

THE SOUND OF A HELICOPTER IN THE DISTANCE shattered the hush of the Nile valley. Gammal and his men rested in the shade of a tent and waited for the aircraft to deliver its cargo.

A large crate dangled from a cable that gently lowered to the ground. Like miniature cyclones, clouds of dust swirled from the desert floor, forcing the men to cover their faces. After a signal from the ground, the pilot released the cable and the helicopter disappeared over the mountain.

"I'm always amazed how you manage to obtain the impossible, Aton." said Gammal.

"A favor from a friend in high places. This one owes his position in the Ministry of Antiquities to me. Come, let us return to the tomb. Tell your men to signal when the new generator is ready. It is time for the past and present to meet. This time we shall succeed."

Two feet of stone stood between Dr. Lawrence and the culmination of his life's work. The laser canon was delivered and set up adjacent to the rear tomb wall under his close supervision. Dr. Lloyd Roberts of InDevCo had accompanied the device and was in charge of the technical aspects of the job. A stout man, Roberts suffered in the desert heat and preferred to move slowly. Dozens of thick, black cables cluttered the floor of the low ceilinged ante-chamber. Most fed into the laser, but three cables powered large floodlights that reflected white light off the sandstone. Dr. Lawrence looked at his watch.

"I know I agreed to be patient, but the promised time for activating the laser has come and gone."

"If even one tiny component is out of synch, there will be no cutting today. Are all the generators on line?" asked Lloyd Roberts.

"Ready."

"Safety glasses on."

All but essential personnel were ordered out of the tomb. Intense red light burst from the laser and bounced off the gleaming sandstone wall. Then the stone surrendered as the light penetrated. The directed energy beam drew such great power that even with every camp generator on line, only minimal laser intensity settings could be used.

"It'll have to be enough," said Lawrence.

Dr. Roberts terminated the beam and inserted a thin ruler into the cut stone.

"One and a half centimeters," he said, looking at Dr. Lawrence.

"Can you drill a clean hole through so I can insert a fiber optic camera?"

Dr. Roberts answered by reactivating the laser.

Soon I will know.

* * *

The cutting proceeded with progress measured in millimeters. Lawrence left the tomb and Lloyd Roberts joined him. They sat under a canvas awning to escape the midday sun and drank warm, diluted orangeade. Dr. Lawrence stared at his glass and turned it slowly with both hands.

"I wanted to thank you for allowing me to be a part of this. I've always dreamed of coming to Egypt on a dig and, well, this is more than I ever hoped for. Can you tell me more about this Pharaoh you hope to find?"

"Katara III ruled during the New Kingdom period when Egypt enjoyed the prestige of being the most powerful nation on Earth. The wealth of the Pharaoh was legendary, and many have searched for his tomb knowing the riches it must contain. But its location remained a mystery. If this is Katara's intact burial chamber, it will make Tutankhamen's tomb look insignificant."

Unaccustomed to the heat, Roberts gulped the drink. "How did you happen to look here?"

"The tomb of an old priest who served Katara and a great deal of luck."

The floodlights and the control panel on the laser lit up as the generators pushed to supply increased power. Without a word, all observers replaced their protective glasses.

Dr. Roberts smiled. "With full power I can make a clean, single cut in a few minutes."

Satisfied with the cut, the beam was terminated. Lawrence approached the wall and inserted a thin fiber optic camera into the hole. He pushed it through for three feet with no resistance, while his men connected the cable to a small television monitor.

"According to the scanners, the wall is two feet thick, so, the extra length of cable should be hanging down on the other side. Power the camera on my count. Three, two, one."

A blurred, gray image appeared on the screen.

"What's that?" asked Roberts.

"Wait until I bring it into focus. Don't forget the light from the fiber is very dim." Lawrence adjusted the camera and they watched the picture clear.

The screen filled with a white object, interlaced with darker shadows.

"Any ideas?" Lawrence asked.

"Pull the camera back slowly and increase the illumination setting."

Lawrence tugged gently on the cable. The picture moved and blurred badly.

"Now, refocus the camera."

The form on the screen cleared.

It was a human skull.

Twenty

STEEL CABLES TIGHTENED AND STRAINED UNDER THE load of two Caterpillar bulldozers pulling the cut section of the thick stone. After completing the cut, the men rolled back the laser and Dr. Lawrence looped cables through thick grommets placed in the center and corners of the stone door.

The stone moved. One cable frayed and snapped, but the others held firm. Finally, the stone blocks moved enough to allow a man to slip through.

Dust clouds drifted from the opening into the dark passage.

Dr. Lawrence donned an oxygen mask and turned to the others in the antechamber. Gammal snapped a photo to continue his visual record. A video camera also recorded the event.

"I claim this find under the power granted me by the Egyptian Ministry of Antiquity."

Lawrence crawled into the narrow passage, and stopped. He had wanted to discover an intact Royal tomb for so long, that now it felt unreal.

His finger hovered above the torch switch, lingering.

Though his eyes perceived the darkness, in his mind, he saw the untouched tomb of Katara. Only his breathing broke the silence. He wanted to light the torch, but a part of him felt so afraid the tomb would be empty, that his finger refused to obey the command from his brain.

All the other tombs were robbed in antiquity. This one is different.

During the many years of opening the tombs of the ancients, the feeling of exhilaration never diminished. Perhaps that is what drove him on. To this.

The torch light burst through the darkness.

Like the new light of a long sleeping star, the lamp illuminated a world of the dead that had remained hidden for over three thousand years. Fifteen foot statues decorated in gold and ebony supported the thirty foot domed frescoed ceiling of the main chamber. The chamber itself contained a twenty foot long barge carved out of mahogany and alabaster. Dr. Lawrence closed his eyes and bit his lip and felt a chill pierce his spine.

This is no dream.

"Thank you, Katara," he said, "for designing a tomb that has withstood the ages."

Without moving from his spot, Lawrence scanned the layout of the tomb. The central chamber was circular, with smaller rooms adjacent like the spokes of a wheel. All were filled with artifacts and treasure. One room was larger and raised from the level of the boat chamber. In the distance, shadows revealed the platform that held the sarcophagus of the Pharaoh.

In all his years of archeology, Dr. Lawrence had never seen a tomb design such as this. Most consisted of a single square chamber, with perhaps one or two additional rooms. This was elegant by comparison.

At his feet lay a human skeleton with a small golden statue of Osiris, god of the afterlife, grasped in the left hand.

"If only you could talk, my friend." His impulse to reach for the idol was strong, but he knew nothing should be touched until all was photographed and cataloged.

"What do you see?" asked Gammal from the antechamber. No one would step in until Lawrence gave permission.

"It's wonderful," he said, lifting the torch high. Hieroglyphics and reliefs adorned the illuminated ceiling with colors vibrant as if they were painted yesterday.

Lawrence marveled at the massive stone wall separating the tomb from the antechamber. From this side, he could see that an ingenious technique had been used to allow each stone to slide into place, sealing the tomb.

The light flickered, then stayed on. He moved under the dome. The Royal barge in the center of the tomb overflowed with ceramic jugs and provisions for the journey into the next world. Bows and arrows, shields, swords and jeweled daggers stowed neatly into its holds. In the small prayer rooms at the periphery of the dome, statues in gold and sandalwood sat atop chests carved of ivory and inlaid with lapislazzuli, turquoise and cornealians. A gilded chariot awaited the Pharaoh's command. In one room, an ebony throne displayed the wings of a large bird sculpted in rosewood on its back, with black and white mother of pearl set into geometric designs on the contoured seat. Dried white and yellow Ostrich feathers guarded each side of the chair to cool the King as he sat upon his throne and ruled the land of the dead. Twelve massive columns that supported the dome had their capitols designed to represent a different month of the year. Each had the likeness of the Pharaoh carved out of a single slab of pink and white marble. Figures of animals, model ships and statues of the Egyptian gods were so plentiful that Lawrence thought it would take years to properly catalog each item.

He stared at the painted dome and recognized the same unusual references to the heavens that they had found in the priest's tomb. The same depiction of the Pharaoh ruling his subjects wearing a very un-Egyptian looking crown.

"Gammal and Dr. Roberts, please join me."

They placed oxygen masks over their faces and entered the tomb. Gammal held a torch, which lit the entry, and they stepped over the skeletal remains. Roberts stayed behind Gammal as they walked slowly into the domed hall. Roberts eyes widened and he stood frozen for a moment.

"Touch nothing," said Gammal. They walked toward Dr. Lawrence, past the Royal barge and the chariot.

"Look at this," said Lawrence, as he studied a wall relief.

"It depicts the king's military victories and shows us how he brought Egypt to the height of her power and prestige."

One painting in particular, interested him: a scene picturing the king accepting the gift of a crown from visitors. The same crown from the wall relief in the priest's tomb and the antechamber of this tomb. Lawrence lingered on this image.

"What is it, Aton? What does it mean?"

"I'm not sure, but we may soon have an answer."

"I never imagined the feeling,' said Roberts. "Thank you for allowing me to share this moment."

"Without you we would not be here."

Roberts smiled.

"Follow me," ordered Lawrence.

Though outwardly calm, Dr. Lawrence was overcome with happiness and emotion. His heart raced with the anticipation of the work ahead. This tomb was the prize of prizes. He knew it would be his last dig.

They stopped before climbing a wide polished marble stairway consisting of six steps.

"If I'm right, the sarcophagus of the king lies in this chamber."

The room was recessed into an alcove, larger than the prayer rooms and open to the dome area to allow the king easy access to his barge. The gilded coffin of the king lay on an ornate stone platform, displaying the unmistakable face of Katara III. A tiny bouquet of dry flowers lay atop the casket, faded colors still evident in the withered petals.

"Probably placed there by one of his wives over three thousand years ago." They stood in awed silence for a moment.

Dr. Lawrence turned to survey the tomb. From here, he could see the entire complex.

So perfect. Unlike Tutankhamen's tomb found in shambles.

"This is it, my friends. Since the rest of the tomb is untouched, I feel it is safe to say that the mummy of Katara lies within this coffin. I'm sure that no expense was spared in the embalming of this king. He probably will be well preserved."

"When can it be opened?" asked Roberts.

"Since there are traditionally three casings, we must proceed slowly. The seal will not be broken until all the tomb contents have been preliminarily cataloged and photographed. Probably two or three weeks."

"I'll have to be satisfied with a photograph. The laser is due back in Zurich by the end of the week. Sorry I'll miss the opening."

Lawrence snapped a Polaroid of the coffin with the tiny bouquet of dried flowers, and handed it to Roberts.

"To remember this day with our eternal gratitude."

The world press descended on the site as word of the discovery spread. Dr. Lawrence achieved celebrity status and conducted daily news conferences to describe the contents of the tomb and their progress in the work of cataloging. He was careful not to mention certain unexplainable facts: the unusual hieroglyphics found throughout the tomb, the unique design of the complex and the skeletal remains at the entrance. Lawrence fed the press just enough information to satisfy the readers and viewers who clamored for sensationalism. The question of the mummy's existence was so commonly asked that he was forced to assign a team to begin the work of unsealing the casket.

The desert sun settled behind the western mountains that bordered the narrow Nile valley. Lawrence sat alone in his tent outside the entrance to the tomb, studying the photos of the wall reliefs. His mind could not accept the only logical explanation.

"See you in the morning, Aton," said Gammal, poking his head into the tent. "Try to get some sleep tonight. You're exhausted. I have personally selected the teams who will guard the tomb. All is secure."

"I'm fine. Good night, my friend," he said following Gammal out of the tent.

The moonless night air cooled quickly and the stars shone like millions of lighthouses pointing the way to Earth. He stared at the black sky until a light shot across the heavens.

Katara was given a gift. A special gift.

Lawrence greeted the two guards who stood watch outside the tomb, and he entered the antechamber. A series of electric lamps installed in each room allowed the work to proceed.

The spirit of the king is strong tonight. The time is right.

Lawrence moved through the tomb and entered the room with the sarcophagus. The team assigned to the task of opening the coffin had breached the outer and middle caskets.

Unlike the first two casings that were wood covered in gold, the inner one was solid gold. A specially fitted hoist attached in four spots readied to lift the massive lid. Cameras were set in strategic locations to record the momentous occasion. It was expected to draw worldwide attention.

The death mask stared at him.

I must be the first to view the king.

For a brief moment, he was thrust back in time to the day of the funeral and the tomb sealing ceremony: the priests sacrificing themselves for their king, the massive stones falling into place forever sealing and protecting the sacred burial chamber from the outside world.

Until now.

Lawrence glanced at the entrance to be sure he was alone, then activated the winch. The machine creaked and moaned as the tension on the cables increased. The cover lifted slowly as he continued to dream of the past and the inexplicable hieroglyphics, the inhuman forms and shapes in the sky and the unusual crown that had appeared in so many wall reliefs. His intellect still prevented acceptance of the obvious truth.

Lawrence studied the image of the Pharaoh carved in gold. He lay in the traditional position with his arms folded across his chest.

The winch struggled under the weight of the death mask. Shadows prevented a clear view of the mummy. He held his breath, checked the winch lines and slowly lifted the Pharaoh's golden image to see the first glimpse of the mummy.

Dr. Lawrence blinked his eyes in disbelief.

The crown rested upon the Pharaoh's head.

For the first time in his memory, he shed a tear.

All his experience taught him to resist the next move, but he could not withstand or comprehend the forces at work. Breaking his own rule, he reached into the casket and gently lifted the royal hat from the king's head, then smoothed the linen wrap that encased the mummy's head.

It's a crown. Nothing more.

He was about to replace it, when light reflected off a tiny metal object in the lining A closer look revealed two small metallic discs positioned so that they rested on the temples of the wearer.

The fragile lining pulled away revealing its secret.

Hundreds of tiny clear rectangular crystals were mounted in rows. Silvery-metallic tubular rings attached to the crown itself formed a circular pattern across the inside, touching the discs that were positioned over the wearer's temples.

"Oh, my god! It's a computer."

Twenty-one

Albuquerque, New Mexico

GORDON YORK THREW THE LATEST COPY OF THE *Albuquerque Gazette* toward the trash can under his desk, but the pages scattered across the floor and the front page landed at his feet.

MESSAGE FROM HEAVEN OR HOAX FROM HELL, read the bold print headline.

The intercom beeped.

"Miss Welles is here and she insists on seeing you."

"Tell her I'm in a meeting. Tell her anything."

A moment later the door burst open and Julia Welles stood in front of his desk.

"I see you don't know the meaning of the word private," he said pointing with his cane to the sign painted on the door.

"I'm from New York, remember? Those things don't apply to me. I have to speak with you. Why haven't you returned my calls?"

"Did you think I would welcome you here again after that piece of trash you wrote about me and the project?"

"I can't blame you for being upset, but that's why I called. I didn't write it."

Gordon retrieved the front page and pointed to her name. "Is there another Julia Welles at the Gazette?"

"Hear me out, Gordon. I wrote a flattering, truthful article about the dedicated men and women I met here the other day. I mentioned you and how the success of S.A.I.L. depended on your unswaying leadership. Unfortunately, that piece was replaced by the drivel you see on the front page. At the last minute, the editor pulled a switch. They had the nerve to put my name on it."

"Why would they do that?"

"A man named Roy Slater. He's the new owner of the paper. A sleazy guy with a lot of money. He wants to turn the Gazette into Albuquerque's version of the Enquirer. Sensationalism and crap. Anyway, that's why I'm here."

Gordon looked puzzled.

"I need a job," she said. "I told them to take their crummy paper and shove it."

"Sorry. We have no need for a fashion reporter."

"I'm not a reporter anymore. Besides, you owe me."

"How do you figure that?"

"Because of you, I got involved with ET."

She pointed to the readout on the computer screen. ENERGY CONTROLS MATTER, flashed continually on the monitor.

"I'm not responsible for your lost job. Sorry, but. . ."

"Don't say no. I can do a lot of things."

"Go back to New York, Julia. You belong there."

"Public relations. You'll need someone to write press releases and handle the TV people."

"I don't think so. We already have. . ."

She handed him a manila folder.

"This is the original article I wrote for the paper. Judge

for yourself."

Gordon read the story.

"It's good." He hesitated. "The best I can do is assistant to Roberta Evans, our public relations person. Everything that goes out of here passes my desk first. Understood?"

"Yes, sir. You won't regret it. Where can I work?"

They were interrupted by an intercom tone.

"York here."

"Gordon, it's Hank. I think you'd better see this."

"On my way. Okay, Julia. Take your pad and follow me. Hank Burton doesn't call me unless it's something extraordinary."

The elevator door opened and Gordon and Julia walked the short distance to the central control desk where Hank Burton and ten other scientists sat converged on a computer screen.

"What's happening?" asked Gordon, sitting in the chair next to Hank. Julia collected momentary questioning stares, which she ignored.

"This just started about ten minutes ago," said Hank. "The directional array is configured exactly as when we received the first message."

Gordon glanced toward the crater outside the lab where the parabolic receivers responded to the computer's directional signals.

The computer's voice broke the silence. "Primary circuits engaged. Directional complex in position to receive incoming signal and boost to maximum output. Secondary stations on line and prepared to accept and process overload data."

Gordon looked at Julia, who was writing furiously, though he knew she didn't understand that this meant a large amount of information was being processed. He said a silent prayer, hoping this new message would help them explain the first. *Energy controls matter* had repeated in his mind for the last two days. Even his dreams were filled with the words. He thought it would drive him mad.

Does it mean that controls on energy really matter? Or rather that Einstein's E=MC2 is the key to...what?

Static filled the central monitor, which displayed an enlarged version of the data that came in on Gordon's computer. Just as Julia looked up, the screen turned solid red, then blue.

"Ready to record data?" asked Gordon.

Hank Burton gave the thumbs up sign.

Gordon entered a series of computer commands and the screen filled with unrecognizable letters and symbols.

"Ladies and gentlemen, what we have witnessed is remarkable and exciting. All of our labors have paid off and I believe we are the first humans to receive communications from another civilization. Now, we must try to understand this data. I'm open to any ideas," said Gordon.

No one spoke.

"When I called this meeting of department heads, I expected some answers. So far all I have is a lot of blank expressions. The question is, can we decipher the coded language or not?" He held up a hard copy of the latest data received from Alpha Centauri Proxima. It contained enough information to fill a small book. "Dr. Hayes, surely our resident linguist can offer some hope in this translation gridlock."

"I'm afraid not. I've never seen anything like this." He looked at his copy of the message. "I'm going to recommend outside consultation. Perhaps the government should be notified. I have a friend who works with the CIA whenever they have a cryptography problem."

"I've considered that myself," said Gordon. "This thing is too big to keep to ourselves, but there's going to be a credibility problem. People have been 'communicating' with alien intelligence for years. How do we prove this is real?" Julia stood up. "Leave that to me."

During the next forty-eight hours, the same illegible message from the heavens repeated four times. Each time the S.A.I.L. scientists traced the origin of the signal to the same place. They waited for the fifth message, but the computer delivered nothing further.

Gordon York sank into his chair and struggled with the daily reports on his desk. "We still haven't figured out why the first message came in English and the second in code or alien language. Nothing else new to report," he wrote, then dropped the pen, spun the chair around and looked at the complex he commanded. He wore a two day growth of beard and his eyes grew swollen from lack of sleep. A knock on the door interrupted his daydream.

"Hope I'm not disturbing you," said Julia. She poked her head through the half opened door carrying lunch and a manila folder.

"Unless you have the answer to the mystery, I'd rather be

alone just now."

"Thought you'd like to see this. It's a fax from New York."

Gordon took the paper and the sandwich.

"What is it?"

"Roast beef. I thought. . ."

"No, I meant the paper."

"An advance copy of the front page of tomorrow's New York Times."

A small article on the bottom of the copy read: *Albuquerque team intercepts extraterrestrial messages.* The article, bearing Julia's name, was the one she had originally written for the Gazette.

"How's that for credibility?" she asked.

"How did you manage it?" Gordon realized the credibility problem now ceased to exist.

"Let's just say I called in a favor. I know proper recognition of S.A.I.L. is all important. We'd better prepare for the onslaught of the press. I allowed them to use our location in the article."

Within twenty-four hours, Julia and Roberta Evans had organized a schedule of news releases and a system to deal with the camera crews and reporters from around the country. One benefit of all the publicity was the chance to assemble a group of experts in language and cryptography. They gathered in the main control area, and Gordon York called for attention.

"I thank you for coming here today, though I know that most of you still don't believe this is truly a communication from another galaxy. As specialists, you've worked individually and collectively in an attempt to understand this new language. At this time, we are no closer to it's translation than we were before. Does anyone have a suggestion as to how to proceed?"

The beeping sound of the directional array filled the room, but no one spoke.

A voice from a man servicing the computer broke the silence. "It's not a new language."

All heads turned in one, synchronous motion.

"Would you care to explain yourself, Mr...?"

"Mike Haywood. I'm a computer engineer and designer with InDevCo on a follow-up call to check on the new system we installed here last month. I guess it worked pretty well."

"You have a talent for understatement, Mr. Haywood," said Gordon. "Won't you please explain yourself now that your credibility is established?"

Mike joined Gordon at the main computer terminal, and ran the tape of the alien transmission.

"There's a lot about this that I don"t pretend to understand, but a good part of it resembles the inside of this computer."

"Sorry, but I don't understand."

"It's an electronic schematic. A computer blueprint. True, it's much more sophisticated and elaborate than anything we have, but I'm fairly certain of it."

Almost every expert in the room protested at the same time.

"Quiet please. This is a radical idea. Okay, Mr. Haywood, let's say for argument sake that you're right, and we have a blueprint. What would we have if we built it?"

"I believe it's a kind of communications apparatus. Many of the alien circuits are new to me, but some of it is similar in design to a device we developed at InDevCo using the new superconductive technology for brain research."

Gordon looked toward the window and observed the crater. Then, addressed the group.

"With the level of technology available to you through InDevCo, do you believe it's possible to actually build this device?"

"If I had the resources of the company to do additional studies of the new designs, I think it's possible."

"Julia, get me Andy Cromwell on the phone. If you're right, Mike, "long-distance calling" will take on a new meaning."

Twenty-two

JAKE REGAINED CONSCIOUSNESS BUT DID NOT IMMEDiately open his eyes. Instead, he concentrated on the kaleidoscope of colors and shapes that inhabited the inside of his eyelids. Voices echoed from a distance, but seemed close by. The strong sensation of a presence overwhelmed him.

My eyes are closed, yet I can sense all of these things. Jake hoped Lane's smiling face would greet him. It was neither Lane nor the lab that he saw, but an electronic scanner with his name on the label marked patient.

"Ah good, you're awake Mr. Parker. We were wondering how long your nap would last."

"Who are you and where am I?"

"Dr. Simmons and this is Subterra Medical Center. Dr. Darby asked me to check you after you failed to wake up in the lab. She's waiting to speak with you."

"Is she here?"

Dr. Simmons moved a computer console into position in front of Jake. Lane's face appeared on the screen.

"Jake, are you okay? I was so worried about you. I'm sorry I allowed you to convince me to implant the modules. They've got to come out."

"But I feel great now. Let's wait a day and see what

happens."

"Absolutely not. You were unconscious for six hours. None of the previous test subjects experienced this lapse. We've got to find out why before going further. These are unknown complications. The removal procedure is scheduled for 1800 hours. I'm sending Eric to bring you back to the lab. Maggie and I will be waiting for you, Jake.

"I suppose you're right. See you soon."

"What are modules?" asked Dr. Simmons, as he removed the console.

"What floor are we on?" asked Jake scanning the windowless room. He attempted to stand, but Dr. Simmons stopped him.

"You're not going anywhere until I get some answers. I don't even know what I'm treating here. Now get back into bed or I'll be forced to sedate you. I want some answers."

"I can't stay here. Get out of my way, doctor."

"Sorry, but you give me no choice." Simmons pulled a derminjector from his pocket and snapped a sedative pellet into the barrel. Jake seized the man's wrist just as he was about to inject the drug.

"Don't try it."

"You're pretty strong for someone who just awakened." Jake easily overpowered the older man, positioned and snapped the injector into the doctor's arm. Jake stood up and placed the doctor in his bed as the struggle ended. Jake grabbed his clothes and went out the door. With the last of his wakefulness, Dr. Simmons pressed the nurses call button on the bedside console.

Jake zipped his pants and headed for the elevator. No

one noticed him and he blended with the visitors and patients that waited with him.

Five people entered the car when it finally arrived. Jake waited until each person had pushed their respective floor button, then he pressed *10.*

The elevator reached the 8th floor and all but Jake and one passenger exited. On the 9th floor, the door slid open and the remaining man left. A nurse in the corridor called to Jake as she rushed to the catch the closing doors.

"Hold it please," she said.

Jake pushed the door close button and he was alone.

When the car reached the 10th floor, Jake opened the ceiling panel and climbed out. He closed the panel as three people entered the elevator. Jake jumped off the car and held onto a support beam as the car descended. The doors to the 11th floor beckoned a few feet above him.

A short, easy climb, assuming I don't look down into the dark shaft.

Slowly, he pulled himself up with a stubborn determination. Finally, he reached the doors. With a great effort, he managed to open one side and pull himself through. The spring loaded door slid closed behind him and he sat propped against the wall adjacent to the elevator. Light from an exit sign above the locked stairway filtered through the corridor. Lane's words, unknown virus, echoed through his mind; the reason she had given for the quarantine on this floor. But something about the story did not hold up.

Call it intuition or just a hunch.

His detective's instinct decided the matter required further investigation.

Jake stood and stayed close to the wall. This section of the floor contained patient rooms that looked identical to the ones on the lower floors. He peered into the empty rooms and moved through the corridor. CLINICAL LABORATORY, marked a set of double doors at the end of the hall. The doors were unlocked and Jake proceeded to the other side, unaware that an infrared motion detector positioned above the door had announced his arrival.

Jake's head throbbed and for a moment, his vision blurred. He leaned against the wall and rubbed the sides of his head. The sensation passed.

Unknown virus? Is this the first sign of the virus?

Then his temples throbbed again, and he remembered the CCEM.

Through an open door at the end of the corridor, a filmy light radiated into the hall. Like a cat overcome with curiosity, Jake approached the door and peered in. Life support equipment filled the room. Oxygen tanks, IV stands, many syringes on the bed stand, electronic monitors and scanners, all functioning and focused on the lone occupant of a bed in the center of the room. Next to the bed, a nurse sat in a chair reading under the dim light of an over head lamp. Jake could not see the face of the patient.

The corridor remained quiet.

He slipped into the room.

For a full minute, Jake stood in a dark, shadowy corner with the unknown patient and the nurse just a few feet away. He moved into the light and the nurse looked up.

"How did you get in here?"

"I won't hurt you," he said. "Who is this?" Jake asked

pointing to the man in the bed.

"My orders are no visitors." She stood up and moved toward Jake.

"I just want to see him," Jake said.

"No." The nurse kicked Jake in the groin and he winced in pain. The move surprised him and he fell to the floor. He recovered just as she was poised to strike. Again she attacked, but Jake stepped back and the assault failed. Jake stood at the foot of the bed. The light shone on the man's face.

"Oh my god," he said.

From behind, the nurse came at him and touched his neck with a metal disc that sent a current through Jake's body, paralyzing every muscle in his body.

Like a bronze statue, he froze in place.

He recognized the familiar face of the man in the bed from magazine pictures and photo albums.

The face belonged to Philip Cromwell.

Twenty-three

JAKE TRIED UNSUCCESSFULLY TO LIFT HIS ARM, AND HIS legs felt like blocks of wood. The light in the room brightened.

"You'll find it impossible to budge from that spot, my friend. The neural interrupter blocks any electrical impulses to voluntary muscles below the cervical level of activation. It's quite effective, don't you agree?"

Jake managed to turn his head.

"You seem to have all the advantages in this meeting. Charles Cromwell isn't it?"

"Very good, Jake. Now I know why mother hired you. You've accomplished your mission and found my father. Would you like your gold medal now or after I've finished with you?"

"What's his condition?" Jake asked looking at Philip.

"Despite what he did to me, I still love him. Can you believe that?" Charles walked around to the head of Philip's bed. "My men found him wandering through Subterra babbling about his new brain. The old fool had the modules inserted without the synchronization program to match them to his brain pattern and he had a stroke."

Jake wondered if Charles still had the implant.

"Your mother still believes he's alive even though the will has been read."

"Poor mother. I do love her so. But she's weak and easily influenced by Andrew. I know all about the will, Jake. Andrew thinks he has the company. All these years, I ran the company through my father. No one knows anything about it except me." Charles' face reddened and the veins in his neck and forehead protruded. He paced in front of Jake and Philip.

"What do you intend to do with us?"

"My father will continue to get the care he needs until I seize power from my brother. Mother will forgive me when she learns that Andrew kidnapped her beloved husband."

"I can help you, Charles. Your mother trusts me and I can convince her that you were right all along. Let me go and I'll speak with her today."

Charles bent over and kissed his father on the forehead. Philip did not move and appeared heavily sedated.

"Why Jake, you must have read my mind. I know you'll be a big help to me. But not that way. You're going to kill Andrew for me after the world learns that he kidnapped father. Mother will have no choice but to turn the company over to me. She'll have her husband to nurse back to health, I'll be running the company and Andrew will be dead."

"I'll pass on that assignment."

"Oh, I feel confident you'll do as I say. I have friends in places that specialize in stubborn men like you. After a short stay at a special resort, you'll be happy to join my organization and do anything I ask."

Before Jake could speak, Charles nodded to the nurse, who approached Jake and placed an additional neural interrupter on his neck.

Jake felt a searing pain in his head, then dropped to the

floor.

"You must eat something, senior," said a small, wrinkled woman who bent over Jake with a bowl of chili in her hand. She held a spoonful of the spicy mixture up to his mouth. "You have not eaten anything for two days." The twinkle in her crystal eyes revealed a mothers instinct though her tattered peasant dress exposed the truth of her hard life.

"Who are you?"

"I am Rosita. I was told to see to it that you stay alive or I will be killed as well. By the blessed virgin, please eat for both our sakes." The woman spoke in Spanish, but Jake understood every word. "You are a very important person, no?"

Jake took the food. The spices burned his mouth, but he was ravenous.

"What is this place?"

"I can answer none of your questions, but if you promise not to try to escape, I will untie you. Do you swear on the cross?"

Jake nodded, and she freed his wrists and ankles.

"There, now you can feed yourself. I must see to the others. I like you, Senior. What is your name?"

Jake was stunned by the question. He had no memory of his own name, nor any past.

"I. . .I don't remember."

"No name, eh? I will call you Juan after my lost son. You remind me of him. Rest now, Juan. I will return later." The old woman stepped through a hatch-type door, turned to Jake and crossed herself, then locked it behind her.

Jake felt a rocking sensation. The walls creaked and moaned. He perspired freely from the stale, hot and humid air. A tiny vent over the door delivered a trickle of salty air.

I'm on a ship at sea.

Jake reached for a glass of water the old woman placed on the table next to the cot, drank most of it and poured the rest over his head. He took off his shirt and pants and sat on the cot. The only source of light in the cell was a single bulb that dangled from a brown extension cord in the middle of a low ceiling. Water dripped from the walls and the rusted beams. Jake rubbed his wrists and ankles where the ropes abraded the skin.

Jake lay on the cot and searched his mind for a memory. There was nothing. No past or recollection of anything familiar. Frustrated, he fell asleep with a dull headache.

The hours passed slowly. Jake lay quietly awake in the cot trying to sift through the thoughts that rambled through his mind. His senses remained sharp; every smell and sound magnified. This made the stench of the bed and the cabin difficult to take. He pounded on the door and yelled for help, but no one came.

During short periods of sleep, strange images appeared. Non-human beings reaching to him. But he always awoke before speaking with them. He heard foreign languages that he clearly understood. But the sleep left him unrefreshed and his head throbbed with a constant, dull sensation; something to be ignored.

With no day or night, Jake lost track of time. He simply lay on the bed and waited for Rosita to deliver his daily food and water. He questioned her about their destination, but she said little, other than to tell him how he reminded her of Juan. He sensed her simple innocence and devotion to God, but did not understand the insight.

Jake awoke to a new sound: Quiet. The vibration of the ship's engines and the creaking of the walls ceased. Like a caged animal, he paced the floor and pounded on the door. Hours passed and no one came for him.

Have they forgotten me?

The hatch opened slowly and two men carrying automatic weapons entered the cell. One man threw a pair of dirty overalls at Jake and ordered him to put them on. The other, motioned for Jake to turn around, and tied his wrists tightly. They shoved him out of the room into a dimly lit corridor. The smell of oil saturated the heavy air.

They led Jake through a series of narrow passageways and up several ladders until the light of the sun appeared through a final hatch. He squinted from the brightness, and realized he was held prisoner in the bowels of a large oil tanker, now tied to the dock of a city somewhere in the tropics. Palm trees and blue water surrounded the port. All deck hands busily readied the ship to unload its liquid cargo into the waiting storage tanks next to the pier.

They continued through the upper decks of the ship toward a gangplank that led to the dock. After a short walk to the road beside the pier, Jake looked back at the ship. The name of the ship was painted on her bow: Sea Titan, with the letters, InDevCo, beneath the name in smaller letters.

Nothing familiar.

Shoved along by his captors, they delighted in hitting him

with the butt of their guns if he did not move fast enough to suit them. An old, rusted car waited at the end of the pier. Jake sat in the back seat with one of the guards, and the car pulled away. He looked back at the ship that was his prison. Another ship tied up directly in front of the Sea Titan also unloaded oil. The name Conquistador Del Mar was painted on her bow. He could not place it, though the name was familiar.

The city beyond the dock area appeared old and neglected as the car sped through the cobblestone streets hitting every pot hole in the narrow road. Children played in front of abandoned buildings. Long lines of expressionless people waited in front of small grocery shops.

"Where are we?"

The guards laughed and spoke to each other in Spanish. Jake understood, but pretended that he did not. They stank of liquor and had few teeth. They were amazed at Jake's perfect teeth, and had never seen anyone like him before. Jake was certain they would remove his teeth if they could.

A billboard appeared on top of a newer building.

"Viva Castro," read the sign.

"Oh, so this is Havana."

The men laughed wildly.

The car stopped outside the gate of a walled complex. Graffiti covered the fifteen foot high prison walls. Electrified barbed wire fencing topped the wall.

The car cleared the security gate and entered the compound. After a short ride, they stopped outside the office of the Commandant.

The guards led Jake into the office and forced him into a

chair in front of a large desk.

Twenty minutes later, a door opened and a bald man dressed in the uniform of a high ranking officer entered the room. He had food stains on his shirt and his belly hung over a belt that strained on its last notch. Thick, black hair protruded from his nose and a cigarette with a long ash hung from the side of his mouth; its smoke forced him to squint. He sat down and picked up a folder, one of many strewn about the desk.

"You are Pablo Munez?"

Is that who I am?

"Speak."

"I . . ."

One of the guards hit Jake in the shoulder with his gun, knocking him to the floor.

"Answer the Commandant, swine."

Jake listened with a vague sense of unreality.

The warden read further, then smiled revealing his many gold teeth.

"I have the sad duty to inform you that our beloved President has signed this order for your execution. Tomorrow at dawn, I will assemble my firing squad just for you, Pablo."

Twenty-four

JAKE HUGGED HIS KNEES INSIDE A STEEL BOX THAT BARELY had enough room for him to move. The pit, the guards called it, when they shoved him out of the Commandant's office after the death sentence.

Sun-wilted palms waited for their daily afternoon shower. The pit sat in the middle of the dirt courtyard for all the prisoners to see. Many had died of heat prostration in this cage, a fact that gave the Commandant pleasure.

Jake stared through the rusted bars at the guards on their rounds. His body ached, every muscle in spasm. Without the slightest idea about the crime he had committed or his identity, he could not quiet his mind. He filled his thoughts with images of distant places that felt vaguely familiar, but gave no comfort in his present predicament.

He closed his eyes to meditate.

Clicking sounds of a key in the lock surprised him. The door opened and a guard pulled him out of the box. He stumbled, but two guards dragged him across the compound.

"Where are you taking me."

Without answering, they took Jake to the Commandant's office.

Charles Cromwell sat in a chair in front of the warden and each smoked a fat Havana Corona. Jake found himself in the seat he occupied earlier in the day.

"Good to see you again, Jake. I understand there was a mix up here today," said Charles. He blew thick smoke from his mouth and it hung in the still, humid air. "Glad I stopped by to check on you on my way to see the President. Can't have them executing you. That would spoil my plans. I've explained to the Commandant about your memory lapse. Sorry about the amnesia, but don't worry, it's a temporary effect of the neural interrupter. You'll have your memory back in time for your return to the states. You haven't the slightest idea what I'm talking about, do you, Jake? No matter." Charles looked at his Rolex and stood. The Commandant stared at the watch, then looked at his own, an old Timex he received when promoted to his present position. "I trust you'll follow your orders, Captain. I'm late for my meeting. I'll check on your progress before I leave tomorrow, Jake. Oh, by the way, Francesca Campbell sends her love. She said you'd remember her. Eventually."

The Commandant stood and saluted Charles.

My name is Jake.

"Take Mr. Parker to cell block four."

The guards prodded Jake as they dragged him through the corridors of the prison to the cell block. Prisoners packed the cells and heckled and jeered. Others lay motionless on their cots and looked blankly at him as he passed.

These are broken men.

He stopped in front of a cell where three men tended to a forth man who lay on the cot and looked so badly beaten that Jake thought he might be dead.

"Move," said a guard, and he pressed his gun to Jake's back.

They stopped at a small cubicle near the end of the

corridor, unlocked the door and pushed Jake in. A man with a long beard sat reading a tattered book. He looked up briefly and resumed his reading. One straw cot, a broken wooden chair, a filthy water spigot and a hole in the corner represented the furnishings of the cell.

"My name is. . .Parker," Jake said offering his hand, his name still unfamiliar. "What's yours?"

The man looked up and stared at Jake.

"How long have you been here?"

No reply.

Jake glanced out the barred window. This cell block was one of many that were clustered together inside the walled compound. Government soldiers patrolled the walls; a good deterrent to anyone with a notion for escape. Jake could see the Commandant's office and the adjoining structure, a white, stuccoed, windowless building. He swatted at the thick swarm of mosquitoes that buzzed in his ears. The stench of vomit and human feces overwhelmed his senses.

"Santiago."

"What?"

"My name is Santiago."

"Why are you here?"

"I'm a physician. I was assigned to the clinic at this prison as part of my service to the government for sending me through medical school. When I refused their orders to torture an inmate, I was made prisoner here until I changed my mind. That was eight years ago."

Jake shuddered at the thought.

Two guards opened the steel door to the cell block and entered the corridor. All the prisoners quieted and clung to the bars of their cells to watch where the guards headed. Jake heard screams as they dragged a prisoner from his cot and took him away.

"Poor devil would be better off dead," said Santiago. "They take him to the infirmary. A cursed place where men lose their souls. They have techniques that rob you of your mind. Each day they torture someone to the brink of death." Santiago opened his shirt. The blistered, red welts told the story. "The scars on my body are nothing. Sometimes when the pain is no longer bearable, I pray for the angel of death to take me into the great void. Only the thought of one day seeing my beloved wife again keeps me from hanging myself and depriving them of the pleasure of my screams. Now, tell me how a man like you comes to this place. You are American, no?"

Jake told Santiago of his trip on the tanker, his amnesia and the close brush with the Commandant's firing squad.

"I am a fatalist, Jake. It is not your time to die."

"Maybe not, but without my memory, I feel half dead."

"Perhaps there is something I can do to help."

Santiago sat next to Jake, who lay on the bed.

"Don't worry, Jake, I've hypnotized many patients. Try to open your mind to my suggestions. You are completely relaxed and I want you to count backward from one hundred. With each number after ninety, you will feel more relaxed. Your eyelids are heavy, and getting heavier with each number. You are completely relaxed. Tell me what you see."

Jake's eye lids fluttered. There was a short pause.

"A city, a beautiful city with thousands of people."

"What else. What do you wear on your feet?"

"Sandals. Made of leather."

"Look around you and describe the place."

"This is the marketplace, but no one is selling today.

People line up along the main avenue to view a funeral procession as it passes on its way to a royal tomb. Palace guards are having a hard time restraining the people, who wail and cry. They loved their King. Priests and officials lead the parade toward the Temple of the Gods."

Santiago did not grasp the meaning of the vision.

"Look at yourself. Who are you?"

"I am Menefter, the Royal architect. I am to be buried with the King, who was my friend. I am afraid."

What is the year?"

"It is the year of the Disappearing Sun. The priest's foretold Pharaoh's death."

Santiago had heard stories of hypnotized patient's recounting past life experiences, but he had never encountered it. His analytical mind refused to accept the dream revelation, yet he questioned his disbelief in reincarnation. Still, with his curiosity more than piqued, he had to continue.

"What do you see now, Menefter?"

A long time passed in silence. Finally, Jake spoke.

"The stones are falling. The tomb is forever sealed. There is no more air to breathe. It is so dark. Pain in my chest." Jake gasped and clutched his chest. Then, he lay calm and quiet.

Jake said nothing more as Menefter. The dimly lit cell remained quiet for a long time.

Jake appeared to be asleep. Santiago made a note in his log.

"When I count to three, you will awaken feeling refreshed and happy. You will remember everything we have said tonight. One, two, three."

Jake opened his eyes and reoriented himself.

Do you recall what you told me during the hypnotic

session?"

Jake nodded.

"What do you think it means?"

"It's a dream I've had on many occasions. I understand my fear of dark, closed places now."

"Do you remember anything of the present?"

"No."

The following day, the guards took no prisoners from the cell block. An anxious Santiago wanted to hear more from his new American friend, and he made notes on scraps of available paper.

Jake relaxed and easily entered the hypnotic state.

"Who are you?"

"I am Menefter, the Royal architect."

Santiago hoped to explore a different lifetime. He knew that in order to reactivate Jake's immediate memory, he would have to bring him through the centuries toward the present. But something more needed to be learned from this time frame.

"Where are you and what is the year?"

"I am at the King's summer palace. I don't know the time. There is feverish excitement during the celebration to Isis and the anniversary of the King's rise to power. Strangers have come to the city. It is said they are very different from us. They bear an important gift for the King. The palace gossips say they are gods and have come from the sky in heavenly boats."

"What is this gift for the King?"

A long silence followed this question.

"It is a crown. A new royal crown. The visitors tell us they have come a far distance to meet us. The crown will give the King powers even the gods could not imagine. But the priests are angry. They say the traditional crown bearing the serpent and the vulture symbolizing the unification of upper and lower Egypt is the only crown the gods will recognize. They are afraid and jealous of this new promised power. They have incited the people to chase the visitors from the city."

"Who are the visitors, Menefter?"

"I do not know, but they have a mystical effect on the people. They are gone now, and the King has convinced the priests to allow him to wear the new crown. I never thought it possible. The King has changed. He sees visions and says he will lead the Egyptian people to greatness and wealth beyond their dreams."

The next day, the door to the cell block opened and the guards entered. All eyes watched as the soldiers stopped in front of Jake's cell, and they unlocked the door.

"You."

They pointed to Jake. As they approached him, he struck one of the guards. The other kicked Jake and held his gun at Jake's head.

"Don't resist," said Santiago. "There's no escape and this will only make it worse for you. Trust me, Jake."

The fallen guard regained his balance and hit Jake in the face with his pistol, then tied Jake's wrists together and led him out of the cell block to the windowless building that Santiago called the infirmary.

They passed through a door with a large red cross on it, into a room with antiquated medical equipment. A ceiling fan slowly moved the hot, stale air. They tied Jake to a blood stained table that resembled a doctor's examination table. Next to the table, two portable cabinets contained equipment with electronic leads and sensors. Stripped and tied to the table, Jake lay still for a long time. A large Palmetto bug flew onto the table and crawled on his leg. He watched the overhead fan and diverted his mind from the screams that came from the next rooms.

A smiling, bald man wearing a stained white lab coat entered the room. "Buenos dias, Parker." He wore thick glasses and his hands were dirty. "Senior Cromwell informed me of his wish that you be more cooperative. You and I will see a lot of each other over the next couple of days." As he spoke, the 'doctor' placed numerous electronic pin leads on Jake's head, chest and testicles. Jake winced as the leads penetrated his skin, and tiny droplets of blood oozed from each site.

"I don't suppose I could talk you into letting me go," said Jake.

"Very good, Jake. You can speak. Now, as I activate these circuits, you will feel some, uh, discomfort. Actually, the purpose of our first meeting is to determine your pain threshold. Shall we begin?"

Twenty-five

JAKE FELT A TINGLING THAT INTENSIFIED TO A BURNING sensation. He closed his eyes, focused his thoughts, and fell into a trance, concentrating on the electrical leads.

One by one, the leads popped off.

"What is this?" the doctor watched with disbelief.

Jake's instincts took over his mind. Two of the leads flew up and attached themselves to the doctor's neck. Jake opened his eyes and he looked at the control panel. The power intensity dial clicked to maximum. The doctor screamed and fell as strong electrical current flowed through his body. He yanked off the electrodes and the leads and the leads danced on the floor with a shower of sparks as they touched one another.

Jake opened his eyes in amazement.

The doctor held his neck, the skin scalded.

"I don't know how you did that but I can promise you pain that will fill the corridors of this building with screams that will be heard in every cell. Guards. Take him away."

Jake's hands were again tied and he was dressed and brought back to the cell block.

Santiago stood anxiously at the door.

"What happened to you?"

"Nothing. I have no idea how, but I managed to avoid

the treatment today." Jake decided not to tell Santiago about his new found power until he understood it himself.

Perhaps when I regain my memory.

Santiago smiled and grabbed Jake's hands. "I am glad you are safe, my friend."

Late that night, after a long session with Jake, Santiago sat up in his bed and wrote his observations on the scraps of paper he had collected on his clean up duty.

"The American continues to surprise me with his detailed recollection of past lives. We have been through diverse and varied times and locales such as a witch's trial, where he wound up buried alive in a coffin, and an African tribal disaster. I have tried to bring him closer to the present each time (though I seem to have little control) so that we may deal with the amnesia. The final identity for the day was an account of the kidnapping and loss of his wife and child, though the memory must be so painful that I don't know if its recounting will be harmful or beneficial. At last we have arrived in the present. After the trance, his memory appeared to be almost completely restored.

"My analysis of the past life experiences has detected an interesting pattern. Almost all the cases involved a leader or military genius near the end of his life. I wonder if his perpetual soul is now finally destined for greatness in this lifetime. Were all of these events merely a training ground for what is to come? I feel certain this is no ordinary man. I believe Jake now has the ability to draw on the knowledge he has gained of his past through the regression therapy, though I am uncertain what direction this will take."

* * *

A violent thunderstorm raged outside the prison. Horizontal rain pelted the courtyard and buildings, obliterating the high towers and outer walls. Santiago thanked God for the storm as the guards rarely took anyone in this kind of foul weather. It meant he could have his final session with Jake with no fear of interruption. He planned the approach carefully, dividing the session in half. The first part would restore Jake fully to the present. The second, a daring departure from the past life therapy; a look into the future.

Jake entered the relaxed state easily. Each time he had revealed bits of information of the past, his own confidence grew.

Santiago spoke softly, pausing whenever a loud clap of thunder shook the building.

"The time is the present. Who are you?"

"Jake Parker. I am an agent with InDevCo on an assignment to find Philip Cromwell, the CEO of the company. I succeeded in finding him, but lost consciousness and awoke on a ship en route to Cuba to be tortured into obeying Charles Cromwell. I now know he kidnapped his own father and has a crazy scheme to force me to kill his brother, Andrew so that he can gain control of the company."

Jake said nothing of the CCEM implant, which he now remembered fully.

"Excellent," said Santiago. "Jake, I want you to open your mind completely. The past is now behind us. We know it has an important impact on the events of the present and the future. We know about the past. We have experienced your lives and learned. You have an extraordinary gift: the ability to expand your vision. I ask you now to do this: look beyond the past and the present. Open your mind to the future. Who are you?"

The pause lasted a long while, broken only by the wind driven rain and the pounding thunder. Lightning flashes illuminated the expression of serenity on Jake's face. Santiago waited for a revelation, for anything.

"I am the Guardian. The time for waiting is almost over. Soon the truth will be known. You will learn how energy controls matter."

Santiago had no idea what this meant. Who was the Guardian? He spent the rest of the night deep in thought as Jake slept.

No further words would ever be exchanged between them.

Twenty-six

SLEEP ELUDED SANTIAGO. THE EVENTS OF THE PAST FEW days had shaken his long standing religious and moral beliefs. He felt good about his decision to defy the government and remained convinced that righteousness and honesty would prevail over evil and inhumanity. He realized something new and startling about himself: he no longer feared death. Santiago now felt free to listen to his heart.

With the dawn still an hour away, Santiago reviewed his notes from the last session with Jake. This encounter looked different than the rest. He did not know how to interpret the message.

Energy controls matter.

A few puffy clouds lingered from the storms of the previous night and a mist in the air tinted the sky crimson as the first rays of the sun filtered into the tiny cell. Dr. Santiago looked up at the sun and enjoyed its warmth on his skin. Jake stirred, and both men turned toward the outer corridor as the door opened. A well dressed man with a cigar in his mouth entered the cell block. He looked into each cell, walking slowly, deliberately. No one said a word, but each man watched him as he made his way. He stopped at the last cell.

"How are you enjoying Cuban hospitality, Jake?" asked Charles. He lit his cigar and blew the smoke into the cell.

Jake got up and walked to the bars. "Why not stay? We just ordered breakfast from room service."

"I see your smart mouth and your memory are back. The prison doctor had an interesting report for me when I questioned his progress with you. How did you convince Lane to give you the Megalon implant?"

"What's a Megalon?"

Jake's Rule #17 — Never let your enemy know your true strength.

Charles' expression changed. His face turned all shades of red and he clenched his teeth.

"Don't fuck with me."

He calmed quickly. Jake watched the transformation in amazed silence.

Charles doesn't have the power anymore.

"Tell me, Charles. Did you lead the Ninja raid that night at the mansion in Newport?"

"Of course. Anything to piss off Mother. Actually, it was great fun, but I considered it more of a fund raiser. Mercenary soldiers don't come cheap these days." Charles puffed on the cigar. "We did quite well that night. Of course, it's nothing compared with the money I've made selling oil to Fidel. I've been able to finance a small army to carry out my plan to take over the company, starting with your precious Megalon lab in Subterra. But InDevCo is only one company. I know I'll be bored with it when I finally get it. Wanting is always better than having. Anyway, I've been trying to figure out how to spread my benevolence to other companies, and that's where you come in. You'll be in charge of a small elite group of men with the brain implant, totally loyal to me. I never thought the bloody thing would work. Always told Lane not to waste her time. Good in theory, but, anyway, with your expanded intelligence, each of you will be placed in a strategic corporate position to make your way up to the boardrooms of the biggest companies in the country. I'll control corporate America."

"Sounds great. There's only one catch. I don't work for you."

"Oh, you will. Dr. Martinez says he has a special treatment in mind for you after what you did to him. I've told him I need you in one piece, but he insisted and promised me you will do anything I ask when he's finished with you, including kill Andrew. By the way, I'll send Lane your best. She and I have a lot of catching up to do." Charles grabbed himself and made a crude gesture. Jake felt his self control slipping.

How terrible that history repeats itself and insane, demented men somehow rise to positions of power and have an important effect on many people.

Charles laughed and turned to leave.

Two interrogation guards, still drunk from last night's party, entered the corridor after Charles left. They swaggered from cell to cell, each inmate breathed a sigh of relief as they passed. Stopping directly in front of Jake and Santiago, they managed to get the key into the lock and open the door.

"Which one is Parker?"

"I'm Parker," Santiago and Jake said simultaneously and without hesitation. The guards laughed and pointed to both men. Suddenly, Santiago pushed Jake onto the cot and charged out of the cell yelling "I'm Parker." He slammed the door shut behind him. The guards were drunk enough not to care which man they took to the infirmary. They strong-armed Santiago down the corridor toward the exit. He turned to look at Jake and smiled. Their eyes locked.

"No, I'm Parker. Don't take him. It's me you want."

Jake knew he could do nothing to help his friend.

The door slammed and they were gone.

Despite the early hour, perspiration poured from Jake's body. He paced the small cell. With his memory restored, he sensed an awareness of the power of his thoughts.

How could I have allowed this to happen?

He cursed himself for letting Santiago catch him off guard before he could help him. It was too late to change the facts. He had to act. To escape.

Night brought only the sound of crickets and distant city noises. Jake lay on the cot alone in the dark cell. Santiago had not returned, nor had anyone else been removed that day. He stared at the ceiling. The stories of his past lives vividly swirled in his mind.

If it's all true, what's the big picture?

Where did his life as Jake Parker fit into the puzzle?

His eyes closed and he drifted into an uneasy sleep with plans of escape and Santiago's smile etched in his memory.

With the dawn came the realization that the events of the previous day were real and not a dream as he hoped. The prison was unusually quiet. No guards appeared in the corridor where they regularly played cards and drank rum.

Jake stood up on the chair and looked into the courtyard. There were no guards at any post, including the towers. In the distance, past the wall, plumes of smoke rose over the city. Faint sounds of gunfire reminded him of fourth of July firecrackers. Santiago spoke of a growing anti-Castro rebellion within the army. "Since Soviet aid vanished," he had said, "the Cuban people suffer mightily. But only when the rebel army is ready would there be outward revolt." Jake recalled the pained look in Santiago's eyes whenever he spoke of the plight of his beloved Cuban people.

The scream of an incoming shell afforded inadequate warning for anyone in the prison to take cover. It exploded in the courtyard and the force of the blast knocked Jake to the floor, where he rolled under the cot. Within seconds, another shell scored a direct hit on the cell block building.

Jake felt the impact of the nearby explosion, then heard the sound of glass and stucco walls crumbling. The shell had landed in another section of the building, leaving Jake's cell with only minor damage to the bars.

He stood up next to the door. Distant screams of agony echoed through the compound. Smoke filled the corridor. Jake examined the bars. They were bent on their frame. He pressed his shoulder against the door and pushed. It moved at first, then the twisted metal locked in place. He pulled and pushed, harder each time, until it loosened slightly. He continued until the space grew wide enough to squeeze through. Once free, Jake turned and went back into the cell. He reached under the cot to a spot concealed under the frame, pulled out a collection of papers bound together by a thin piece of white string, and put them in his pocket.

Santiago's journal.

Thick smoke billowed in from the breached end of the building. Jake ran through the cell block and stopped in front of a cell where a headless corpse lay sprawled on the floor in a pool of blood.

The heat and smoke grew intolerable. Now, the fire raged closer, fed by a ruptured gas line somewhere under the building. The smell of burning flesh mingled with the unmistakable odor of propane. Jake heard the screams of those trapped under fallen concrete debris.

By now, anyone who could run fled from the worsening inferno. With no time to try to save other inmates, Jake headed for the exit door and ran out of the building into the courtyard. The only cover from the fire and the incoming shells sat in the middle of the courtyard: the pit. He scrambled toward it and crawled inside the steel cage as the gas ignited and the cellblock exploded into an immense fireball.

After the explosion, Jake sat in the box waiting for the possibility of another blast. When he ventured out, the cellblock had vanished; leveled to smoldering debris and rubble.

I've got to find Santiago.

He headed toward the windowless Infirmary building, where flames already danced from its roof.

Jake ran into the deserted building and found his way through the narrow hallways. Thick, acrid smoke scorched his lungs, and he coughed hard. The building shook with each new explosion. He recognized the laboratory sign and followed it through a maze of corridors until he came into a room with at least a dozen men lying on examining tables covered partially or completely with white sheets. One by one he uncovered them, the revulsion growing more intense with each discovery. Some were mutilated so badly that the remains could hardly be called human. Movement attracted his attention. He drew the cover back slowly.

"Santiago, can you hear me?"

A blast rocked the building and debris fell from the ceiling. Visible flames consumed the rooms around him. Shelves full of bottles toppled over covering the floor with shattered glass and unknown chemicals.

Santiago said nothing.

Jake felt a weak pulse as he looked at his friend's broken, naked body. His finger nails were removed and his chest covered with fresh cigarette burns. High voltage charred the bottom of his feet and his neck. Jake lifted Santiago's head slightly.

"I've got to get you out of here, to a doctor." He knew as he spoke that it was impossible. Still the words came out.

The fire raged closer.

Santiago opened his eyes. With the last of his strength, he whispered, "Journal . . . Maria."

"Your journal?"

Santiago nodded.

"I have it. Here."

Jake read the last entry. ENERGY CONTROLS MATTER.

He looked at Santiago, his eyes fixed and empty.

Jake replaced the papers in his pocket.

"Rest in peace, mi amigo." He covered his friend.

Jake ran as the flames consumed the building. He turned

back for a last glimpse.

Never again to be used for human torture.

Inmates fled through the gate into the street outside the prison. Nearby, the sound of gunfire grew louder and closer than before. Flames engulfed most of the prison buildings.

Deserted shacks lined the street next to the prison. Prisoners and residents ran through the streets trying to get away from the inferno and the gunfire. In the distance Jake saw a government transport truck headed for the prison. He ran into a nearby house. The truck roared by and stopped in front of the prison gate. Soldiers jumped out of the open backed truck and fired on anyone in the street. Jake realized that had he hesitated another moment in the infirmary, he would have been caught and killed.

Jake sat alone in an empty house. He had no money, knew no one in Havana, and was in the middle of a revolution. Still, he vowed to find a way back to the States.

He took the journal and read the latest entries, including a letter addressed to Santiago's wife, Maria, with yesterday's date.

My darling Maria,

A day does not pass when I do not think of you and our life together before the terrorist dictator imprisoned me. I have lost some of the resolve I had when brought here all those years ago. The lack of news of you and the slow progress of the rebellion is disheartening. I pray for the time when we will be united and for the day when our people will be free. I have met a most interesting man. His name is Jake

Parker, and we are cell mates. During the time we spent together, he helped restore my faith and I no longer fear death. He has a very special gift which I have never encountered: the ability to reach into the past and draw strength and knowledge. His intellect has somehow been expanded beyond human standard and I believe his potential is unlimited. I feel strongly that he is destined for great deeds. I was blessed in knowing him and perhaps playing a small part in helping him to discover his destiny. I feel this so strongly that if the time came, I would sacrifice my life for him.

I don't know if I will ever see you again, or if you will see this letter, but there is hope in the writing. I pray you are well and can continue to fight for our people to the end.

Eternal Love,
S

Jake looked up from the page.

I must find Maria. She must see the last words of her husband.

Government troop carriers roared by the tiny house where Jake hid in the corner of a long deserted kitchen. He passed the time reading Santiago's notes of the regressive sessions where he had revealed his past lives. It seemed unbelievable, though Jake remembered most of what he said while hypnotized.

Somewhere in these notes is the answer.

The city in flames ignited the night sky. The parade of soldiers past the prison had stopped. Jake left the house.

I must find Maria Santiago.

I must stop Charles Cromwell.

Twenty-seven

THE GIANT SILVER 747 EGYPTAIR JET LIFTED EFFORTlessly off the ground from Cairo airport. Dr. Stanley Lawrence looked out the window at the endless sand dunes of the Sahara desert as the passengers settled in for the long flight to Kennedy airport. He knew the hastily made decision to leave the country carried great risk.

Suspended like a blanket from the cloudless sky, a brown haze cloaked the city. Lawrence watched the sphinx and the pyramids disappear from sight. He thought about the last time he left the country twelve years ago to speak as the guest lecturer at the opening dedication of a new Egyptian exhibit at the British Museum in London. He knew this trip was different; this excursion might be one way.

When the plane emerged from the perma-smog, sun burst into the cabin and the sky cleared to cloudless blue. Lawrence accepted a glass of orange juice from the stewardess and settled in his seat, ready to continue the journal started with the discovery of the tomb and the crown. He wrote in the cryptic code he had developed over the years that he used whenever he feared the danger of his notes falling into competitors hands.

As I record the events of the past weeks, I find it

difficult to believe the magnitude of the find. The discovery of the intact tomb of Katara III was the fulfillment of my dreams as an archeologist. The treasures of the tomb will enrich the lives of all who see them. The new wing at the Pharonic Museum in Cairo will be a fitting place to display the glories of Katara.

I still have a thousand questions about the king's crown and its surprising contents. During the days that followed the discovery of the tomb, I examined the crown in secret in my laboratory. Not even Gammal, my trusted friend and assistant knows of its removal from the mummy and from the country.

Despite my best efforts, I failed to discover the purpose of the device inside the crown. Also, I was unable to activate it in any way, if this is indeed possible after all this time.

After realizing I required help, I decided to contact Dr. Roberts from InDevCo again. He provided valuable help during the opening of the tomb, and I know he can be trusted. Discretely, and without giving too many details, I phoned him and he agreed to help again. I accepted his invitation to utilize the state of the art facilities at his disposal in New York, as the chances of success with the crown are improved.

With the cataloging on schedule, I knew the time was right to leave, my sudden departure explained by the death of an aunt in New York. I admit my surprise at the ease of leaving the country. For once, I thanked the hoards of tourists that come and go with ease, for I appeared as just another visitor leaving with a trunk of souvenirs. The special lining of the secret compartment of my trunk is designed to show up on the scanners as normal contents. I tried not to act nervous when the dogs went up and down the aisles of luggage placed outside the plane. Fortunately, the trunk is air tight. Each passenger had to point to his belongings before it would be loaded. If discovered, this particular souvenir would be confiscated by the Department of Antiquities, who take a dim view of anyone removing ancient artifacts from the country. I shutter to think of the punishment for such a crime, as I know it to be severe.

When we arrive in New York, I hope to go directly to Dr. Robert's lab, so that I may finally find some answers to this mystery.

Lawrence put down the pen and closed his eyes. The sleeping pill he swallowed after take off had its effect. He placed the journal in his brief case and reclined the seat, hoping the journey would be over when he awakened.

Twenty-eight

GORDON YORK AND JULIA WELLES SURVEYED THE CITY skyline for the third time as the plane circled, waiting for clearance to land at LaGuardia Airport. Though this was his first visit to New York, the scenery felt familiar after listening to Julia and reading the Triple-A guide book he obtained before the trip. The long flight afforded him the opportunity to reflect on the events of the past days.

After the experts determined the alien communication to be a schematic and that the device could be built with existing technology at InDevCo, he assigned his best people to accompany him to New York to oversee and assist with the construction. A communication network link would be established to monitor and interpret any additional new data received from space.

"Penny for your thoughts," said Julia.

"The future."

"That covers a lot of territory. Can you narrow that a little?"

"I've spent a good part of my life organizing and running S.A.I.L.. I never gave much thought to what came after first contact."

"You don't think humanity is ready for this?"

"I know we're not, but it's too late to turn back now.

We'll rush head first into the unknown as we always do. Only in this case, it could mean the end of life as we know it."

"I can't believe you're having second thoughts."

"But it's only reasonable if you look at the facts. We get instructions to build an alien device and plunge headfirst into it without asking the right questions. What if they're not the benevolent, peace loving creatures we hope for? I suppose there's an undeniable and irrepressible curiosity in all of us. The harder the puzzle the more we want to solve it. The difference here is that no one on Earth has the answer to this one yet."

"You're scaring me."

He took her hand. "I'm sure it'll be fine. Besides, you're a New Yorker. I thought you weren't afraid of anything."

"Don't believe it. It's a lie perpetuated by the chamber of commerce. The truth is, we're afraid of everything. Especially the dark."

Julia squeezed his hand tightly as the plane landed.

"I always hate this part."

"Welcome to New York," announced the captain.

Twenty-nine

JAKE AVOIDED THE MAIN STREETS OF HAVANA AND distanced himself from the prison. Smoke from many fires clung to the horizon and the sound of gunfire and mortar blasts could still be heard. But the frenzied action slowed with nightfall. Jake slipped into a narrow alley between two abandoned buildings. Small cars and troop carriers occasionally rumbled past him. He wondered which side prevailed in the fight for freedom.

The sound of a door slamming across the street forced him into the shadows. Laughing loudly, two uniformed soldiers walked out of a house. They leaned on a parked car and lit cigarettes. Unseen, Jake knelt close to the building and listened to their conversation.

"Life will be good after the dictator is dead."

These are rebel soldiers.

They spoke of a plan to infiltrate the government stronghold using stolen Colonel's uniforms, and wipe out the weapons dump. Without the Russians to resupply them, they were sure the government would fall. One of the men wore the stripes of a high ranking Castro officer, and pointed to various areas on a map of the city, which he placed into the glove compartment of the tiny car. Then, the men went back into the house.

The street remained quiet for a long time. Jake slowly approached the car and opened the driver's door. He reached under the dashboard, found the ignition wire, and pulled it from its attachments. Within a minute, the tiny engine turned over as he connected the ignition wire to the starter.

With darkened headlights, he drove the car out of the neighborhood, and stopped in a deserted alley over one mile away. The map appeared quite detailed and he memorized it instantly. He took out Santiago's journal, including the letter to his wife. The address read, Maria Santiago, 27 Calle de Sueno.

Street of Dreams.

Jake found Calle de Sueno four miles from the area where he stole the car. The street appeared deserted, and barely wide enough to drive through. Small, decaying houses that lined Calle de Sueno had no windows and corrugated metal roofs. Graffiti covered most walls, and garbage lay in torn plastic bags or loosely strewn about the yards where cats fought each other for the best morsels.

Jake circled the block twice, straining to see the faded house numbers. Finally, he spotted number 27 and pulled the car in front of it. Jake exited the car, silently walked to the door and knocked.

No response.

He knocked again, then opened the door slowly.

"Anyone here?" he asked.

No answer.

He walked into the house, which consisted of three rooms; a living room with an old couch and two chairs, a small bedroom and a simple kitchen. The bedroom had two beds, one a child's. Toys lay on the floor. Jake searched his memory, certain Santiago never mentioned a child.

On the dressing table, a wedding picture of Santiago and Maria caught his eye.

Just as Jake turned to leave the bedroom, he heard a sneeze. He pulled open the flimsy curtain that covered a closet, but it revealed only old clothes and shoes. Another sneeze. It came from underneath him. Jake kicked the torn carpet exposing a trap door. As he opened the door, a woman with a child in her arms stared up at him. She appeared plain, with straight brown hair and a tight face drained of color. The boy looked about eight, and held tightly onto his mother. Jake had never seen so much fear in two pair of eyes.

"Are you Maria Santiago?"

"Please, don't hurt us. We know nothing," the woman said, trembling.

"Don't be afraid. I won't hurt you. I'm a friend of your husband. We were in prison together. I'm an American."

Jake offered his hand. Maria hesitated, then she and the boy climbed out of the shelter.

"My name is Jake Parker. I have a letter from your husband."

"Is he coming home?"

"I'm afraid Santiago is dead."

"Dead?" She crossed herself and said nothing for a minute. Tears welled in her eyes and dropped onto her cheeks. "I knew it. I felt it." The boy cried too, but only because he watched his mother.

"He never even knew he had a son," she said.

Jake knelt on one knee. "What's your name?"

The boy stared at Jake, silent.

"His name is Jose," Maria answered.

"Well, Jose, you have your father's eyes."

"I haven't heard for so long. What happened to him?" asked Maria.

"Your husband died with honor fighting the government soldiers while we escaped from prison."

Maria sat at the table and read Santiago's journal and letter by the light of a candle.

"I must ask a favor of you," said Jake.

"What can I do? I have nothing to give you. No money."

"Help me get home."

"I cannot. There is no one to help."

Jake paced the floor. His mind raced, searching for an answer.

"There has to be a way out of here. What about a boat or a helicopter? Where does Castro keep his helicopters?"

"In the central military base near the dock area of the city. The people call it El Lugar del Muerto.

The place of death.

"Many go there for questioning and have never returned."

"Show me where it is." Jake brought the map from his pocket.

Maria pointed to the location of the base. It had already been marked on the map by the rebel soldier.

"It is suicide to try to break into that place, especially now with the rebel uprising."

"If I'm right, there'll be confusion at the base. I should be able to. . ."

Maria interrupted. "There is a way. Wait here."

She ran into the bedroom and returned with a military uniform. "This was Santiago's. He wore it at his graduation. The first and last time. I don't know why I saved it all these years. Take it. I know he would have wanted you to have it if it can help you escape."

Jake took the captain's uniform. Though slightly faded, it looked almost new.

It just might work.

"When I return to the states, I'll send for you and Jose."

Jake put on the uniform and stood at the door. He kissed

her on the forehead, then patted the boy's head.

The boy whispered in his mother's ear.

"Jose has something he would like to give you."

Jose reached in his pocket and pulled out a small, carved wooden bird, one wing larger than the other. He handed it to Jake.

"It's beautiful. Did you make it?"

Jose nodded.

"He loves to work with his hands and wants to be an artist some day. He did it from a picture. It's an eagle. Does not the Eagle stand for freedom in your country?"

"Yes, it does." Jake knelt. "I'll carry it with me always, as a good luck charm. Thank you, Jose."

The boy smiled.

"I must go now."

"Via con Dios," she said and made the sign of the cross.

The tiny Volga started with difficulty, and he headed toward the waterfront. Traffic had increased with the sunrise, but the Volga fit in with the other rusted, nondescript Russian gray vehicles on the road. Military traffic increased as he approached the base, with primarily troop carriers and artillery guns headed toward the countryside to engage the rebels.

Jake pulled his car onto the end of a long line of vehicles waiting to enter the base.

They'll ask me for papers.

Finally, his turn came. A momentary rush of adrenalin charged him with the courage to continue.

"Papers," demanded the guard, who's large belly barely fit through the narrow opening of the security booth.

Jake handed him the map and concentrated his thoughts.

The guard took the paper and looked at it. He glanced at Jake and looked again at the map.

"Is there a problem, Sergeant?" asked Jake.

The man wavered and scratched his head.

Jake knew he had him.

"No sir. I just thought. . .never mind. Clear." He waved Jake through the gate.

Jake smiled and drove through the gate into the compound. Through the rear mirror, he watched the confused guard stare at him as he drove away.

The base swarmed with activity. Soldiers loaded trucks with supplies and ammunition. Jake abandoned the Volga behind a storage shed and continued on foot.

The area contained mainly barracks and bins and Jake used them for cover. Suddenly, he heard footsteps coming toward him from around a corner. The path dead-ended, leaving him with no way to turn back. He forced a rusted lock on a door that looked forgotten, and ducked into a building as the guards passed.

Jake glared at stacks of explosives, automatic weapons, grenades and crates of ammunition. There were rocket launchers, laser and infrared aiming devices. Soldiers were hard at work in the front of the building, loading the trucks that lined up and waited their turn. Jake slipped silently out the door and ran toward the next secure cover. So far, the location of the helicopters eluded him.

He could see the waterfront now. Large cranes lifted cargo containers from a ship. Nearby, an oil tanker lay silent in her slip. The name on the bow jolted his memory. Conquistador Del Mar, the ship he saw taking InDevCo oil from the platform in the Gulf of Mexico.

On the dock next to the ship were three Russian helicopters resting on their pads, guarded by only four men.

I need a diversion.

He doubled back to the ammunition dump and entered through the back door. Alone, Jake opened the crates one by one, and within a short time, had assembled the parts for a small bomb. He set the timer for fifteen minutes, placed it on top of a crate of rockets and slipped out the back door.

The same four guards stood watch over the helicopters. Jake crouched at the corner of a barracks building closest to the pads. He looked at his watch.

Four minutes to go.

"Get up slowly, hands together over your head," a soldier ordered. Jake winced in pain as the sharp jab of a gun barrel in his back surprised him.

The guard pushed the gun harder into Jake's back forcing him to walk toward the helicopters. Jake guessed only seconds remained until the blast. He had to use it to his best advantage. The initial surprise would afford only a brief advantage.

The guards standing near the aircraft spotted them.

"What have you found, Carlos?"

The explosion caused a small fireball and diverted their attention. Moments later, a much stronger secondary blast shook the ground and knocked them off their feet.

Jake expected it and recovered quickly. He stood up, turned to the the two guards nearest him, and knocked them out with their own guns. Before they could react, Jake turned, kicked the guard who had previously had him at gunpoint, then pinched a neck trigger point in the remaining two men.

Pain.

The two screamed in agony as Jake concentrated his mental energy on them.

Damn, it worked.

Alarm claxons sounded throughout the base. Fire from the explosion mushroomed hundreds of feet into the air and additional smaller blasts still shook the ground. Jake climbed aboard the closest helicopter and looked at the control panel.

"Shit," he said. "It's in Russian."

Jake's Rule #28 — When in doubt, look under the seat. There's always good shit under there.

He reached under the seat and found a manual written in Russian. Jake scanned the entire book and committed it to memory in seconds.

A minute later, the engine started and the huge rotor lifted the aircraft. Jake watched the rotors on the other helicopters turning.

He headed toward the open sea. A warning light on the control panel flashed its message in red: LOW FUEL.

Jake guessed the craft were slated for service and refueling before joining the fight against the rebels. He hoped the other helicopters were also low on fuel.

The computer alert signaled an incoming missile. The other ships closed in and fired. Jake dove sharply and reduced speed, leveling off just above the water. The missile sped overhead. Now, he took the offensive and turned 180 degrees, surprising his opponents. They veered off to avoid a collision, but Jake achieved a computer lock on the lead ship and fired a heat seeker. Seconds later, the missile found its mark and the Cuban pilot disintegrated with his ship. Another warning flashed, reminding him of the critical fuel status.

The second ship positioned itself for attack. Jake ran a weapons inventory and realized he had no additional missiles and only a few rounds of ammunition remained.

On the defensive and with no fuel.

Jake suddenly thought of a stunt he performed at air shows in the Midwest where he had learned to fly. He pulled the ship up sharply just as his opponent fired on him. Making a 360 degree loop, he hoped to pull out of it just behind the other ship. He prayed the engine did not stall. Only luck prevented a direct hit as the enemy missile missed by inches. Jake pulled out of the maneuver in the exact position he hoped and fired his last rounds into the enemy ship.

With no further fire power and the Cuban still aloft, Jake knew he had no more time. Flying on an unknown reserve, Jake noticed a stream of smoke trailing from the other ship. A bullet had penetrated the fuel tank and whatever fuel reserve the Cuban pilot had, now leaked out. Jake pulled up next to the crippled ship. Blood streaked the windshield and Jake saw the Cuban pilot slumped over in his seat. He watched as the Russian helicopter splashed hard into the water and sank quickly.

Fuel now spent, Jake's engine sputtered and finally stalled. The shoreline appeared about five miles from his present position. Jake grabbed a life jacket.

He managed to auto-rotate and set the helicopter down gently on the water. It took on water so fast that he barely had time to escape. Bubbles rose as it sank beneath the surface.

Jake floated in the calm, warm water.

Despite his best efforts to swim toward shore, the current carried him further out to sea. He saw boats in the distance, but couldn't reach them or make himself seen. An occasional flying fish reminded him of the teeming life that filled the sea beneath him.

The sharks will come.

Jake reflected on the experiences of the past days. He had learned new things. Not only about himself, but about the nature of life. He stared blankly at the distant horizon. Maria and Jose entered his thoughts. The boy would never know the love of his father and wouldn't understand why his father died. Jake thought of the lie he told Maria about Santiago's death.

No one would contradict the story. What purpose did it serve to tell her he had been tortured to death for the pleasure of a demented doctor?

Wind whipped the surf into a frenzy of waves. Jake snapped out of his reverie and realized another helicopter hovering overhead caused the storm. The bright sun and glare from the water prevented him from seeing the aircraft clearly.

At least a prison cell is dry. Until they execute me.

A harness gently dropped into the water beside him. He slipped it around his arms and waited. The craft ascended as Jake relaxed and allowed the winch to lift him out of the water.

Thirty

"WELCOME ABOARD, 'CAPTAIN' PARKER. YOU KNOW, I'm really getting tired of plucking you out of the ocean, little brother."

"Harry, I can't believe it's you."

"Of course its me. Don't I always come to your rescue?"

Harry signaled the pilot to leave.

Jake removed the harness and he hugged Harry.

"How the hell did you find me out here?"

"Thank Lane. She contacted me after you disappeared and we've worked on your rescue together. She told me everything about the implant. Pretty impressive. Did you know she added a homing signal emitter chip to it? We've been tracking you since you arrived in Cuba. It took us three days to find you because a huge solar flare caused a satellite link malfunction. Once we located you, we had no way to get you out. Until today. By the way, the signal strength is down 70%. We barely picked up the signal even this close. What gives?"

"Damned if I know, but I sensed the difference too. Maybe the batteries need recharging. Lane will know. Where is she? I've got to see her."

"New York. Some kind of top level project, very big and hush-hush. Rumors are flying around. Crazy rumors."

"Like what?"

"First contact."

"You mean with aliens? Maybe just like the game we played as kids, where we traveled to other planets and met monsters from space."

"This is for real, Jake."

"You're serious aren't you? How do you know all this?"

"I have my sources. Never to be revealed."

"When do we get there? I've got to see her."

"We're booked on the 12:30 flight to Kennedy out of Miami. Now, would you mind telling me how you wound up in the ocean off the coast of Cuba?"

"Luck. Just dumb luck."

Jake reached into his pocket and took out the tiny carved eagle, then turned toward the disappearing coastline.

"Thanks, Jose."

Thirty-one

GORDON YORK AND JULIA WELLES GATHERED THEIR carry-on bags and left the aircraft as ordinary citizens. When they exited the jetway, they were celebrities. A crowd of reporters pushed forward.

"Dr. York, is it true that you're going to head the team that is assigned the task of constructing the alien machine?"

"Have the ET's told you anything about themselves?"

"Are they coming to Earth?"

"I have no comment at this time," said Gordon. He grabbed Julia's elbow and somehow managed to make it to the down escalator and the baggage claim area.

"How could you do this, Julia?" Gordon asked. "You know the importance of the black out."

"This isn't my doing. You can thank your friends at InDevCo. My publicity releases never mentioned a trip to New York. Now will you please let go of my arm? You're hurting me and I don't let my enemies do that, let alone my lovers."

"Sorry, I thought. . .never mind."

Once outside the terminal, Gordon placed the luggage into the trunk of a waiting taxi.

"Take us to the InDevCo building in Manhattan."

Dr. Lawrence entered the airport terminal after the ordeal of customs and immigration. He retrieved his trunk, intact and without incident. Glad to be ignored in the frenzy of airport activity, he felt safer on U.S. soil. Although exhausted from the long journey, Lawrence decided to go directly to the lab and begin the examination of the crown and its uncommon contents.

The cab driver loaded the trunk. Lawrence looked around instinctively, expecting to be arrested at any moment for smuggling. But no one noticed him, and the cab pulled into the normal heavy traffic.

"Manhattan, please. The InDevCo building."

Two taxis arrived at the entrance to the InDevCo building in mid-Manhattan. Lawrence looked at the crowd of reporters and cameramen waiting at the door.

How did they find me? Got to get away.

Before he could tell the driver to leave, a man and a woman got out of the cab in front of his and the press people surrounded them. He watched the couple push their way through the persistent reporters and enter the building.

Lawrence paid the driver and left the cab with his trunk in tow on a small dolly. The reporters ignored him and he walked into the building as if invisible. He stopped at the security desk.

"Yes please, I have an appointment to see Dr. Lloyd Roberts. My name is Stanley Lawrence. Dr. Lawrence."

The receptionist keyed her computer console. A video image of Dr. Lawrence with verification of his appointment appeared on the screen.

"Please wear this coded ID badge while you're in the building, Dr. Lawrence. It'll allow you to pass through the security screens. Dr. Roberts is expecting you on the 55th floor."

Dr. Roberts smiling face greeted him as the elevator door opened.

"Stanley, good to see you again." They shook hands. "What brings you all the way to New York? You sounded so secretive on the phone."

"Can we talk in private?"

"Of course. Follow me."

The two men passed through a scanner and entered an office. Gold script letters on the door identified Dr. Roberts as assistant director of Research and Development. The door closed behind them.

"I must admit you've piqued my curiosity. I presume you've brought something from the tomb for me to examine. I'll warn you, Stanley, I'm only an amateur Egyptologist compared to you."

Lawrence lifted the trunk onto a table and opened it with a key he kept hidden in his shoe. He pulled the false bottom away, revealing the wrapped treasure. Slowly, he opened the linen.

"I thought it's illegal to remove artifacts from the tomb."

"It is. But this is no ordinary relic. I discovered it on the mummy of Katara III soon after you left. I know it's genuine, since I broke the royal seal, and I was the first to open the sarcophagus," he said, holding the crown.

"It's beautiful, Stanley."

"The best part is not its unique shape nor the jewels, but rather what's inside." Lawrence turned the crown over and revealed the computerized contents. "This is exactly the way I found it. I failed to discover its purpose. I'm hoping you can help me."

Dr. Roberts remained speechless for a moment, then said, "It's unbelievable. If anyone else had shown me something so outlandish, I would have them thrown out. How old is it?"

"I estimated the age from the tomb writings at around 3500 years. Also, we carbon dated one of the statuettes."

"Are you saying the ancient Egyptians had computer technology?"

"Not at all. I believe they had extraterrestrial visitors who gave them this device. The hieroglyphics also confirm this. Many legends have proposed this for years. I suggest to you now, that here is the evidence."

"Fantastic. Tell me, Stanley, are you aware of the latest news concerning the supposed messages from space received by a team of scientists using our new superconductive computers?"

Lawrence shook his head. "We don't get much news of the outside world in the desert."

"Briefly, they picked up transmissions from a distant galaxy that turned out to be a message. We recently deciphered the message as a blueprint for an alien communications device." Dr. Roberts picked up the crown and looked inside. "Don't you think it's a coincidence that you and the blueprint arrived at the same time?"

"I don't believe in chance, Lloyd. But I don't have an answer to your question. Right now, I'm more interested in beginning the examination of the crown."

"Before we do, there's someone I've got to speak with immediately."

On the 59th floor, Dr. Mike Haywood and Gordon York sat in front of a video monitor. Julia spoke on the phone to the InDevCo press office and arranged a regular schedule of news releases to quiet the reporter's demands.

A tone sounded and the screen lit up.

"Good afternoon, Dr. Darby. Are you ready for us?"

"The latest data is available now. I'll expect you in ten minutes," said Lane.

Gordon and Mike Haywood stood to leave.

"Take care of the press, Julia. Mike and I will be with Dr. Darby in her office if you need me."

She nodded, and spoke into the phone.

Minutes later, they exited a secured elevator and entered a lobby. A large sign marked InDevCo Research & Development hung on a wall behind the secretary's desk.

Mike flashed his security clearance badge.

"Dr. Darby's expecting us and he's with me," he said to the receptionist anticipating her questions. Gordon showed his security badge and the secretary opened the door to the lab with a remote release.

They walked through a wide corridor past rooms filled with superconductive Lorestronic computers. Mike opened double doors that led into Lane's office. She spoke to her secretary and smiled when she spotted them.

"This must be our friend from New Mexico. Dr. York?"

"It's nice to meet you Dr. Darby. I'm anxious to see the progress you've made in the design. Do you have a prototype?"

"Not exactly. We've got a small problem. Please come in and I'll show you what I mean."

Lane indicated seats in front of her desk for them. Sitting down, she turned to a Lorestronic console. The lights in the office dimmed and the shades closed on the panoramic windows that lined three sides of the office. A panel on her desk opened and a blue light glowed from its center. Small fragments of light raced around the surface and after a minute, formed a complicated maze of patterns.

"Dr. York, these configurations are the basis for the new computers you have in your lab. The superconductive energy travels at the speed of light without the slightest resistance or loss of efficiency. From this we developed low resistance electronics or Lorestronics."

The swirling light patterns fascinated Gordon.

"The alien schematic that you brought to us uses a design very similar to our Lorestronic circuits. If you came to us a year ago we would have no idea what this schematic meant. What you see forming in front of you is a computer generated holographic image of the alien device constructed by the computer. Our best people designed a new software package to allow us to feed the data from the schematic into the Lorestron computer. This is the result. Actually, it bears a remarkable resemblance to a cerebral cortex expander device we developed using this same technology."

The hologram took shape, with every circuit visible through the skin of the device.

"Looks like a futuristic Walkman," said Mike Haywood.

The 3-D hologram floated and turned in front of them. Lane entered additional commands and a human skull appeared to demonstrate how the equipment fit into place.

"Two electrodes touch the temporal area and a third one extends to the base of the skull toward the brain stem, all connected by a ceramic frame that houses the latticed circuitry," Lane said.

The human brain glowed red to show the areas expected to be affected.

"It's fantastic," said Gordon. "Do you have any idea what it is?"

"We think it's a telepathic communicator, but there's no way to be sure until we build and test it," said Lane.

"Dr. Darby, you mentioned earlier that there's a problem."

"Yes, and it may be a show stopper. Please observe the device as I command the image to invert itself."

They watched the hologram turn inside-out. The computer displayed the entire apparatus with one section of the connecting circuitry missing.

"The vital missing link, gentlemen. We don't have any idea how to build this component, which is the power supply for the entire unit. According to our computer, the technology to construct this particular component does not yet exist. We have no idea what to do next."

They stared at the image of the impossible cosmic radio.

An intercom tone broke the silence.

"No calls, Pat," ordered Lane.

"Sorry to interrupt, but it's Dr. Roberts on line. He says its urgent."

Lane activated the vidphone and Lloyd Roberts face appeared.

"Yes, Lloyd, what can I do for you?"

"I have something here you will want to see. Immediately."

"Maybe later, Lloyd. I'm in conference now and. . ."

"I know you're working on the alien schematic. I'll come to you. This can't wait. I promise you won't be disappointed."

The secretary announced their arrival. Dr. Lawrence carried the wrapped crown.

"Gentlemen please, over here," Lane said.

"Sorry to interrupt your meeting. May I present the noted archeologist and Egyptologist, Dr. Stanley Lawrence.

Dr. Darby is the head of our research and development department. This is Dr. Haywood."

Mike Haywood introduced Gordon York.

"Now, Lloyd, what is so important that it couldn't wait?" Lane asked.

Dr. Roberts stood and took the wrapped crown from Lawrence.

"Recently in Egypt, Dr. Lawrence made a startling discovery: an intact Pharonic tomb outside the Valley of the Kings. A tomb far richer than Tutankhamen's. But the tomb revealed an astonishing secret that makes all its treasure pale by comparison." Dr. Roberts unwrapped the crown.

"It's beautiful, Lloyd, but I . . ." Lane said.

Lloyd Roberts removed the ancient computer from its 3500 year old receptacle and held it next to the hologram of the alien communication device that still spun slowly around.

Lane ordered the computer to add a holographic simulated section to the missing link.

The hologram of the alien radio and the crown's computer were identical.

Thirty-two

A YELLOW CHECKER TAXI STOPPED IN FRONT OF A houseboat tied up to an abandoned pier at the end of West 32nd street in Manhattan. Jake stepped out of the cab. "Thanks for the ride," said Jake.

"You live here?" asked the driver.

"I'll see you later, Jake. You can buy me dinner," said Harry.

Jake stepped on board and opened the front door into a room filled with model ships. His passion for nautica dictated the decor of the place. Posters and photos of old cruise ships covered every wall, with memorabilia on shelves and tables. Jake acquired a piano that once sat in the Grand Salon of the Queen Mary. It occupied a place of honor on a raised platform in the center of the living room. While playing it, he imagined elegantly dressed passengers gathered around the piano, listening to Bach and Mozart.

"Welcome home, stranger," said a voice from the kitchen.

"Lane, is that you?" asked Jake. He rushed into the narrow galley. Lane stood next to the stove stirring a pot of simmering tomato sauce. She wore an apron over her white lab coat. Pots and dishes cluttered the counters.

"Oh, Jake, I thought I'd never see you again."

She turned toward him and he kissed her, both hands

softly holding her.

"I've thought of this moment for a long time."

"When I heard you were on your way home, I wanted to surprise you." She stirred the sauce.

Jake pressed the front of his body against her back and held her around the waist.

"I've missed you," he said, and tickled her left ear lobe with his tongue.

"You know what that does to me," she said, leaning her head back onto his shoulder, her eyes closed.

He whispered in her ear. "I want you."

She smiled. "But my sauce. . ."

"Can wait."

Jake unbuttoned the top of her blouse and draped his arm lightly about her shoulder, caressing her breast. She faced him and they pressed their mouths together, tongues exploring, breathless and urgent. He felt her heart pounding in unison with his own.

"We've done this a thousand times before," he said, taking the wooden spoon from her hand. "I know every inch of your body." The memories opened before him as if a curtain ripped aside.

"What about. . .the food."

"Later."

Jake picked her up and carried her up the short flight of stairs to the loft bedroom. He placed her gently on the bed, and removed her lab coat, blouse and skirt. She unbuttoned his shirt and opened his belt. Their clothes gone, he lay on top of her and kissed the side of her neck, working his way down to firm nipples crowning the soft breasts that he cupped in his hands.

"Don't move," he said and got up.

"Where are you going?" She could see his naked body in the mirror as he left the room.

Jake returned in a minute with a bottle of champagne.

"What. . .?"

"Shh. Don't talk."

He drizzled the cool wine on her breasts and stomach, then licked it lightly in a sensuous exploration.

Lower and deeper, probing.

She moaned.

"How did you know. . .my fantasy?" she asked, eyes closed.

"I know everything about you now. We're a part of each other."

The magic of his mouth and fingers overrode her inhibitions, and she met the full force of of his passion with an equal force of her own.

They sealed themselves together.

Lane rested her head on his chest and tickled him lightly. Jake closed his eyes but did not sleep.

"What did you mean when you said we've done this a thousand times before? she asked.

"It's difficult to explain."

"I have time." She poured champagne into a beer glass. Jake sat up and sipped the wine.

"When I arrived in Cuba, I had total amnesia. It almost got me killed. My cellmate in prison turned out to be a dissident doctor who knew hypnotic regression techniques that eventually restored my memory. During the sessions, an amazing thing happened. Vivid dreams that I've had many times came to life. I recounted experiences from previous lifetimes that always repeated the same theme: you and I are together and Charles shows up to destroy us. Time after time, in one identity or another he always managed to separate us and murder me. Then when you wouldn't go with him, he killed you too."

"I could make a joke but I see you're serious about this," said Lane.

"Deadly serious. You and I are old soul mates, Lane. We keep playing out this drama and Charles always wins in the end. I've got to break the cycle. Charles has to stop interfering in our lives."

"I don't think he'll be bothering us in the near future."

"What do you mean?"

"Charles invaded Subterra and his men took over the entire complex, including the Megalon lab. He's demanding that Andrew surrender himself and give up command of the company. He's completely mad."

"I knew it," Jake said and got up.

"How could you know?"

"Charles is the one who had me shanghaied and brought to Cuba. He's selling InDevCo oil to Castro to raise money for his army. On one of his trips there he visited me in prison to gloat about his plan to kill Andrew and take over the company. Taking Subterra is the first stage of the operation. By the way, he no longer has the CCEM power."

"Well, he has the Megalon lab, but I don't think it'll help him. After we inserted your CCEM, I changed all the security access codes again. Speaking of brain implants, is yours still active?"

"I think you know the answer. You never told me it had a limited power supply."

"I didn't know you'd get kidnapped. I planned to remove them after you passed out in the lab. Did Harry tell you about the homing circuits?"

"I guess I ought to thank you for that surprise. I'd probably still be in the water. Can you recharge the modules?"

"Not without my equipment in the Megalon lab. There might be another way, but it's risky."

"Remember Jake's rule #32 — *When a beautiful woman offers a risky proposition, run the other way.*"

Lane laughed.

"No one will force you to do anything. You can walk away from the entire situation," said Lane.

"Can't do that. I have too much at stake here. Charles has to be stopped if we want to save the company and you and I are to stay together. So you see, whatever risk you are referring to is unimportant. If I fail, this performance will end and the next one begins. Do you understand?"

"No, but it doesn't matter. If you believe it then. . ."

"Listen, remember that recurring dream you told me about, the one where you see yourself in front of a burning house. Your fear of fire is rooted in these dreams because Charles has always had you burned."

"I'm a scientist, Jake. You're asking me to believe a hypothesis that can't be proved. It's wild."

"Then don't believe it. But allow me the luxury of

following my instincts. Tell me what I must do to recharge the modules. If I have to face him alone, I want whatever advantage they can give me."

"The company's in charge of a project that's a little unorthodox. Actually, compared with this, your story is normal. Around a year ago, InDevCo sent some of our new Lorestronic computers to an organization that searched the heavens for life. We did it more for a tax break than anything and Andrew knew the project director. Recently, they picked up a legitimate signal. It turned out to be a complete set of instructions for building an extraterrestrial communication apparatus. Many of the circuits are similar to the design of the CCEM. I believe it will allow its user even greater brain power than our original module."

"You've constructed an alien communication device that you want me to test?"

"Pretty crazy huh?"

"Nothing surprises me anymore. When and where?"

"Tomorrow in my office. We're putting the finishing touches on it now. By the way, in his ramblings, Charles mentioned that he had an important hostage. Any ideas?"

"I know exactly who it is. I'm starved. Let's have that dinner now."

"Not until you tell me who it is."

"If I tell you, promise it won't change anything about my plan to infiltrate Subterra alone."

"Promise."

"It's his father, Philip."

Thirty-three

THE AROMA OF FRESHLY BREWED COFFEE DRIFTED FROM the houseboat's galley. Jake opened his eyes slowly. A burst of new sun reached through the skylight above the bed. Lane appeared carrying a tray with hot coffee and blueberry muffins. Jake pretended to be asleep. She quietly placed the tray on a table next to the bed, pulled the blanket down and kissed his neck.

"Time to wake up, darling."

"Can't I sleep a little longer, Inga?"

She could not see the smile on his face.

"Inga. Who the hell is Inga, you bastard?" she slapped his behind. "One of your wives in a previous lifetime?"

He turned quickly, laughing, then pulled her to him and kissed her.

"Go ahead and make jokes. That's the last time you get breakfast in bed."

"Smells great. Let's eat."

Jake sat up, sipped the strong, bitter coffee and bit into a hard muffin. "Microwave?"

"Of course. Tell me. Did I give you breakfast in bed in any of our past lives?"

"Sometimes, but mostly we just did other things."

Lane sat on the bed, and her expression changed. "Do you think Philip is still alive?"

"Definitely. Charles claimed he loves his father. Personally, I think Philip is an insurance policy. Charles is insane and dangerous, but not stupid. We must never underestimate him." Jake looked at the clock. "Time to go. Wouldn't want to keep your people waiting."

Mike Haywood and his team worked with Gordon York and Stanley Lawrence through the night, assembling the circuits for the alien apparatus according to the schematic. By morning, they had a reconstructed facsimile of the device found inside the crown. Mike read the results of a series of tests they had performed on the crown.

He held the crown and pointed to the colored jewels. "According to the dynamic spectral electron flow analyzer, the jewels on the outside of the crown contain ultra-sensitive photovoltaic cells capable of producing sufficient electrical energy to power the device even from the dim light of a candle. Once hooked into the rest of the machine, they should glow when exposed to light. Must have been magical to the ancient Egyptians. No wonder they thought Pharaoh was a God. The damn thing lit up whenever he used it."

"Tell me, Stanley, did you find any references in other tombs to additional visitations by our alien friends?" asked Gordon.

"None whatsoever. I've explored hundreds of tombs all over Egypt and translated thousands of pages of ancient texts. Never have I found any other mention of this event. I consider it a one time occurrence."

"Wonder why they never came back?" asked Gordon.

"Maybe we'll find out. Lane called to say that she has a volunteer for the first test. They're on their way right now," said Mike.

Jake and Lane held hands in the back of the cab. Only the driver spoke as he cursed the traffic and wild maneuvers of other taxis.

"You're anxious about this, aren't you?" asked Jake, finally breaking the tension.

Lane just smiled.

"Come on, loosen up. It'll be fine," he said.

"You're the eternal optimist. I guess that's one of the things I love about you."

The taxi pulled in front of the InDevCo building and Jake paid the driver. Lane's apprehension eased. She realized Jake's determination to go through with the test and face Charles, meant nothing she said could change his mind. The scientist in her knew the equipment had to be tested. That part of her romantically involved with Jake said, "let it be someone else." But there was no one else.

The security guard greeted them. "Morning, Dr. Darby. Dr. Haywood asked me to tell you to go directly to the Delta-3 lab. He said you'd know what that meant."

"Thanks, Ken. Mr. Parker's with me."

The guard accompanied them to the secured elevator.

Moments later, Lane greeted her assistant in the laboratory. She introduced Jake to Mike Haywood, Gordon York and Stanley Lawrence, and explained the reason for each one's presence.

"I've briefed Jake on the entire program, and he's agreed to be the first to try the alien communicator. One reason I have accepted him as a volunteer is his experience with a similar brain expansion module that we designed to utilize unused portions of the cerebral cortex. From our computer simulations, this device probably has a similar function. Of course, this is speculation. We all know the only way to find out. Okay, Jake, lie down here." She pointed to a table covered with a contoured cushion. Suspended over him, an array of sensors responded to Dr. Darby's commands and lowered into place. Assistants attached leads to Jake's head and chest.

"We'll monitor nearly every bodily function with these Med computers, Jake. At the first sign of a problem , the test will be discontinued."

"Why the big video screen?" asked Jake.

"Most of the cranial leads will monitor brain functions, but these over the temples will be in contact with the crown's sensors. They're hooked into a neuronal matrix image enhancer. Simply put, it means we'll see and record everything you do, Jake. Any questions?"

"When do we begin?"

Mike Haywood rolled a cart next to Jake with the Pharaoh's crown resting on a pedestal.

"Pretty interesting hat," said Jake.

"You must be completely relaxed and clear your mind," said Mike.

Jake recalled the hypnotic sessions with Santiago. Lane monitored the drop in his heart rate on the ECG.

Mike looked to Lane, who nodded.

Two assistants placed the crown on Jake's head and gently lowered it into position.

"You should be honored, Mr. Parker," said Stanley. "The last person to wear that crown was a Pharaoh of Egypt, 3500 years ago."

"Of course, the circuitry is a little different and the power inputs are stronger," said Mike. "Okay Jake. We think it's activated by thought. You have to turn it on."

Jake closed his eyes. Mike switched on a bright overhead light to power the photovoltaic cells.

The jewels on the crown glowed faintly as the static on the video screen cleared. Faces appeared and disappeared, images of fire, then, water. Ships of all sizes. More faces.

Children laughing and crying.

"EEG registers sleep," said Lane. "Look at his eyes. He's experiencing REM sleep."

"Then we're seeing his dreams?" asked Gordon.

Lane realized that part of what she saw could be the characters Jake spoke of in the past life experiences. She watched the continued parade of strange faces on the screen.

"Analyzing this should be most interesting," Lane said. She watched the screen so intently that she missed a change in the EEG. Jake slipped into a deep coma-like state. The jewels on the crown glowed brightly now.

Jake felt more at peace with himself than ever before. While he appeared asleep, he relived all his past lives in vivid detail and in rapid succession. His childhood flashed by. When he reached the present, Jake floated above his body and observed the entire lab. He felt a wonderful sense of well being.

In the next moment, the lab and all familiar Earthly references vanished.

Jake watched the landscape pass as if he flew in a jet a few feet off the ground; rolling hills carpeted with flowers of every color; trees laden with ripe fruit shaped like square oranges and stripped with bright reds and blues; sheer formations that rose out of the ground like geysers frozen in stone. Blue-green water fell thousands of feet from the summit of the spires to pools full of fat fish that sparkled. Three suns lit this landscape; one in constant partial eclipse, one, a red giant, and the last, a sun resembling Earth's. The combination blanketed the planet with an orange glow.

In the distance, geometric structures towered to the sky reaching higher than he could see. Next to these were cities covered with vast domes.

Jake entered a city.

Huge maintenance drones adhered to the sides of the buildings and scoured them clean as the lifeless drones climbed upward in their endless task. Lights flashed in the distance. Beyond the city, a vast expanse of clear, turquoise water extended to the horizon. He breathed clean air scented with hints of pine and lilac.

I've found paradise.

Jake stood inside a dome resting on a single pylon in the center of the city. From here, the entire city spread out around him. Columns surrounded the circular arena with smaller rooms positioned like the spokes of a wheel.

He waited silently.

The light in the arena dimmed, and a lone holographic figure materialized before Jake. It appeared humanoid, but with a large, protruding head and small extremities.

"Greetings, to a traveler. Welcome to Velon. Communication is possible through the use of the Telepathor that neutralizes even the greatest distances. I am the guardian of this place. There is no one else. I alone tell the story of my people.

"Our race was an ancient one, much like many others scattered through the universe. In those early times, we made war on each other and poisoned our planet with the wastes of our technology. We advanced mentally and saved ourselves from extinction by realizing that our planet's regenerative powers were not inexhaustible. We came to terms with our problems and solved them, devoting this newfound intelligence and our resources to free ourselves from planetary boundaries. Our newly expanded minds enabled us to develop technology that propelled us through the galaxy faster than the speed of light. We searched for other intelligent life. Many such places exist, and our explorers left behind Telepathors with the leaders of the greatest of each civilization so that we could communicate and share new friendships.

"Time passed and our minds grew stronger. No longer did we need the Telepathor to reach out. We evolved and controlled our surroundings with the energy of pure thought. Our world became the center of a vast network of planets that we controlled and watched. Touched by our minds, chosen individuals on these planets became leaders and their essence passed from one generation to another.

"Still our minds grew stronger. We shed our material possessions and controlled every aspect of our environment with thought. Our minds enabled us to combine the energy of pure thought and matter into one entity."

Energy controlled matter.

"But the restraints needed to properly utilize this power gradually disappeared. We destroyed each other in the quest for supreme power over our world, the most important planet in the universe. The result of our achievement in ultimate intellectual power was total extinction.

"Three millennia have passed since the last Velonian activated this program and created me as the guardian of time. A constant signal beacon is beamed to all planets in the galaxy visited by our people: all places where Telepathors originally left behind for communication may lead to development of the same technology that doomed us. The message is a warning to advancing civilizations: Do not allow thought energy to control matter.

"Traveler. As the last of my kind, I bid you safe return to your home."

The apparition vanished.

Lane realized the mind link had terminated. Jake opened his eyes.

"Do you remember anything?" she asked.

"Every sight and every word."

"Then the message is a warning," said Gordon. "Don't let energy control matter. We only received part of it."

"Right," said Jake. "If we allow ourselves to use this technology to expand our minds, it will lead to our doom just as the Velonians fell prey to their own hidden weaknesses."

Mike Haywood interrupted. "I don't agree. If we're aware of the dangers, we can prevent misuse of this power. Besides, it took thousands of years for them to reach the point where their civilization destroyed itself. We could make good use of this technology now. Why worry about what might happen in the future? Man may destroy the planet with a nuclear war way before that time."

"We must act responsibly," said Stanley Lawrence. "Whatever we do today will have a profound effect on future generations. Perhaps, Katara had good reason to bury the Telepathor with him."

Each person had his own opinion, voiced with increasing forcefulness.

Lane shouted. "Wait a minute. Who among us can make a decision like this? None of us has the authority to destroy or utilize this technology."

Jake listened and smiled. He sat up and removed the leads from his head and chest. The group drifted away from him, the heated discussion about the new technology now more important than the messenger. Without a word or a touch, Jake focused his thoughts on the crown.

It rose silently from his head and came to rest on the table beside him.

Thirty-four

JAKE STRETCHED ON A COUCH IN LANE'S OFFICE. SHE ordered a portable med-computer brought in and proceeded to examine him.

"I'm telling you, I feel fine. I'm better than fine. That trip to Velon energized me. What do you think about it?"

"I'm still numb. I can't believe instantaneous telepathic communication is possible over such a vast distance. Any chance it's a hoax?"

Jake shook his head. "No way."

"Just the same, I want you to check into the medical center on the 20th floor for overnight observation. I'll call Dr. Kennaly and he can. . ."

Jake stood up. "I can't wait that long. The Telepathor recharged the CCEM, but it will only last a short time, maybe 8 hours. I've got to get to Charles now, with or without your help."

"Doing this alone is suicide. Let me send a force of our security people with you."

"No. That'll never work. But there is a way you can help. Show me whatever blueprints or maps of Subterra you can find."

Lane sat at her desk. "Computer, display holographic visual of entire Subterra complex in scale."

A detailed image of the city appeared and floated above the desk.

Jake sat down and studied it.

Lane pointed to the main entrances. "Charles' men control all the travel tubes from the entrance access terminals, here and here. Even if we did recapture one of the terminals, he could shut down the tube system from central city control."

"That means I've got to get down there without alerting him," said Jake.

"Impossible. The place is impregnable. Charles planned this well. We have no choice but to give him what he wants."

"Andrew's a dead man if he goes down there to deal with Charles. What about the ventilation system?"

"There are surface air collectors every 500 feet and 4 main ducts that distribute fresh air to the city. That might work, but there are two problems. First, by the time you climbed through the duct and reached Subterra, you'd be exhausted. Second, there's a high speed turbine fan at the bottom of the air shaft that would chop you into little bits."

"Any other ideas?" Jake asked.

Lane studied the hologram. "I think the vent system is the only way. Computer, display schematic of Subterra ventilation system." The hologram appeared. "Now explain maintenance schedule for this system."

"The main vent shafts are cleaned by remote capsules that constantly traverse the length of the ducts."

"Computer, are these capsules big enough to hold a man?"

"Affirmative, but that is not its purpose. Travel tubes are designed for human transport, and are available through main access terminals."

"There it is. Not real comfortable, but you'll reach the end of the shaft. Now, when you get to the bottom, the intake fans work on an automatic cycle. Ten minutes on, one minute off. The fans are all computer coordinated so the caverns always have fresh air. You must deactivate the fan, then cut through a wire mesh gate and you're in."

"What else?" asked Jake.

"That's it. The only problem, we don't know where Charles is in the city."

"Leave that to me. Okay, I'll need the things on this list ASAP." Jake made notes and tore a page from a pad on Lane's desk.

"A helicopter will be waiting for you on the roof in twenty minutes. You'd better come back to me, Jake." She wrapped her arms around him.

"You and I are soul mates, Lane. Stopping Charles will break a cycle that should have ended eons ago. Charles, or whatever he called himself in the past, will never again come between us."

He took her lips in a soft, moist kiss.

She closed her eyes and savored the moment.

"Don't go, Jake."

"I'll be fine." Jake turned. "I'm doing this for us."

"What can I do from this end?"

"Just before I go in, I'll signal so you can alert your teams."

"We'll be ready and waiting. One more thing. I'd love to see Philip again."

He smiled, winked at her and left the office.

* * *

Jake sat in the pilot's seat of the InDevCo helicopter and looked at his watch. A man in a company uniform ran from the cover of the roof elevator and handed Jake a black attache case. The wind from the rotor blew off the man's hat.

"You're late," Jake said to him. He opened the case and checked its contents: a force field belt, a Lorestron gun, the 'Dick Tracy watch,' as he called it, and all of the smaller items he requested. Jake gave the thumbs up sign, and the man disappeared into the service elevator.

Jake set the navigation computer with the proper coordinates and the aircraft lifted off the helipad.

The helicopter landed in a clearing surrounded by dense woods. Jake wrapped the belt around his waist, the watch on his wrist and put the gun in his pocket. A small back pack contained rope and other items. With all systems shut down, he left the aircraft in search of the vent opening.

"It's camouflaged as a tree," Lane had told him.

Jake walked into the forest and listened. The sound of rushing air came from a nearby tree. Jake moved closer, and felt the powerful suction. He opened a small control panel in the trunk of the tree and pushed four buttons in sequence. A large intake grill slid open. Jake looked up into the hollow tree and found the shaft cleaning module. He pressed the release; the pod descended and stopped in front of the grill opening. Jake climbed into the capsule and activated the release again. The door closed and the robot descended into the dark air shaft.

Jake calculated the travel time at one hour and he relaxed in the cramped quarters. He knew the capsule would automatically ascend once it reached a certain point near the bottom, so exiting at exactly the right spot was imperative.

Time passed slowly. His thoughts took him back.

Was I really on another planet?

He sensed the feeling of exhilaration and power fading already.

The capsule stopped with a jolt. Jake kicked out the bottom and slid into the shaft. The turbine fan had just stopped.

He set his watch alarm for 59 seconds, reached into his back pack for a small bottle, and carefully poured its contents over the motor housing of the fan. The corrosive acid worked immediately as the covering burned away, revealing the core of the motor. Jake poured more acid on the wiring.

His watch signaled the end of the off cycle.

The turbine started on schedule. Slowly at first, then, it picked up speed to full power. Trapped in the shaft, Jake grabbed onto the bottom of the rising cleaning module to escape the hurricane force suction of the fan. The pod carried him slowly away, but the wind blast pulled him and he lost his grip. Just as he fell, the acid worked on the final inner wiring and sparks showered from the motor housing.

The blades of the fan slowed and turned only with momentum. Jake glanced at the capsule as it rose out of sight.

No turning back now.

Once the fan stopped completely, he stepped through the giant blades and used a small wire cutter to cut the mesh that covered the fan on both sides.

Jake found himself at the junction of four narrow, dark tunnels. He recalled the holographic image of the city in Lane's office.

Tunnel 14 leads to the city center.

Using only the light from his own flashlight, he easily traversed the length of the tunnel in fifteen minutes. At the end, the Subterran sun provided enough light to allow him to cut through a final wire barrier.

The streets of the city appeared vacant. Transport tubes lay quiet in their terminals. Charles had succeeded in turning the once vibrant metropolis into a deserted shell. A team of security guards passed on patrol. Jake hid behind the corner of a transport tube terminal and listened to their conversation. A moment later, he fired a pulsed double burst from his Lorestron gun, stunning both men simultaneously. Jake dragged them behind the building and tied them together. Then he removed communicators from their belts.

"Repeat your message, F-5. Do you need assistance?" central security asked. Jake looked at an assignment grid map in one of the guard's pockets.

"F-5, Beta section is clear. Proceeding on patrol," Jake said. He placed his watch next to the communicator and read its frequency. Within seconds, he had the source and distance of the signal triangulated.

The City Command center. Charles is there.

Jake made his way toward the control center carefully avoiding Charles' security patrols. He knelt next to a fountain across from the command building and looked at his watch.

14:20. Ten minutes before InDevCo inner core agents attack Charles' position at transport terminal one.

At 14:35, Jake watched at least twenty heavily armed men rush from the building toward the transport terminal. He waited until they all cleared the area. Two guards remained. Jake focused his thoughts on these men as they stood guard outside the front entrance.

Stun the man next to you. He is your enemy.

They fired at each other.

Jake approached the building and stepped over the bodies of the guards. The corridors appeared deserted. He drew his gun and proceeded slowly, searching each room.

Charles is here. I can sense him.

Jake climbed the stairs to the top floor and the computer control room. He kicked the door open. A man sat alone at the main control console with his back to Jake and looked at three large video screens that displayed the scene at the transport terminals and the surface. Charles had thrown all his men into these areas believing that any attempt to remove him from Subterra would start from there. The video screen in the center showed a fierce battle at surface transport terminal one.

"Very impressive set up," said Jake. He aimed his gun at Charles.

Charles spun in the chair, the stoic expression on his face unchanged. "Why, Jake, what a surprise."

"Order your men to surrender."

Charles stared at the blue aura around Jake.

"Are you God? If you are, I've been waiting for you. I want to be your partner." He took a drink from a coffee cup. "This is poison, you know."

Jake tried to reach deep into Charles' mind, but he found only hatred and confusion, scrambled thoughts and turmoil.

"Come with me, Charles. We can help you."

Charles slowly pulled a gun set to kill from a drawer, and pointed it at Jake from under the desk. "You still don't get it. This is my kingdom and I have final say over the life and death of my subjects. You will bow before me."

Before Jake could answer, Charles fired his Lorestron gun. The point blank blast struck Jake and knocked him down, but the force field belt absorbed the killing energy. Jake survived, and Charles ran from the room before Jake recovered and returned the fire.

At the front entrance of the building, Jake caught only a fleeting glimpse of Charles as he fled into the tube station. Jake took off in pursuit, and arrived in time only to see Charles speeding away in a travel pod. Jake summoned the next pod and programed the computer to follow.

At the end of the tube tunnel system, the pod stopped at a small station. The window of the capsule clouded with condensation. Jake stepped out of the pod and the intense heat struck him like he had walked into a wall. Cautiously, he entered a large cavern. All around him pits of boiling mud bubbled and spewed sulfurous fumes into the air. The temperature gauge on his watch read 128 degrees.

This is the hot spring cave; the source of electricity for the city.

Charles disappeared, though his capsule had stopped directly in front of Jake's. Sweat poured from Jake's body. He knelt behind a rock for cover. He sensed Charles' watchful eyes.

Beyond the mud pit, thousands of steam pipes collected superheated water that turned a turbine in the generator building, creating abundant electricity for the city. Jake walked cautiously around the cavern, using the pipes and boulders for protection. Stalactites of every size hung from the roof of the cavern. The calcite projections glistened with water in the artificial light provided by the generator. Occasional bursts of steam exploded with loud hissing noises as excess pressure in the system vented.

A voice from behind cut through him.

"I have no more time to waste on you, Jake."

Jake turned to face Charles, but felt momentarily dizzy in the intense heat. Charles' expression exposed his hatred and disgust.

"Goodbye."

Charles pulled the trigger.

Nothing happened.

Jake fired his gun with the same result.

"Looks like the heat affected the trigger mechanism," Charles said and circled toward Jake.

Hoping to gain the initiative, Jake lunged at Charles, pinning him against the pipes on the outside of the generator building. The move failed and Charles used his superior physical strength to reverse their positions. Jake sensed only intense hatred from Charles. It blocked Jake's thoughts.

I'm losing the power.

Suddenly, a burst of steam erupted in Charles face, momentarily blinding him. Jake moved away, but Charles reached for him and ripped the force field belt from his waist in an attempt to pull him back. Jake fell to the ground and Charles leaped toward him. They rolled toward the boiling mud lake, locked in combat.

Each man had his hands wrapped tightly around the other's neck. Charles used his great strength to pin Jake to the ground just at the edge of the boiling mud pit. Jake fought to keep his head up. He felt the rising steam and hot mud singe the back of his neck as Charles forced him closer to the seething cauldron.

Jake gasped for air.

Can't breathe. Mustn't let history repeat again. Got to stop him.

Jake looked at the ceiling of the cave. His vision blurred. The smell of sulfur nauseated him.

Energy controls matter.

The familiar words repeated in his mind.

At once he remembered and understood the Velonian message. They controlled their environment with their minds.

Brain energy controls matter. I have that power.

The light appeared to dim and the stalactite formations on the cave ceiling glowed with a misty aura.

Summoning his consciousness and strength, Jake focused his mental energy. A small crack formed in an overhead stalactite. The defect grew until the razor sharp projection came loose and fell.

Charles released his grip.

His eyes registered the shock of the impact. He reached around and removed the stony dagger that struck him.

Charles stood and staggered toward the travel pods.

Jake sat up and rubbed his neck. He coughed from the noxious fumes and his nearly collapsed windpipe. Exhausted and drenched in perspiration, he regained his composure, and followed Charles.

The two travel pods sat in their tubes. Jake searched the immediate area, but saw no one. Drops of blood collected on the ground near the pods. With only one tube into this remote area, Jake's pod, its door open, blocked Charles' pod. The bloody trail led into an area of smaller connecting caves.

Good thing I locked the pod computer entry code with a password.

Jake followed the lead of blood away from the generator building and into a labyrinth of caverns where the stalactites grew much larger than near the mud pits. Blue green luminescent algae growing on the ceiling and walls cast a glow in the caves. Water dripped from the walls and collected in pools. Jake choked from the thick air, heavy with moisture and sulfur, though the temperature felt much cooler here. He fingered the gun in his pocket, hoping it would work in the cooler temperature.

Jake heard a cough in a nearby cave, and pressed himself against the stone wall. Cautiously, he moved toward the triangular shaped opening of the grotto, entered, and shined the light from his flashlight. Charles lay on the ground next to a small pool of black water. Only the sound of dripping water broke the silence.

"Et tu, Brutus?" Charles asked, extending one arm. He propped himself against the wall. Blood saturated the side of his shirt. "ÒWhy would noble Brutus, my best friend, wish to harm mighty Caesar? Why such foul play?"

"You must pay for the crimes of your malevolent immortal soul. For too long you've inflicted misery. Now, you are like a malignancy that must be excised from the cycle of life and time."

"I will always be Caesar, and you, always my slave."

"Not anymore. I'm ending this ancient game, and you're going back to hell."

"Never."

Charles took his gun and fired. Jake dropped to the ground and the blast impacted above him with a shower of sparks. Jake grabbed his gun and returned the fire, but the shot went high and Charles crawled behind a rock.

"I always win," said Charles laughing. He fired wildly.

Jake fired back, fell to the ground and rolled out through the narrow entrance to the cave.

That's the only way in or out.

Jake closed his eyes and summoned the last of his mental energy. He concentrated on the rocks above the entry.

Must focus. Energy controls matter.

A low rumbling shook the caves.

The vibration increased until the ceiling formations swayed. With a thunderous crash, the largest of the stalactites fell, completely obstructing and sealing the grotto entrance.

"That's for Menefter and Ashanti."

Jake's rule #31 — Happy endings are always better than sad ones.

Thirty-five

JAKE SPOKE INTO HIS WATCH TRANSMITTER, NOT KNOWING if the signal penetrated to the surface from such a great depth. "Come in, InDevCo command. This is Parker. Do you read?"

A welcome voice replaced the static.

"We've been expecting your signal, Parker. One moment while I patch you through to Dr. Darby."

"Jake, are you okay? What's happened down there?"

"I'm fine, but I'm afraid Charles won't be coming home. I'm heading back to the control building to reactivate the main elevators and open the entrance. Tell your men to be ready. After that, I'll try to help out from this end. Do you copy?"

"Yes. Good luck and see you soon."

Jake stepped into his travel pod and fell into the soft seat. His body ached. The struggle with Charles left him exhausted. He entered the destination code into the computer and the pod sped away from the hot spring cavern toward the city. Like the first rain after a drought, the air from the capsule ventilation system cooled his overheated skin.

Jake sat in the seat behind Charles' desk in the main control room. The monitors continued to show scenes of the city and the transport tube terminals. The complex array of computer banks managed all life in Subterra.

He spotted the panel that controlled the power couplings; the transport terminal systems flashed red. Slowly, Jake reactivated the circuits and the panel changed to green. The vidphone displayed the face of an angry man.

"Control, what the hell are you doing there? The power just came on in this entire sector. If you don't shut it down, InDevCo security will be right in our laps in a few minutes. Damn it control, come in."

Jake did not answer the call, but instead grabbed his gun dashed out of the building, and headed for the transport tube station.

When he arrived at the terminal, the battle raged into the lower levels. InDevCo forces took advantage of the restored power to enter the security check-in area, where their advance stalled. Charles' men outnumbered the InDevCo men by five to one, and pinned them into a small lounge. Jake approached unseen and used a nearby support column for cover. The air was thick with particle beam bullets. Jake knew that he had one chance only to surprise the enemy.

He positioned himself behind Charles' men with the InDevCo forces in front of them. After judging he could get no closer without being seen, he reached around the column and fired.

Two of Charles' men fell immediately. The others turned, shocked to be caught in a crossfire. The momentary pause in firing allowed the InDevCo men to advance their position. Jake now had approximately twenty men shooting at him. He froze, unable to retreat or advance.

Got to focus my thoughts. The power is. . .gone.

As more InDevCo men arrived from the surface, they pushed further into the security area. Jake fired and hit a man who appeared to be the field commander of Charles' forces. With their chain of command broken, the trespassers faltered. Jake saw two mercenaries run into the tunnel leading to the observation deck. He followed and hugged the wall, inching his way toward the end of the dark passage. He stopped just short of the entrance to the observation area, which appeared deserted. Jake knew this to be a dead end, yet the two had disappeared. Suddenly, a stun blast surprised him from behind a small bend in the terrace. He took a direct hit in the right shoulder and fell to the floor. The two men approached cautiously.

It's Pat Young and Eddie Garcia from the oil rig.

"He's dead," Young said and kicked Jake in the ribs.

Jake surprised him, grabbed Young's foot and forced him down. In the next moment, Jake rolled over and fired at Garcia, stunning him.

Jake stood and lifted Young by the throat. "I've dreamed about this day, boy," he said and punched him in the stomach. Young slammed his fist into Jake's injured shoulder. It connected, and Jake fell to the floor, writhing in pain. Young picked Jake up and dragged him to the edge of the terrace. Using both his hands, Jake slammed Young's ears hard. Young released his grip. Jake swivelled and kicked him with all his strength. Young struck the guard rail and flipped over it. Jake heard the fading scream as Young fell to the bottom of the cavern.

Jake emerged from the tunnel holding Garcia in an arm lock. The fight was over. Charles' men gathered in the lounge, their hands held high, surrounded by InDevCo security.

"Take this scumbucket away," Jake said to an InDevCo agent who approached him.

"How bad is it?" he asked pointing to Jake's shoulder.

"Hurts like hell. Good thing I moved out of the way when he fired."

"Looks like you didn't move fast enough. I'll call the medic."

"No, I can't stay. There's something I need to do."

Jake headed toward the transport tube station again. His shoulder throbbed, but one more objective of this mission remained.

Jake again found himself in front of the quarantine sign on the top floor of the medical center. He thought of the possibility that Charles had moved Philip.

In his arrogance, Charles would never consider failure. I'm certain Philip is still here.

Slowly, with gun drawn, Jake opened the door and stepped into the corridor. He fired at the video cameras and motion detectors fixed on the ceiling along the way. He walked uninterrupted through the quiet corridor.

The inner apartment appeared unchanged from his previous visit.

A woman sat in a chair next to the bed with her back to Jake. A man lay motionless in the bed. Thick carpet silenced his footsteps as he entered the room. The nurse held a syringe and withdrew a clear solution from a tiny bottle. Just as she wiped the man's skin with alcohol for the injection, Jake turned on the light.

"Freeze, lady. Touch him with that needle and you'll die today."

She turned, startled. "Who are you? How did you get in here?"

"Look, I've had a bad day." Jake touched his wounded shoulder and winced. "What's in the shot?"

"Why, it's just his sedative. Mr. Charles told me to administer it every eight hours or the patient gets violent."

"Mr. Charles won't be giving orders anymore. Get away from the bed."

Before she moved, the nurse activated a silent panic button on the floor. She placed the hypodermic on the stand next to the bed and turned away as ordered. Jake approached the bed, felt for a pulse in Philip's neck and lifted his eye lids.

"Good thing he's alive." Jake activated his wrist communicator. "InDevCo command. This is Parker. Do you read?"

A door opened silently behind Jake.

The man that walked through the door towered over Jake. His abnormal height and weight gave him a distorted appearance. Before Jake could turn to see him, the giant pinned Jake's arms to his sides.

Jake turned his head and looked at the man.

"Who the hell are you?" Jake asked.

The behemoth squeezed Jake's injured shoulder, lifted him off the ground and tossed him across the room like a basketball. The gun flew out of Jake's hand and slid under a dresser on the opposite side of the room.

Dazed, Jake forced himself up and charged. He hit the

giant feet first and they both fell to the floor. Pain seared through Jake's body as he landed on his shoulder. The body guard recovered in an instant.

Jake noticed Philip stirring as the sedative wore off.

The sedative.

Jake lay on the floor next to the bed. He reached out and grabbed the syringe just before the huge man lifted him, ready to throw him across the room again. Jake rammed the needle into the man's neck and pushed the plunger hard. Hardly feeling the pinch, the man continued to pound Jake despite his efforts to break the hold.

Suddenly, the monster loosened his hold. He stumbled toward the door and the nurse. Clutching her arm, he collapsed to the floor on top of the helpless, screaming nurse.

Jake could barely stand. He grabbed the bed and pulled himself off the floor.

"Harry was right. I've got to find a safer line of work," Jake said. "Can you hear me, sir?"

Philip's eyes opened, but he said nothing.

"Your wife is anxious to see you."

Philip nodded, and Jake hoped he understood. He touched Jake's arm and a tear ran down his cheek.

"InDevCo command, do you read?" Jake spoke into his watch.

"Command here. What happened to you, Parker? We received your call signal ten minutes ago."

"It's a long story. Notify Mrs. Cromwell that her husband's safe. We'll meet you at the emergency surface security clearance area. Do you copy?"

"We copy that. See you there, Parker."

Now more alert, Philip sat up as Jake pulled a nearby wheelchair next to the bed.

"I don't know which of us needs this more right now, sir," he said to Philip, who still did not speak. Jake wondered if his silence was due to the stroke or the long period of sedation.

Once on the surface, Jake pushed Philip slowly toward the nearby clearing. A few minutes passed and they heard the sound of an approaching helicopter. It touched down and two women stepped out. Jake moved toward them. Ruth Cromwell ran to Philip. Tears streamed down her cheeks. She embraced him.

"I never gave up on you. Never."

Philip held her arm.

Lane dabbed her eyes with a tissue. A medic checked Philip's vital signs, nodded and smiled to Ruth.

"What about me?"

"What happened to you?" Lane finally asked, placing her arm around Jake. "You look terrible."

"I. . .never mind. Maybe I'll tell you about it sometime in this lifetime."

Ruth Cromwell turned to Jake and took his hand. "Oh Jake, I don't know what to say. Thank you for giving my husband back to me." She hugged him.

"I'm sorry it had to be at the expense of your son."

"We never realized it, but we lost Charles a long time ago. By the way, I think this belongs to you." She handed him an envelope with his name on it. Inside, was a cashiers check for one hundred thousand dollars.

"Now I'm the one who's speechless. Thanks."

"You earned it, Jake. If ever there's anything we can do for you, just ask."

"There is something." Jake wrote two names on the envelope. "I gave my word I would try to help these people come to America. Can you use some of your Washington connections to help them?"

"I'll do what I can. Are they friends?"

"The best." Jake reached into his pocket and found the carved wooden eagle.

They said their goodbyes. The medics placed Philip on a stretcher inside the aircraft and Ruth boarded the chopper. Jake and Lane watched as the ship flew into the distance toward Newport.

Lane realized Jake could barely stand.

"You really do look awful," she said. "Do you want to go to the hospital?"

"No way. Let's go somewhere quiet where you can nurse me back to health."

"I know the perfect place for your recuperation. A little abandoned barn in the middle of the country not too far from here. We can discuss the first day of the rest of our lives together. I love you," she said.

Jake lifted her chin and kissed her lightly.

"I've loved you for 3000 years."